Kaitlyn Jones, Reuniting Fate

By
Kathleen J. Shields

ISBN-13: 978-1-941345-08-5 Paperback
ISBN-10: 1941345085 Paperback
ISBN: 9781301359790 Smashwords eBook

ERIN GO BRAGH Publishing
Canyon Lake, TX
www.ErinGoBraghPublishing.com

Chapter 1

One week after that amazing goodbye at the White House with Jonathan Stangard, Kaitlyn found herself dressed in training gear and uniform, standing at attention in a line with twenty other men listening to the Warrant Officer go over the rules here at CovSec's formal training.

"I am Chief Warrant Officer Rivera. I have earned the title Chief Warrant Officer because I am a technical expert and a combat leader and trainer. Through progressive levels of expertise in assignments, training, and education, I'll administer operations, and integrations in various systems and equipment across the full spectrum of activities. I'll teach you about emerging technologies, survival skills, I'll make you confident war fighters. I'll refine your technical expertise and your physical capabilities and hone your skills making you into elite fighting machines."

For a week now Kaitlyn had been looking forward to this day. The excitement of something new, of learning new skills, of moving forward with her life was alive in her body, but there was something else on her mind as well that she just couldn't escape from no matter how hard she tried, Tom. How she had tried to forget him, to mourn and move on after his death, but that dream she had a week ago just would not leave her mind. Trying to determine that the dream was more guilt for being with Jonathan than of Tom actually being alive, Kaitlyn was unable to convince herself.

All week long her mind kept bringing her back to that dream, and back to instances in her life that point to the possible fact that that dream very well could be true. Starting from the beginning, she knew it was her dream, her ability to see into the future that saved Tom's life from the car crash.

1

Her dreams have never let her down and the fact that it was a dream that told her of her father's demise and a dream that told her about her real mother's final days as a hostage.

But it was more the investigator inside her from the police force in San Diego that brought her to think back to the rationality of the dream. She never truly believed Tom had died that day in the bar, he was too strong, too fast and too smart to have been shot. It was that belief that made her drive across the country to San Diego and to retrieve his file from the police force. It was that file that encouraged her disbelief of his death with its strange lack of information, no witnesses, no video tapes, no finger prints and no body. Kaitlyn knew it was strange that the morgue cremated the body before there could be an autopsy or investigation and with no body for closure, there was no proof that he had actually died.

That fact added to the words Victoria said that night about Tom acting strange before the bar brawl. How he seemed to know he wasn't going to be there for her any longer and how he walked away from her and into that fight like he knew something bad was going to happen. Victoria was certain Tom didn't die even though she saw his still body on the floor and the blood pouring from his chest, and Kaitlyn was certain as well.

The dream Kaitlyn had a week ago was vague. The surroundings were unfamiliar and hazy, none of her dreams had ever been so unclear like this one. It was this reason that led her to believe that it might not be true. A desperate attempt of her mind to express her guilt for actually forgetting about Tom for a night. Kaitlyn was standing in a line of men, under the baking summer sun in the heat of the day and she knew her mind had to be playing tricks on her. She had just shook the dream from her mind for the last time when a harsh yet cooling wind kicked up the dust of the dirt road below her and blinded her and everyone else standing in line.

As a helicopter flew overhead, lined up its decent and landed, everyone's attention was drawn towards the sky to watch as it came in. Everyone stood at attention, still, even after the wind from the blades tried to knock them over. Each person standing there tried to prove that he or she was the most tough, that they weren't worried, that nothing could scare them or knock them down. Kaitlyn however just stood there and stared as the doors of the helicopter opened and a man wearing a major's uniform emerged from inside, followed by two other men in army green camo. CWO Rivera continued speaking over the noisy entrance, as he introduced the Major who had just arrived.

"Now, please give your full attention to Major M. he will be here supervising you recruits and determining if you are proficient enough to stay here."

The Major walked up to the podium to address the team. Kaitlyn looked up at the man standing before her and her team, and her eyes widened. Her mouth opened just slightly and she felt tears whelp up into her eyes. Her face burned with emotion. She felt as if she couldn't speak, move or even breathe anymore. As she looked at and recognized the broad face of a man whom she had longed for, for so many years, her body began to shiver.

She could have been wrong about this, delusional because of the hot afternoon sun, confused because of the dream, maybe even lonely enough to want to believe it, or excited about what she was doing to want to share it with Tom. But this couldn't be Tom. He had died almost three years ago. It was a very close resemblance, too close for comfort, but Kaitlyn kept trying to ignore the similarity even convincing herself that when the man spoke she would determine that he definitely was not Tom due to some foreign accent. But finally the man spoke and the deep booming voice that came from his mouth was undeniably, indubitably and unquestionably, Toms.

"Good afternoon class. I am Major M. I am in charge of supervising your daily progress and determining if you are fit enough to hold the title of CovSec agent. When we're done with you, you'll be some of the damn finest government agents the nation has ever had the pleasure of NOT knowing. If you don't survive you'll be considered nothing and we won't miss you at all. Only the best pass this course and only the best survive. Let's hope you're the best because I hate losers!"

Kaitlyn felt so many emotions fill her all at once she wasn't sure which one to express first, or if she wanted to express them at all. She was standing there in shock, her mouth dropped from a slight open shock to a drop jawed gape which made her look like she had just seen a ghost, a look that for a brief moment caught the Major's attention. He caught her eye for a second, a long second that seemed to last but then, he looked away as if he didn't know her and ignored her the rest of the initiation.

Kaitlyn knew Tom didn't have a twin brother and although some people say everyone's got a doppelganger, there's a person out there that looks exactly like you somewhere else on the planet, no one could look this good and sound this good, to pass so easily as the Tom she knew so well. After he looked away she blinked and brought her jaw back up, continuing her stance of self-awareness and pride yet she was definitely anything but. She was utterly and completely shocked and she couldn't even form a question in her mind as to where to start first.

After Major M finished his speech and walked away, CWO Rivera distributed training assignments. Kaitlyn watched as Tom walked away and once dismissed herself, decided to find out the truth. She felt in her heart that it was

Tom, but she had to talk to him, to find out for sure once and for all or she would be so completely distracted she would never make it through training. As if she were stalking him she followed his path until she came to an area where no one was around except she and Tom. Then she called out his name, his real name. He had introduced himself as Major M, which wasn't Tom's last name, but just the beginning letter and too much of a coincidence to ignore.

"Tom." She called out waiting for him to turn.

He stopped walking for just a moment, but didn't turn around. Then he continued walking like he had heard nothing. She wondered if he had heard her but didn't know where the sound was coming from. Of course he didn't look around, but she kept following nevertheless. If for some reason he was supposed to be dead to anyone who ever knew him before, she didn't want to break his secret now. He turned a corner, she waited a moment and then turned the same corner he did. As she walked in she saw it was an empty alley between two wood buildings, that didn't lead to anywhere but a tall wooden fence. She walked in a little more, confused as to where he went, when he leaped out from the shadows, wrapped a hand around her neck and threw her against the wall, pinning her there.

There was strength in his eyes and he almost didn't look like the same person as before, but she could tell it was. He was either an exact clone of Tom, or the real thing. There was no other explanation. He looked into her eyes and although her heart was racing and she contemplated fighting back she waited to see if he said anything first. Finally he spoke.

"Who are you working for?"

Even more shocked now she became speechless. He asked again, this time drawing a knife to her throat. "Who?"

Choking with her words and thoughts all she could think to say was, "Tom?"

He stabbed the knife into the wall less than an inch from her head while still pinning her against the wall with his other hand, then he reached for her brown button down shirt and ripped it open. A ravaging excitement swept through Kaitlyn for a split second but the shock and now fear was more prevalent and all she could do was gasp. Her eyes were fixated on his eyes but he avoided eye contact, he was searching her body. Forcefully he spun Kaitlyn around, pinned her left arm against her back and began patting her down. Kaitlyn was so confused she couldn't even think about fighting back, her mind had stopped working completely, she was just plain stunned.

Once he was finished with his pat down he spun Kaitlyn back around again, holding her against the wall still, but finally looked her in the eyes. He spoke again.

"No wire?"

Kaitlyn shook her head no. Then he released his grip on her. Under any other circumstance Kaitlyn would have reacted now. Done anything, but she was still too terrified. Still uncertain. Still stunned silent.

"What do you want?" He demanded, now taking his knife from the wall next to Kaitlyn's head and sliding it back in its holster. Kaitlyn had been thinking about this day for five long years but she never once thought it would go like this. Her mind was racing and yet she couldn't grasp one word to say. She just kept staring at him curiously, eyebrows scrunched in concern and fear, mouth still open slightly. She wasn't sure now she was standing in front of the person she thought she was. If this was Tom he had changed.

"What do you want?" He demanded louder, the tone of his voice making Kaitlyn shiver to the bone. The only word she could think to say was, "Tom?"

"Yes."

"You're Tom?"

"You've gotten slow?"

"Why are you acting like this?"

"Acting like what?" He demanded quickly losing his patience.

"Like an asshole." Kaitlyn remarked, beginning to feel the adrenaline firing up.

Tom stepped back and looked at her with complete disillusionment. He looked at her as if she just talked back to the teacher and knew she wasn't supposed to.

"I had heard you were coming I just hoped it wasn't true."

"Why?"

"You know damn well why!"

"No I don't!"

"We can't work together. It's a proven fact."

Kaitlyn paused. "Okay one, I didn't even know you were alive, this is a complete shock to me."

"Yes and you show it well."

Kaitlyn wanted to growl but attempted to keep her composure. "And two, what do you mean we can't work together?"

"If you are that naive then I'm wasting my time even talking to you. So when will you be transfering out of here?" He spoke with pure determination.

"Transfer? Why?" Kaitlyn said with a little too much innocence in her voice.

"We won't work together, I will not let anything interrupt my duty."

"Spoken like a true soldier, except you forget how well we do work together. Or are you concerned that we're going to hop in the sack like before and you're not going to be all you can be?" Kaitlyn was beginning to become irate.

"Mock all you want to but you know I'm right!" Tom yelled.

"Oh do I?" Kaitlyn growled finding her true anger. "My Tom died, three years ago. I've grieved. I've moved on, and I'm just as furious to see you alive as I am that you expect me to give up this opportunity. If you want to transfer be my guest. But I'm going to make it through this training with flying colors and become one of the best secret agents the states have ever seen. And if you get in my way, mark my words Tom McKinney, I will send you right back to your grave. And trust me I know exactly where that is!"

Tom was angry at first. He looked like he wanted to say something back, he huffed angrily, teeth grinding, but he paused, collecting his thoughts. He hadn't heard his own last name in three years, it struck a nerve. Finally, he changed his tune.

"I'm sorry Kaitlyn. I never meant to hurt you. I never thought that you would hear about my death much less take it to heart."

"Take it to…?" Kaitlyn half laughed. "Tom I contacted you, or at least I tried to. You never answered, otherwise I would have known for sure that you weren't dead!"

"I know you tried to contact me, I refused to contact you back."

"But why?"

"I had to die! I had gotten myself in too deep with some really nasty groups and when CovSec contacted me they suggested I die in the face of the public to rid myself of those death threats and assassination attempts and to become someone with no connections to pedestrian life or I would put everyone I ever knew in danger."

"Fine. But I'm not anyone. You could have told me."

"We parted in different states of mind. And you hadn't tried to contact me since then. Why should I find you and tell you something extremely top secret when I had no idea what your frame of mind was?"

"Well you didn't try to contact me any of those times either. You were the one who sent me away. You were the one who dropped communication. You were the one who...."

"Okay I get it! I screwed up! I sent you away to learn a life lesson. What do you want from me? I did what I thought was best for you at the time. And if you remember correctly I came back to you later asking for another chance and that time you dropped me!"

"Of course I did! You think I'm going to let you push me away and then take you back later? Why is it always all about you? Why I'm following you? Why I'm angry at you...." Kaitlyn gripped.

"What do you want to do then?" Tom gripped bitterly.

"I just want to do what I came here to do."

"Well we can't. I'm not supposed to have connections to the outside world. It's why I had to die."

"We'll I'm not part of the outside world anymore. And I'm not going to die!"

"If you make it through training you too will have to die in the face of the nation, so that way there are no connections to the world to get in your way. I died so that way my mother would have no connection to me. No connection to tie me to her and cause her problems if that information got into the wrong hands. I never even considered you because we hadn't spoken in five years, normally or telepathically. I figured you were over me."

"Well you figured wrong." Kaitlyn said with a little too much shock in her voice to suit her. "I may have walked away from you, but you were also the one who said we had this connection, this soul-mate type of bond that was always in the back of my mind. No matter how crappy my life was I always remembered that bond, that connection and it made me feel better. I guess that sounds pretty pathetic to you, but it kept me going."

9

Tom stood there in front of her. Understanding every word, taking it completely to heart and he wanted to take her into his arms and comfort her, just like those many years before when they were rather close, but suddenly she turned, like a viper to its' prey.

"But my life's great now. And just because you're here means nothing. You mean nothing to me in the big picture. You got it? I'm here for one thing, Tom, training. After that I'm out of here and out of your life again, just the way you like it. Play like you don't know me if you need to, but trust me, you screw this opportunity up for me by saying something about our past and I will hunt you down and trap you like the dog that you are!"

And with that she spun around and walked away. She didn't turn around and look back at him. She walked away with the same intolerance that Tom had grown to love so many years ago. And he smiled, she hadn't changed a bit, she moved past her confusion and right into a strength-building anger, and yet she had grown so much since he had last seen her. So many close calls recently had prepared him for this moment but nothing he could have imagined would have brought these emotions long ago bottled away back to the surface again. He had wanted to be strong, not wanting to get in her way, not wanting their past to interfere with either of their jobs, but even now after seeing her, after touching her again, a spark lit in him and he knew he was in for a very bumpy ride.

Chapter 2

The following day Kaitlyn was standing at attention with the rest of the team, when CWO Rivera walked up to greet his battalion. He was giving directions for the day when Major M. walked up to listen. He didn't even look at Kaitlyn for the first ten minutes, forcing himself not to make eye contact, he didn't even know if she was looking at him. A few moments later Rivera sent the order for the class to warm up on the training field before they began the CrossFit training.

The training field was filled with the traditional physical training course, climbing walls for strength, rope swings for endurance, tires for balance; everything you'd think would be in a training field. Then they reported for CrossFit. CrossFit is principally a strength and conditioning program that delivers high intensity functional movement to defined and rigorous training. There are a plethora of techniques and exercises they work on but basically it is fine-tuning and embellishing upon the abilities an agent already possesses.

Rivera was busy supervising all when General Harrison walked up to Major M and him.

"CWO Rivera, status report?"

"Excellent. We've got some real troopers here this time."

The three men watched the team of twenty climb walls, leap hurdles, cross bars and whatnot for a few moments when the General spoke; his attention focused on Jones.

"How's she doing?" He asked pointing his attention to Kaitlyn who was busy crawling hand over hand across the bars. Tom looked over at her for the first time this morning and found himself get lost in her beauty for a moment.

Rivera answered casually. "She's just as good as any of the men."

"Major?"

Tom watched her for a moment. "She seems like she is capable of more but she's holding herself back."

"How do you mean Major?"

"Look at the way she's almost doing a double step there, and do you see how she kind of lifts herself upwards when crossing under the bars? She's trying to get a bit more out of this it seems." Tom knew Kaitlyn well. He knew how much she enjoyed physical activities, how she seemed to thrive on obstacle courses. He also knew that she could handle it and he was curious as to how much more she could give.

"Good eye Major M, I see it too. Rivera, I want all these men to get the right training, but she is our key. She doesn't have the look of an agent, she doesn't look as strong as she is, she doesn't have the physical characteristics that most would preconceive... This makes her a prominent candidate for undercover missions. I want you to work her especially hard. I'm even going to allot some time for Major M and her to work separate from the class, for additional training."

"Sir?" Tom coughed, caught off guard by that last comment the general made.

"That's right. When the other trainees are off on individual training, I want Jones to report to you. I'll have high-level CrossFit exercises for her to begin with and then we'll progress further from there."

"Yes sir." Tom spoke not quite sure how Kaitlyn will react to that news. He wasn't sure that was a good idea for the two of them but what could he say? The General was right, and it would be excellent for Kaitlyn. Unfortunately, he wasn't sure it'd be excellent for him.

"Rivera call her over here, I'd like to talk to her."

"Yes sir." He said then looked up to Kaitlyn. "Jones!" He called out loudly. She looked over at them, not that she hadn't been ever since Tom arrived. She leapt down from the bars and jogged over to the three men.

"CWO Rivera, General Harrison, Major M.." She acknowledged. The general held out his hand and shook hers.

"Lieutenant Jones, glad to finally meet you, I've heard so much about you."

"All good I hope sir." She smiled.

"And modest. Answer me this, how much can you bench?"

"Respectively 250 sir."

CWO Rivera coughed almost as if wanting to declare 'Bullshit!' but Tom knew better. In her prime in high school any weight he had her try she was able to do, she surpassed the machines, he wondered if she still had that strength in her, the strength of six men. Maybe he would find out.

The general raised an eyebrow to Rivera but then continued. "We've been talking about you and we all agree, we want you to get additional training."

"Am I not doing well in the class sir?"

"On the contrary, you're doing exceptional. So much so that you may become detrimental to the others. I've decided that you and the Major should train together. Special tasks force requires teams for high-level missions and when the Major here returns to active duty I'd like to place the both of you together.

"Excuse me sir?" Kaitlyn spoke out of turn.

"Do you have a problem with that Lieutenant?"

"No sir." Kaitlyn erupted formally. "I'm sorry sir!" The General continued. "Okay, my secretary will put together a special schedule for you two. Next Monday report to my office at o-seven hundred and we'll discuss this further. As you were."

13

Kaitlyn looked at Tom for a moment before saluting and returning to the training field. She noticed the three continue to watch the group for a few minutes more and wondered what had instigated all that. Tom must have said something, but what?

Once the General and Major had left, Rivera called everyone back over . "Alright, Looking good. Pretty good warm up huh?" He said as he waited to hear if anyone spoke, no one did, but the looks on their faces expressing concern of, 'if that was a warm up, what's next?' then he said it. "Welcome to Hell Week! Hope you all are ready because if you're not, too bad." He then sent them out to perform off the wall, extraneous assignments encouraging them to push themselves to levels never before imagined. As the team started the first assignment, jogging uphill, carrying a hundred-pound bag, a ten-mile run in the heat of the day, Rivera stayed next to them, riding along on a golf cart.

"Is that the best you can do people?" He pressed them to work harder.

Hell week was considered one of the worst forms of torture imaginable, which was what this organization considered a good method of weeding the babies from the best. It is a twenty-three hours a day, push you to your limits and keep you going, physical suffering, psychological torment and emotional anguish formed to mold a person into steel bending, strong as they come super agents who will be able to handle any situation ever thrown his or her way. You have to be able to show you can last in extreme cold and heat without showing any signs of weakness or shock. You have to be able to endure a capacity for hardship, the same that you would encounter in real world missions. This week is designed to discourage complete individualism, encourage teamwork and whack the competitiveness right out of your system.

When lunchtime passed by and they didn't stop, some men began to worry. When dinner time came and went and still they weren't allowed to stop, the rest of the class began to worry and when the lights went on and night was looming overhead and everyone expected they'd at least be able to stop for rest and they again weren't allowed to, some of the men began feeling they'd never be able to make it. About midnight, they were sent to their cabins. They were given one hour to eat, sleep, clean up, pray or whatever else they felt they needed to do to make it through this week. At one in the morning, as silent loomed throughout the field and everyone was asleep, the siren sounded waking everyone bringing them out for middle of the night field maneuvers. Aerobic activities first, jumping jacks, ten thousand pushups, and a billion steps of running in place until everyone was ready to collapse and when everyone was downright exhausted, they were given ten minutes to eat their morning rations before hitting the field again.

About eight that night a physician came out and gave a brief physical to everyone, making sure they were okay. About midday Wednesday many of the men were discouraged, the few that could feel the end of the week drawing near, were skeptical at best. They were trained to ignore distractions; react to commands either by codes or whistles. They had no choice on whatever they did, they had to accept the challenge and perform it. The students were highly competitive, trying to prove themselves to the CWO as well as the other men in the group. Trying to prove that they were the toughest, the strongest, and the most capable for the job. The competitiveness made them all work harder than necessary, but the competitiveness went even further than who the toughest man was. Being there was a female here, the men worked even harder than they were willing to; trying to show off. Kaitlyn was holding her own, keeping up with

15

the best of them, in fact she was surpassing a few men who were already struggling and falling behind. Tensions and emotions were high and it was everyone out for themselves.

"Alright ladies," Rivera began, "Today we're going to have a much easier day." The men smiled a little at hearing that. "Today we are going to do a bit of landscaping." He paused for effect. "You are going to go out into the woods over there, find good size rocks and put a nice outline down both sides of that road there." The team leader pointed as the men turned their heads to look. The road was easily 10 miles long. "The entire road. And I want it done by thirteen hundred."

The task seemed long and daunting but divided by twenty workers shouldn't have been that difficult, however, it got that way. The rocks weren't really heavy, they weighed 20-50 pounds apiece depending on the size. The larger the rock the less it would take to trim the road but the heavier it was to carry that distance from the woods. After a few hours of high paced walking and heavy lifting everyone began feeling the burn. The time went by quickly which brought to their attention that they'd need to work faster to be able to finish the task. By the time one o clock rolled around the task was done and the men were exhausted. They were dismissed to lunch and were directed to report back in half an hour. When they returned, the team leader was waiting.

"Good job ladies." He began, the men smiled. "Now put the rocks back." The mens eyes flipped to each other as they were certain they had heard wrong. Rivera continued. "I changed my mind, we don't want all these rocks cluttering the road edge, so take all of the rocks back to the woods and disperse them. I don't want to see large piles of rocks. And we'll need it done by the time the other classes return from their field maneuvers at sixteen hundred so get busy!"

Each day was filled with other daunting tasks, grueling physical projects that led to long arduous days. By the end of hell week, every muscle imaginable and even the muscles the team didn't know they had were sore but the excitement of the coming week and the knowledge of special assignments and specialized training was just around the corner seemed to get the men through it.

Kaitlyn however knew she'd be working one on one with Tom and she wasn't quite sure how to prepare herself emotionally for that. He had died, then he was alive, then she was angry at him and now she hadn't seen or talked to him all week and had absolutely no idea what he thought about this project. Had he suggested it? Did he want to work with her? They worked so well together, or did they? Kaitlyn remembered quite a few good times, so much love, so much passion... would it be like that again? Or had Tom changed? He seemed different when they met in the alley, he was certain they couldn't work together, he suggested transferring out of there. Kaitlyn figured he didn't have as nice memories as she did.

Of course they had bad times also, and their arguments were always overly emotional. Maybe it was because they were telepaths, maybe it was because of their history, but whenever emotion was involved, and it always was with the two of them, loud arguments were sure to follow. Would it be like that now, Kaitlyn pondered. She'd just have to go in with an open mind and an open heart and hope for the best. If he worked her she knew she'd enjoy it. If they proved to work well together, she knew things would be fine, but if he had any reservations going into it, she knew it would affect everything.

"Reporting for duty." Kaitlyn announced as she marched in the target room where Tom was setting up. Tom turned to face her, felt a smile start to spread across his face and quickly wiped it away. He was determined to make this professional pairing work and he had spent all week trying to push any emotions or feelings he may have out of his mind. He didn't want to mess this up for either of them and he knew that if they started arguing like they had a tendency of doing it wouldn't take long for the General to find out and that would not be ideal.

Tom took an automatic rifle in his right hand and secured it in his left palm and turned to face her.

"Colt M4 Carbine Automatic Rifle"

"I have had some weapons training." Kaitlyn said trying to show off as well as begin a conversation.

"Good for you." He said which made her half smile until he finished his thought. "However, the weapon training you got at the police force and secret service is child's play in regards to what I'm about to teach you. We've got a lot to get through in a short period of time. We've got weapons knowledge, weapons safety, timed weapons assembly, demolition tactics, land warfare, gun proficiency and tactical shooting, all with top secret weapons that don't technically exist."

"Cool." Kaitlyn smiled then repeated what Tom had started with "Colt M4 Carbine Automatic Rifle...

"5.56mm, lightweight, gas operated, air cooled magazine fed with a selective firing rate that can be sighted from the shoulder. Shoots 700 rounds per minute."

Kaitlyn nodded expectantly looking forward to firing it. Tom paused, tossed it to her which she caught with both hands, then Tom pressed a button on the table and timed target practice began with cardboard cutouts popping up at various levels and areas of the course. Kaitlyn took ten shots in twelve seconds then safetied the gun and stood at attention. Tom pressed another button to bring in the targets and noticed near perfect accuracy. He smiled. Kaitlyn tossed the rifle back to him, he turned, placed it back on the table and then turned back around with another gun in hand.

"TAC 308 Bolt Action Rifle..."

As Kaitlyn went through target practice, Tom reminisced. He remembered the day he first saw her after all those many years. The day of the presidents attack. Tom remembered that day well, he was fighting for his life, trying to keep his team safe, trying to take down the assassins and keep the secret service from killing him and his team. When Tom turned to fight the next threat, he realized it was Kaitlyn. His eyes caught hers for only a second as he hesitated, she swung at him, not knowing who he was and as he ducked he noticed an assassin behind her about to attack. Without thinking anything, he warned her telepathically that someone was behind her and when she turned to take down the assassin, he disappeared into the chaos.

He hadn't told Kaitlyn about that day, he wondered if she ever thought about it, if she figured out it was a telepathic message or if she simply thought it was someone verbally warning her. But now was not the time to prance down memory lane. Tom was in the process of training Kaitlyn and the task was exhilarating.

"Excellent."

"What else you got?" Kaitlyn smiled

Tom turned, faced the table for a moment making his next decision then picked up a rather large weapon and turned to face Kaitlyn.

"SACO MK-19 Automatic Grenade Launcher."

"Now that's what I'm talking about!" Kaitlyn smiled.

"To be worked up to."

Kaitlyn pouted. Tom smiled took the entire gun apart in record time then spoke.

"Timed weapons assembly."

"Kaitlyn went to work."

Each day Kaitlyn learned about new guns, new tactics, new techniques. Each day she thrived, enjoyed every moment of it. As they progressed from weapons knowledge to land warfare and the physical aspects of her job were brought into play she was truly in her field. Tom would show her a maneuver and she would duplicate it. As she graduated one aspect he would bring in the next. Before Kaitlyn knew it they were doing laser guided tactical maneuvers in the field against each other.

Tom was very good at what he did and Kaitlyn enjoyed thoroughly trying to live up to his expectations. She was truly excited about this but there was something missing. Something that always helped them meld into one psyche, become less like a team and more like an individual but Tom had not brought it up and Kaitlyn wasn't sure how to. She knew he hadn't forgotten how to but maybe without practice after all these years or not having a reason to use it he'd forgotten he could, but how would she bring up the telepathy and was it even a good idea?

As Tom began to explain the procedures for the next maneuver he could see that Kaitlyn was split, listening to him but thinking about something else. He paused for a moment, waited a second and when Kaitlyn realized he had stopped talking she spoke.

"Sir?"

"We're training the way every CovSec agent trains. Deviations of the supplied material are not..."

"Deviations? I'm not in a class of twenty. I'm doing one-on-one hand to hand combat with a Major. I'm pretty confident that that's a deviation right there."

"You know what I mean."

Kaitlyn stood there wondering for a second and then... "It's as if you were reading my mind."

"Well that's preposterous agent. People can't read other people's minds, it's a scientific fact."

"Hmm?" Kaitlyn hummed loudly as if she were trying to get him to say more.

"The procedures I train you will be the same as every other agent learns. Deviations of proven techniques will only get other agents killed if they can't 'read your mind'"

Kaitlyn realized with that she had her answer. No telepathy. Unfortunately, with that knowledge, she also realized Tom was not willing to go down any past memory lanes. She had hoped their working together again would draw out some of those past demons so they could work through them, but apparently Tom was not ready to do that... yet.

Tom and Kaitlyn seemed virtually inseparable to the rest of the team though. The other men had their opinions on the situation and with nothing much exciting to discuss on the training field, rumors and accusations were all they had as entertainment for the moment.

Working together all day and keeping it professional was very difficult for Kaitlyn. Each time their physical assignments would draw on a little longer than expected, Kaitlyn felt that emotion begin to build. She wanted him to hold her. She wanted to be in his arms, but he wanted to keep it professional. How could she keep it professional when all she wanted to do was kiss him? She shook it off. She had to.

She knew of only one way to keep from falling in love with him again. One way she could keep it professional with this man. Others weren't a problem. Others she didn't care for. But with Tom, the man she had loved, the man she wanted to get to know again with all of her heart and soul, she had to keep it platonic. The idea angered her. And that anger was exactly what she needed. Every time it seemed Tom held her in an attack stance for too long she pushed away. She was doing what she could to make sure they didn't grow close. To Tom, however, it had begun to get quite annoying.

He was spotting her for a (DTFS) double-twist-flip-shoot, a gymnastics-type move that would take her from a high area like a building or cliff, help her safely land on the ground, drop and roll, and then aim and shoot at the suspect. This was a move that she had pretty much gotten but Tom was being too particular on her dismount. He kept yelling at her about not placing her feet in the right place, that in a fight one false move and no matter how good you are, this move could crack your ankle. Kaitlyn however was growing more and more annoyed at him. She had performed the maneuver a dozen times now and she was growing tired of it. She was expressing her intolerance with attitude and Tom had seen enough of her insubordination. He walked up to her, still angry and grabbed her calf, lifting it up in the air and nearly knocked her off balance, she saved her balance, standing on one leg and began to yell at him.

"What the hell is your problem?"

"What the hell do you call this?" Tom countered still holding her leg up in the air.

"Assault!"

"I call this tacky, wasteful. I'm wasting my time training you! You just don't get it do you?"

Kaitlyn had heard enough by now. She took her free leg, the one she was balancing on and with a slight twist, jump twisted around and kicked Tom upside the head, making him let go of her leg and nearly fall over. Kaitlyn fell to the ground but immediately leapt back to her feet to ready herself for retaliation. After Tom saved himself, in non-thinking retaliation he swung a sharp hand at her to slap her down. She caught it in her face, but sent one right back at him. The both of them stopped and looked at each other, hate seething through their gritted teeth. Silence filled the room for a moment as the two of them collected themselves.

Tom was so angry he almost sent a punch her way but stopped, yet not before Kaitlyn reacted to block his punch. By then it had started all over again. Tom sent a retaliatory punch, she blocked and sent one back at him, before they knew it they were in a drag down fist fight, kicking, screaming and not too far into it, hair pulling and wrestling. They were beating each other up good, and Tom was beginning to win, he had Kaitlyn pinned to the mats and was about to finish her off when the general walked in.

"What the HELL is going on in here!!!!" He yelled at top voice acquiring Kaitlyn and Tom's attention. They looked up at him, Tom's hair still clutched in Kaitlyn's right palm his neck pulled awkwardly back. Tom had her pinned underneath him, her right leg and left arm pulled awkwardly behind her back. Slowly they let go of each other, and separated, then stood up.

"I repeat! What the HELL is going on?"

"We were… training sir. I guess things went a little too far." Tom answered nervously.

"A little too far? If I hadn't had walked in just now… what were you planning on doing with her Major, after you had her pinned down like that?"

"Nothing sir."

"Nothing? According to her bloody nose and the scratches on your face, arms and legs, it doesn't look like nothing Major. You sir are dismissed, I want you to report directly to my office I will deal with you later."

"But sir, we were…"

"I don't want to hear it Major. My office! Now!"

Tom nodded and left, looking more like a beaten tiger than a man who had been so angry earlier. Kaitlyn stood there not sure what to say or do, when the General walked up to her.

"Are you alright?"

"I'm fine sir. I can take care of myself."

"Is that right? What were you planning on doing just then if I hadn't walked in?"

"I could have gotten him off of me sir, granted it would have been difficult. However, if he would have been someone worth killing I would have done it by pulling just a bit harder on his neck until it snapped."

"I see. And why were the two of you fighting like that?"

"We've been under quite a bit of stress lately sir. Working almost non-stop for the past two weeks. He has his way of doing things I have mine. We were disagreeing with each other and things got a little out of hand." Kaitlyn explained honestly.

"I see." The General nodded. "And you are okay?"

"Yes sir, perfectly fine sir."

"Good. Now, I want you to realize something Agent Jones. Major M is in charge of training you. He has been through the program and you have not, so your way of doing things is a mute subject. The next time you get out of line or disrespect him or any other of our officers higher ranked than you, you will be penalized. Do you understand me?"

"Yes sir."

"Do you really understand that Jones?"

"Yes I do sir." She admitted bitterly realizing the truth wasn't quite the get-out-of-jail excuse she needed.

"I have given you quite some leniency since you came aboard because I can see your full potential, but if you can't accept the levels of leadership here, you have no place in this organization. Now I'll ask you again Jones, do you understand that?"

"Yes sir!" She answered like a true soldier. The general nodded and dismissed her to the showers. Then he left to go to his office. Once he entered Tom stood up and addressed him.

"General sir I should explain my actions."

"Major." He nodded as he shut the door. Tom started right in on the explanation he had been preparing.

"I take full responsibility for what happened this afternoon. It was my fault for letting things get out of hand and accept whatever punishment you deem necessary."

"Relax Major. She told me everything."

"She did?" Tom asked as he stood at attention. The general sat and motioned for Tom to do the same.

"My question to you Major is, do you think she is worth it?"

"Worth it sir?"

"She is insubordinate, a loud mouth, she has no concept of rules and regulations. She may not be worth our time in training her and I need to know from you is she worth it?"

Tom sat there stunned. Kaitlyn took the fall for their fight. She allowed herself to be penalized for his actions to what? Save his reputation, his job? He didn't know what to say.

"Sir, I haven't, I mean, I don't know her well enough to make that decision but what I do know is her potential greatly out numbers her mild down falls."

"Mild? Have you seen her on this base, she has this attitude about her. She gets on everyone's nerves, even the cooks! I have half a mind to shove a good helping of resolve down her throat to straighten her act out. The problem is the brass have seen her and love her spark. They think she's all that and a box of chocolates."

"Bag of chips."

"Major?"

"All that and a bag of chips. The box of chocolates was from Forest Gump."

"Whatever. All I need to know is can you continue training her without this abuse? I can't have my two best agents killing each other."

"We can work together." Tom assured as he half smiled. He hadn't thought about it much but all in all everything had come around full circle. They were once again being paired together and it made him feel warm. It didn't stay long though because he had to stay on track. The general finished what he had been saying with these simple words.

"I'll have my eye on you two!"

Later that night as Kaitlyn crossed the field to get to the cafeteria she saw from afar as Tom entered the cafeteria. She hadn't heard from him or anything from anyone else regarding the incident in the gym earlier that afternoon and was very curious to find out what happened. The fact that Tom was still here and she hadn't been punished any made her think everything was fine. As she entered the cafeteria she decided to rest her worries and go ahead and ask Tom about what had happened in the General's office. She walked up behind him in the line and struck up a conversation.

"So how did it go this afternoon?"

"What do you mean?" He asked as he turned to see who was talking to him.

"With the general? Did you get in trouble?"

"First off this isn't high school, I don't get in trouble, and I don't worry about getting detention. I am responsible for my actions and the actions of my trainees, not you! And I don't appreciate you down playing my authority to the General!"

"So I guess he was angry?" Kaitlyn said sarcastically as she looked around for the nearest exit.

"He had been considering transferring you out of here. Is that what you want?"

"Hell no. You know that."

"Well your attitude speaks volumes against that. He was ready to boot you out of here and I stopped him."

"Why? I thought that's what you wanted."

"It was."

"What changed?" Kaitlyn asked curiously.

"I did." He put his tray down and pulled her outside. He spoke to her quietly, almost in a whisper. "I realized you might have been partially right. All of these years I was telling you to grow up and actually I needed to do so as well. I'm sorry."

"No, you were right. Your sending me away did help. I realize now how foolish I was, how crazy I was acting back then, and how if you hadn't done what you did I would probably be dead or in jail. I owe you an apology."

"So we agree, we were both fools. Can we also agree to start fresh? If we're going to make this work there needs to be no foul issues between the two of us. We're supposed to not know each other shy of the day we met on this field and I think it best we keep it that way."

"I agree. So you want to go back inside and eat?"

"Yes, that would be nice."

Chapter 3

Unbeknownst to Kaitlyn and Tom, they were the gossip of the camp and the other guys from the formal training course. Everyone had their own duties but they all knew something special had been assigned for Major M and Agent Jones they just didn't know what, hence the gossip. Their almost too friendly training relationship gave for exciting conversation. So they added their own rumors to the speculation.

A guy and a girl, spending that much time together, touching one another during hand on hand training, couldn't keep things strictly platonic, especially since every guy there had had their own wet dreams about Kaitlyn. Sure there were other women there on the base but most of them made little to no effort accentuating the fact that they were women, in fact almost all of them tried so hard at being one of the guys that they began to look, act and even talk like one of the guys, which did nothing for their social life, if time ever gave way for that kind of thing.

As Kaitlyn and Tom returned to the cafeteria, a couple of the men at one table elbowed others at the table and spoke low.

"Amazing isn't it? How the Major there can have such a close relationship with a trainee and not be ridiculed from the brass?"

"The General paired them together for special ops."

"Yeah, great cover story, except it doesn't jibe." One of the guys added. "Jones is a trainee just like us, she should be in all of the same classes as us, and yet she has been pulled aside for 'special training' with the Major and no one questions this?"

"Sounds more like you are jealous of her."

"Maybe I am. I came here for special training. I want to leave here knowing all I can as I am sure all of you are as well, so why does she get special attention? Why does this female hang out with the Major?"

The friendship thing between Kaitlyn and Tom worked out well. They worked together, hung out together, laughed together, spent off time together and were quickly becoming the friends they once were. Although the closer contact seemed to bring up those old feelings of love, but each time that came up, they nuzzled them back down again as if they didn't exist. They weren't going to let things like that destroy the potential they both held dear here at CovSec.

However one night while they were out walking together, the moon was right, the stars were twinkling, and Kaitlyn's eyes met Tom's just right. He leaned in and kissed her without thinking and she accepted it tenfold. They held each other in that kiss for just a moment until he finally pulled away.

"I'm sorry."

"For what?"

"I shouldn't have done that."

"Why not?"

"Because we shouldn't be involved that way. It's not right."

"What's not right about it? You're a man, I'm a woman, and we've been in close contact with each other nonstop for four weeks."

"I know but look at what happened to us before." Tom inserted remembering all of the bad times they had in high school.

"What? It brought us closer together? Fulfilled our every fantasy? Connected us spiritually, physically and supernaturally? I remember a time when you told me it was natural, more than natural. You were afraid then, like you are now, but the reasons are different. You know the truth. You've just chosen to forget it."

"I haven't forgotten it. I don't think I could forget that if I wanted to, and trust me I don't." He smiled at her remembering every sensual night. "I just don't want to screw things up like last time." Kaitlyn looked at him and smiled.

"There was a time that I thought I would never get another chance to talk to you, to see you." She said referring back to the day she found out he was killed.

"I know. It was difficult."

"You have no idea how difficult."

"Actually, I do." Tom added with painful emotion.

"What do you mean?" Kaitlyn asked curiously. Tom paused wondering if this was the right time to tell her. Everything in his soul believed that it was.

"Well, contrary to what you may believe Kaitlyn, our love is stronger than…" He paused, how do I say this? He took a deep breath, "I really don't know how to put this except straight forward. I can feel your emotions."

"What do you mean by that?" Kaitlyn asked curiously, not quite understanding what he was saying.

"Many years ago, when we were in New York and we were arguing, something happened to me. I don't know how exactly or what really, but somehow you transferred to me telepathically all of your emotions. As we stood there arguing I suddenly felt your pain. I felt your sadness and hurt, your fears and your determination. I was able to, for the first time, feel exactly how you were feeling and I understood you. I became Empathic. I knew that I should have told you but you were already so angry with me I couldn't bring myself to say oh by the way I'm feeling your emotions now, hope you don't mind."

"Uh-huh." Kaitlyn hummed listening intently yet extremely curiously.

"When you were trapped in that house I felt your fear, I was able to figure out where you were and what you were doing through your emotions, enough so to find you and save your life."

"You said that I had contacted you."

"Technically, you did." Tom paused wondering how she was taking this but he had done such a good job at blocking those emotions from his mind that now he couldn't access them. He continued explaining. "When you found out about my death that day, I felt every ounce of pain, hurt, fear, anger and grief you had. I felt it all, experienced it just as you did."

"What do you mean? Did you cry when I did?"

"I was in control of my own emotions but I felt yours as if they were my own. You see, the morning you found out about my death, I felt your denial. I felt you deny it, and then I heard you as you tried to contact me telepathically on the side. I could sense you traveling to town your anxiety at returning to your hometown, continuing the attempts to contact me as you secretly felt when you arrived you would prove the papers wrong.

I felt your heart break when you got there, I felt every ounce of grief you had as you spent the night trying to figure out what you were going to say at the church the next day. And then that day," He paused remembering it well. "God, you have no idea what you did to me that day!" He paused tears whelping up into his eyes, but he sniffed them back, blinking frantically until there wasn't a threat of them coming.

"I had to put myself into solitary confinement to keep from breaking down in front of everyone! They would have thought I was nuts. The extreme amount of emotion you sent to me that day, nearly killed me, I can't even believe you survived, but I should have I guess. I felt the nervousness, the fear, the denial, the anger, then the breakdown. When your heart crumpled, so did mine. When you lost all control of your body, your lungs, your heart your tears, so did I. The pain was so unbearable I almost wished I *had* died. I earned a new found respect and admiration for you that day, and when you blacked out and the emotions stopped coming, I realized how strong you really were. And I fell in love with you all over again. The next most painful thing I ever had to deal with was keeping myself from contacting you then, and every other day after."

Kaitlyn fell silent. Tears were streaming down her face as she remembered that day, and when Tom was done he pulled her into his arms and he too broke down crying. Kaitlyn couldn't say a word; she suddenly realized just how strong their connection was as she too felt just a small bit of Tom's pain that very second. Kaitlyn couldn't deny her feelings any more. As they kissed again, this time she gave him her soul and as the night progressed they moved on to his apartment and closed the door.

She stood in front of him. Candlelight danced in the background. He held her close to him, delicately kissing her lips, then her nose then her eyes. She was completely relaxed, eagerly waiting to see what was going to happen next when he rolled his right hand through her hair. He then slid his left hand up her back until his entire forearm rested against the curvature of her spine. His palm spread and open, bracing her steady, his forearm leading her to his will. He pressed her body onto his. As her body straightened, her head slowly fell back, her eyes and lips opened just slightly. He kissed her again, leaving a longing on her lips for more, then proceeded down her neck.

He then slowly leaned her over the bed. Using his left arm as a one armed push-up he slowly brought both of their bodies onto the bed, stopping only once to pull her to the center ever so carefully. Then he leaned to his side, rested on his left elbow and began caressing her body again, leaving her in that state of utter longing and vulnerability. She never remembered him taking such utter care and protection of her; they had never made this kind of love before.

Ever so slowly, he touched her. Always kissing her with the gentlest of tongues, until she moaned, wanting more, wanting it all, and yet he was teasing her. He was tantalizing her, making her body crave him, wanting every part of him until finally she couldn't stand the wait any longer and she reached for him. That night there was no rest and as morning came, the dull orange light entering the room through closed shades, they finally fell asleep.

She was walking down the field looking carefully at a guest map and then up at the nearing buildings when she stopped. She looked up at the mid day sun and then down to her watch. She knew she was running late but that didn't help the fact that she just had to be lost. She was looking around for a guide when someone spoke behind her. "Can I help you?"

"I'm looking for the training office." Came the reply from a voice Kaitlyn knew oh so well.

"Susan?"

Susan turned and looked up from her map. "Kaitlyn? Oh my God!" Susan laughed as she went to hug her best friend. "What are you doing here?"

"Me? What are you doing here?"

"Well you know how I was in charge of procurement for that defense department?"

"I think so."

"And you know that machine I had been working on to help train others?"

"Kind of."

"Well they liked it so much they asked me to come up with more things for them."

"More of what?"

"Oh that's hush-hush you know. Top secret etc. It's silly but these government agencies like their cloak-and-dagger stuff."

"Well that's great." Kaitlyn smiled curiously. "So you're going to be here for a while?"

"Just the week, then I'm being transferred to the Denver office for instruction."

"Wow," Kaitlyn paused "That's pretty amazing." This was the kind of thing Kaitlyn never expected to happen. She knew Susan was doing well. She knew she had talent, but to be here, now, for that reason?

"So what are you doing here?" Susan stopped and looked at Kaitlyn up and down noticing something seemed different.

"Training for a top secret organization, I could tell you who they are but then I'd have to kill you." Kaitlyn smiled and Susan laughed.

"I can't believe we'd meet again here, at a place like this!" Susan exclaimed.

Just then Tom walked up. "You forgot your badge." He said as he handed it to Kaitlyn and then looked at Susan. Not recognizing her at first he watched her as her eyes widened and her mouth dropped open. Just then she leapt at him, wrapping her arms around his neck.

"Tom McKinney I can't believe it! You're alive? You're alive!"

Tom pushed her away and looked at her again. Panic filled him at first. He didn't know her but she knew him. She knew him well, but who was she? Then as she flicked her curly blonde locks and it surprisingly came to him. "Susan?" He said with pure shock.

"In the flesh."

"Well this is funny." Tom spoke with hesitation.

"Funny doesn't cover it, who would have thought we'd have a high school reunion right here in the middle of a top secret organization."

Just then Tom stiffened. "Why are you here?"

"Oh, well, as I was explaining to Kaitlyn I created this machine, well actually it's more of self defense training device but, oh I won't go all into it, besides I can't – the need for secrecy and all. Needless to say I'll be here through the week so we are going to have to get together." Just then Susan looked at her watch. "Oh man, I'm running late, do any of you know where the training office is?" Tom pointed to the building as Susan gave him another hug. "Oh I can't wait to practice my telepathy with you guys. This is going to be great!" Then she ran off.

Tom stood there dumbfounded for a moment, not having expected to see anyone he knew here, especially Susan of all people, the cheerleader... and then it hit him. "What did she just say?" He looked at Kaitlyn carefully.

"A lot of things, she talks rather quickly." Kaitlyn backed knowing this wasn't going to be good. Knowing exactly what Susan had said and it made her cringe at the idea that she said it out loud and that she said it in front of Tom.

"She wants to practice WHAT with us?" Tom's eyes closed hoping this was all just a bad dream.

"Tom now don't get upset."

"Kaitlyn, what is she talking about? Tell me I didn't hear what I thought I heard."

She could hear the panic in his voice. "Tom you were dead." Kaitlyn began trying to explain but she could sense his frustration and panic building by the millisecond. "I discovered she had the gift, we practiced together..."

"She's a... she's a"

"It shocked me too when I found out, I mean who would have thought Susan could use so much of her brain right?"

"Kaitlyn I can't even begin to fathom this..." Tom turned to walk away but couldn't move. His worst fears were coming back to haunt him and he couldn't even begin to understand the emotions that were flooding through him.

"She knows. She's one herself. She knows about the risks, she knows you never wanted anyone to know about you. I'm sure she wouldn't tell anyone."

"You're sure she wouldn't tell anybody? Kaitlyn she was the biggest gossip in school! You've damned us!"

"Tom you're over reacting. She's grown a lot over the years. She knows that this is serious."

"She talked about it out loud!"

"Tom take a breath. It'll be fine. Who's she going to tell? Who would believe her?" Kaitlyn attempted to play down the situation.

"Kaitlyn," Tom rolled his fingers through his hair. "I can't handle this. Take care of it." Then he walked away. As Kaitlyn watched him walk away she wondered what he meant. She was certain she just needed to emphasize to Susan how important it was for secrecy although the way Tom said that just now made it sound that he wanted her to kill Susan. Either way she had a pit in her stomach that just dropped.

That night as Kaitlyn was meeting Tom for dinner in the mess hall she received a telepathic transmission from Susan.

"Where you at?"

"Mess hall."

"Perfect I'll be there in a minute."

Kaitlyn spotted Tom and knew she had to tell him. She walked up to him quickly, grabbed his arm and pulled him to the side of the room. A few of the guys from their training group saw and began to talk amongst themselves.

"There they go again. You'd think they'd try to hide it better."

"It's as if they want to get caught."

"Have you noticed how lenient he is with her? Hell, I'd sleep with him too if I could get a break."

Just then they all noticed the Major yank his arm away from Jones and step back.

"Tom it's not that bad." Kaitlyn spoke quietly.

Everyone hushed and suddenly Tom realized they were making a scene. He quickly grabbed Kaitlyn by the upper arm and led her out of the building.

"Trouble in paradise." One of the guys said as everyone else began to talk amongst themselves.

"Well if it wasn't official before it is now, they are definitely involved."

"His first name is Tom?"

"Kaitlyn I told you to take care of it."

"I hadn't heard from her all day, I figure we could talk to her about it tonight and get it all straightened out."

"Kaitlyn I don't want..."

"Hey you two what's up?" Susan exclaimed as she pranced up to them.

"Hi Susan." Kaitlyn smiled shyly as Tom stood there in silence.

"Are we going in?"

"Susan we need to talk."

"Sure. About what?"

"About not talking."

"Oh, you mean the telepathy?" Susan said brightly. Tom turned and threw his hands up in the air.

Kaitlyn pulled Susan aside and whispered quietly. "You know how I told you that I don't want anyone else to know about me?"

"Yes." Susan said telepathically.

"Well Tom feels even more strong about that decision when it comes to him." Kaitlyn answered back telepathically.

"But why? I mean it's this great gift you should be able to share it with others."

Just then Tom cut in, hearing their conversation through his telepathy. "You can't trust others. You have no idea who will use the knowledge of this ability against you."

"Like how? Ooh, I'm going to talk you to death?"

"Susan this is serious." Kaitlyn spoke silently.

Just then CWO Rivera and another guy from inside the cafeteria walked out and saw Tom, Kaitlyn and Susan standing there staring at each other.

"You find that weird?"

"Not really." Just then Tom threw his hands up in the air and turned his back on the two females.

"You find that weird?"

"A little." Then Tom turned back around and flicked his hand against his head and up into the air. "Is his mouth moving?"

"Nope." Both men stood there for a moment watching the shenanigans when Rivera spoke one word. "Charades?"

"Sure, that'll work. I'm going to bed."

"Yeah, me too."

The next day during afternoon training Tom walked over to CWO Rivera and nodded his greeting.

"Major M. sir, how may I assist you?"

"Just supervising. Proceed."

Rivera perked up and barked out his next orders to the class.

38

Kaitlyn was doing everything she was told to do, performed her tasks properly and to the best of her ability, but towards the end of class she noticed that Tom was talking to Rivera quietly. The next thing she knew Tom barked out her name so loudly it made her jump. "Jones!" He spoke as he watched her jump then leap to her feet to salute him. "What kind of push-ups do you call those?" He asked as she stood there.

"Sir?" Kaitlyn questioned thinking, they're just push-ups.

"Your form is off, your back's not straight and your knees were bent. Fifty more done properly this time."

"Sir yes sir." Kaitlyn answered and resumed doing flawless push-ups.

As she began, Tom kneeled down in front of her to watch as he struck up a telepathic conversation.

"You've been wanting this haven't you?"

Kaitlyn found herself start to pause but realized she needed to continue performing those push-ups, Tom was trying to distract her and she knew it.

Tom telepathically spoke again, "I expect you to answer me when I ask you a question."

"Yes sir." Kaitlyn said back telepathically.

With a loud booming voice Tom yelled out, "You just bent your knees again, add ten more to that!"

Kaitlyn said nothing aloud but spoke telepathically. "Are you testing me?"

"Damn straight." He answered quietly. "You think this Susan thing is harmless? Just wait until you are in the middle of something really important and she butts into your mind with a perky, hey what's up?"

"I don't see what the big deal is." Kaitlyn countered.

"What is that?" Tom yelled aloud, "Slouching shoulders? Ten more!" Then he added telepathically, "That's what the big deal is. You can't speak telepathically without it interfering with your bodily tasks."

"It's not interfering, a little slouched shoulder is not a big deal."

"You did it again," He barked, "Ten more!"

Kaitlyn paused angrily.

"Problem Jones?"

"No sir!" She bellowed then resumed her flawless push-ups.

"If you were lining up your sights with a target and only had one shot, was in the process of squeezing the trigger when you were contacted and it put you in the slightest disarray and you missed the shot that could be a huge problem. If you insist that this Susan thing is not a big issue then prove to me now in front of all of these men watching that you can have a telepathic conversation with me without it affecting one single muscular structure in your body besides your brain."

"Fine." Kaitlyn thought.

"Ten more!" Tom yelled aloud.

"Tell me your rank." Tom spoke silently.

"Special Agent Kaitlyn Jones."

"Sloppy, ten more!" He barked.

"What is the general's last name?" Silently.

"Harrison."

"I saw your elbow flicker Jones!" He barked aloud. Then silently; "What does the CWO stand for?"

"Chief Warrant Officer." She came back telepathically.

"Keep your shoulders straight!" He yelled aloud. He could see Kaitlyn was becoming tired but he was trying to prove a point.

"What does CovSec stand for?"

"Covert Security, sir." Kaitlyn answered silently focusing on her form as she did.

"Better." Tom spoke silently. "Rounds and Feed System of a Beretta M9 Pistol."

"Fifteen nine-millimeter rounds."

"Did I see some hesitation?" He asked aloud.

"No sir!" Kaitlyn answered aloud, her elbows shaking ever so slightly.

"Ten more!"

"Give me the specs of a Heckler & Koch HK XM25 IAWS." He spoke silently.

"The HK XM25 Individual Air-burst Weapon System is a semi-automatic, multi-shot, shoulder-fired 25mm grenade launcher categorized as an "air-burst weapon" system designed to neutralize out-of-view targets."

"Better. Go on."

Kaitlyn continued her push-ups throwing extreme focus on them as she paused mentally to collect her thoughts on the weapon in question. "Twenty five by forty millimeter grenade, four round magazine with a sixteen hundred and forty foot effective range and has a delayed munition detonation capability."

"Good focus, I heard a delay in your response though. "Sights?"

"Thermal and Optical."

"Good job." Tom spoke silently with a little aggressive funning mixed into his thoughts. "All right Jones, finish up those push-ups then report to my office when you are done." Tom spoke aloud while he resumed a standing position.

"Sir, yes sir." Kaitlyn spoke not faltering on her push-ups.

"You may resume CWO Rivera."

"Thank you sir. Anytime you want to terrorize my men be my guest."

Tom smirked at that as he walked away.

About half an hour later Kaitlyn walked in through the door to Tom's office. "Jones, good. Close the door." Kaitlyn did so as Tom spoke telepathically, "And lock it."

Kaitlyn did so as Tom stood from his desk and walked over to her. He pulled her into his arms and kissed her passionately on the lips. She wrapped her arms around his neck and lifted herself onto his pelvis. He wiped the office supplies from his desk with one arm and laid her down upon it. He quickly removed her shirt as she worked on unbuttoning his pants. They were making hot passionate love on the desk when there was a knock at the door about ten minutes later.

"Major, are you in there?" His secretary called through the door.

"I'm busy right now." He spoke through deep breaths still going at it wildly with Kaitlyn.

"I understand sir, but the General is out here and he'd like to have a word with you sir."

"Oh, shit." Tom whispered as he fell off of Kaitlyn who was busily trying to find her pants and shirt. Tom called out through the door. "Just a minute." He quickly tried to get dressed, but then he realized all of his office supplies had been thrown to the floor. He quickly tried to pick them up, replacing the phone, a legal pad, and his nameplate. But it had taken too long.

"Major M! I don't like waiting!" The general voiced angrily. And a moment later Tom and Kaitlyn heard keys in the door and then the door swung open. As the General walked in, Tom dropped his pen holder and Kaitlyn clutched her shirt closed. The both of them looked shocked, guilty and were completely speechless. The general stared for a moment, noticed the sweat on Tom's desk and Kaitlyn's bra in the corner. It didn't take a genius to figure out what was going on. Finally he spoke to Kaitlyn.

"Thirty seconds. Get yourself put back together and then leave." He turned and slammed the door closed behind him and Tom and Kaitlyn stood there still in shock for a moment longer. Then Kaitlyn looked at Tom with eyes opened wide. "Oh God!"

"It'll be all right."

"What's going to happen?"

"Not sure." Tom admitted as he squatted down to the floor to gather his supplies. Kaitlyn bent over to help him clean up his office, but he took her by her arm and pulled her up.

"I'll get it. You should finish getting dressed and go. The less time you're in here the better." Kaitlyn nodded, but was still worried about the consequences. What was going to happen? Would they be punished? Separated? Kicked out? Or worse yet was Tom going to be angry with her?

As Kaitlyn walked out the door, the General just glared at her, his stare following her as she walked straight through the office and out of the building. Then the General walked into Tom's office and closed the door. Tom was still scrambling to straighten up when the General spoke.

"How long has this been going on?"

"This is the first time." Tom lied.

"Was it good for you?"

"Sir?" Tom asked, very uncomfortable with the question.

"Was it good?"

"Yes?" He said questioningly, still wondering where the general was going with this line of awkward questioning.

"Are you asking me or telling me?"

"Um, telling you sir?"

"Good. Because it was the last time." The general spoke with such sureness it made Tom's heart sink.

"But sir!"

"She'll be shipped out of here in the morning."

"No! Why?"

"I've seen what these kinds of relationships do to agents. It impairs your judgment and gets people killed in the line of duty. We can't take that risk."

"But sir…"

"That is the end of it Major!"

"No it is not!" Tom back-talked standing up at his desk, his palms flat on top of it.

"I beg your pardon?" The General stood anger seething through his teeth.

"It won't happen to us sir."

"I can't take that risk Major and you know it."

"Then I'll leave. Don't punish her."

"Can't take that chance, she is a liability to any of our men. She has to go."

"How about a compromise?"

"Major I've made my decision."

"A simulated test, I've seen them done. Put us together in it. If at any time one of us flounder and doesn't go by regulations or if one of us ends up getting killed in the drill, then the both of us will leave. No questions asked."

The general stood there for a moment. "You believe in her that much do you?"

"I trust her with my life, completely!" Tom said surely.

The general looked at Tom for a moment and thought about this. "You'd bet your career on her?"

"Yes sir."

"Is she worth it?"

"Everything and then some."

With hesitation, the General relented. "All right Major, tomorrow morning 6am. Two hour simulation, laser tag design, either one of you screw up and you're both out of here."

"Thank you sir."

"Don't thank me yet Major, you are the ones who have to do this."

As Kaitlyn made her way across the field to her room Susan called to her telepathically.

"What are you doing?"

"Susan now is not a good time."

"Why? What's going on?"

Kaitlyn didn't want to tell her so she changed the subject. "What do you want?"

"I think I have just done something exceptional but I think Tom's going to be a bit angry about it."

"Join the club." Kaitlyn came back.

"What?"

"Nothing. What did you do?"

"I think we should meet."

Kaitlyn peered at her watch then sighed. "Okay, where are you?"

Later that night Tom went to Kaitlyn to tell her the news. Kaitlyn was sitting on her bed but she wasn't in the mood for anything fun. She had been frazzled about what had happened in his office all afternoon and was even more stressed out about what Susan had told her. He could tell by her face that she needed some good news and quick so he jumped right into it.

"Good news and bad news."

"What's the good news?"

"Most people want to know what the bad news first."

"I'm not most people."

"Good news is, he's not going to kick us out of the base, yet."

"What's the bad news?"

"That is if we pass the simulation test tomorrow morning."

"No problem, I've run that test a dozen times."

"Yeah, but not with every guy on the base shooting at you."

"Every guy on the base? That would be almost two hundred men!"

"Yeah, the thing is; it's a live laser simulation. It's like our FTX Final Training Exercise. We have to make it through the course wearing full body gear and gun and we have to do it on a timed strategy. Catch is, if we screw up, get shot or cause the other person to foul up we're going to be booted out of here fast. The both of us."

"No stress, I like that." Kaitlyn half smiled.

"I know we can do it."

"I know. I just wish we didn't have to." Kaitlyn was still worried about what Susan had told her but knew she needed to face one challenge at a time. If she and Tom were kicked out Susan's news would be meaningless, so the plan was to deal with tomorrow and when that was over, then decide if she should tell Tom the other news.

The next morning everyone seemed ready to do this. The men had been informed that it was a special assignment and to give no mercy. Kaitlyn and Tom were then given their weapons; they geared up, and were given the lowdown on the route to take.

"Your task today should you choose to accept it, is simple. It's your traditional LTPMAS, Locate Target, Perform Mission and Arrive Safely. At the end of this ten-mile course is a prisoner. This prisoner is being held by twenty men with whom you will need to distract or deactivate in order to free the prisoner. Then you must safely return the prisoner back here, otherwise known as head quarters. If you, your partner or the prisoner in anyway gets hurt or killed, marked by the laser, your mission will be over and the before mentioned consequences will be enforced. Is this clear to you?"

Kaitlyn and Tom both answered in unison, "Yes sir."

Then the gun was shot and the simulation began. Kaitlyn and Tom ran towards the hurdles and prepared for the guerrilla warfare to begin. Once they saw an opportunity they took it. A shot was fired at them and they took their shot on cue. Moving through the obstacle course one hurdle at a time, covering each other, and taking out men one at a time, they worked together perfectly. If a man tried to run up to them, they tackled that man down; one by one they merged towards the center of the field. And then suddenly the stakes grew; a hundred men in military gear came charging down the hill towards Kaitlyn and Tom. The both of them split up and took defensive maneuvers keeping in close contact with each other via telepathy.

Men came to the left, to the right, Kaitlyn shot like a pro, but quickly was backed out of her hideout and was flushed to the front, but she fought like it meant everything which it did. She leapt to the top of a tall boulder and shooting her laser, knocked man after man out of the game, then as she saw they were nearing her, she performed the DTFS that Tom had trained her, getting herself out of the line of sight for a gun and placing herself on the ground at just the right angle to aim and shoot, knocking out three other men before she ran behind a boulder where she waited. As two men charged over, she shot the both of them down and then scrambled to a new place.

Tom on the other hand had taken the initiative to be forward, he ran right into the crowd knocked down ten men, used their bodies as a live body shield and shot himself another twenty before dropping the body and running for cover. He then leapt behind a rock, spun around like he was racing for the base on a baseball game and shot out four more rounds, dropping four more men.

Men were dropping like flies as their sirens suits were binged by the laser. Men walked off the course feeling ashamed at getting shot so quickly into the course, but laughing at the others who didn't last as long as they did. Everything seemed completely crazy, bodies were moving all over the course and Kaitlyn and Tom were having a tough time keeping up, but they were doing good. Damn good.

As they neared the end of the course, arriving on time and together just shy of the prisoner depot they quickly and silently motioned out a game plan. From a quick glance they could see that the twenty guards posted around the depot were split up as five men per side, four sides. Tom decided to take the sides and the back and clear out the men from the darkness of the forest, Kaitlyn's task was a little more forward. She ran out of the forest, her gun and hands held high in the air as she screamed in utter terror.

"Cougar! Wild Cougar in the forest! Chasing me!"

Suddenly and just like she assumed, the men took a defensive move, aiming their guns to shoot the animal, defending one of their teammates, defending a woman. Kaitlyn ran right past them, dropped and shot all five of the men before they knew what was happening, then she walked inside just in time to see Tom clearing the wall and landed right next to her. They pulled the prisoner from the prison depot then began calculating existing enemies.

"How many shots have you taken?" Tom asked as he pointed to Kaitlyn's gun. She quickly glanced at it, did the math and spoke.

"Seventy two, at least eighty percent hit." She said explaining that she had taken seventy-two shots and out of that eighty percent of those shots were hits or approximately 58 men down. Tom quickly did his estimates and spoke.

"I've gotten about one hundred and five, leaving approximately thirty-seven men remaining, they'll be hiding waiting for us before they strike, keep your eyes open and alert.

"Yes sir!" Kaitlyn said as she ran slightly behind the prisoner in order to watch the prisoners back. As Tom heard a laser shot sound, he yelled for Kaitlyn and the prisoner to get down, Kaitlyn leapt atop the prisoner to shield him from any flying debris. Then they quickly ran at a crouched position into the forest for cover. Tom took control of the prisoner this time and Kaitlyn took the lead and as she led them through the forest Tom noticed something out of place. A trap had been set for them and he quickly warned Kaitlyn about it telepathically. Kaitlyn looked around, she saw the string and trigger device and quickly disarmed it, then yelled clear. They were making great time and were just about through the forest when Kaitlyn got a flash.

Immediately sensing that a tree was starting to fall and that Tom and the prisoner were in its fall path she yelled.

"Tom look out!" At the same time raising her hands and without thought sent out a telekinetic pressure plate that caught the tree and paused it in mid fall. Tom had just turned to see the falling tree with a punch of adrenaline and fear he hesitated then saw it pause. He turned towards Kaitlyn as his body tugged at the prisoner to roll out of the way and in seeing Kaitlyn holding up the tree's fall with telekinesis rolled towards her and bumped her as he cleared thus making the telekinetic pressure pause enough for the tree to continue its fall.

"What the hell was that?" Tom yelled into her face.

"I don't know! It just happened!"

"We'll discuss it later!" Then Tom grabbed the prisoner and continued through the forest leading the way.

The prisoner, however, Lieutenant Todd Butcher could not forget what he had just witnessed. Everything was happening exceptionally fast and there could have been anything that kept the tree from falling those few nanoseconds, but he couldn't erase Tom's voice from his mind when he overheard Tom yell at Kaitlyn. Sure it could have easily been a captain yelling at his subordinate for triggering the release of the trap but not even Todd had seen the trigger and there was something about the way Tom had yelled at her and the particular words that he had said that made Todd Butcher wonder if there was something more to this woman that everyone else didn't know.

Finally it was down to five men, and three hundred feet. They were playing like it was real, moving in carefully, sending signals to the others to move around to the side all the while adding telepathic additions to the plan.

"They're surrounding us, we may need to fight hand to hand."

"No problem, bring them on." Kaitlyn yelled. Just then she heard the yelling call of a man charging her way. She leapt out towards the sound, and pounced on him, knocking the gun from his hand and slamming down the manual button on his suit knocking him out of the game, but as she was doing that another guy ran up behind her, grabbed her by the neck and spun her around facing Tom, he poked out from behind the wall ready to shoot but stopped when he saw Kaitlyn. He knew the three other men weren't far behind, so when Kaitlyn telepathically told him she had this one, he back peddled and slipped back behind the wall taking the prisoner with him in his care.

"What?" Todd spoke quickly. "You're not going to help her?"

"She can get out of that. We'll meet her by the jeep." He answered surely and then took a quick glance in both directions and ran them towards the jeep.

"Show yourself or she dies!" the man called out, but before he could really finish what he was saying, Kaitlyn had taken his arm into hers, twisted him over her shoulder and stomped the manual switch down knocking him from the game. She then too progressed towards the jeep knowing the plan well.

Tom on the other hand was fighting off two other guys, from behind the jeep door as he drove it towards Kaitlyn, as he neared her she quickly dove aboard atop the prisoner and got into position to take down the remaining two men who were running after them. When those two lasers were sounded and they ceased their pursuit, Kaitlyn and Tom gave each other a high five in congratulations to each other for a job well done.

Their final task was to transport the prisoner from the jeep to the other side of the finish line where they would be safe and although they were pretty sure they had gotten all of the men they both knew that in a real world mission there could always be more men waiting and they couldn't guess the job was over until they knew for sure it was over. They drove the jeep to the end of the dirt road and were about to get out and take the final steps when Kaitlyn got a premonition of the very last guy, aiming and just about to shoot at them. She crouched down behind the jeep door just as she sent a telepathic message to Tom to do the same, he grabbed the prisoner and leapt out of the way just before the laser whizzed by him.

Then the man charged out to find them and that's when Kaitlyn and Tom simultaneously leapt out of the jeep, knocked the gun from the guys' hand and knocked the button down, sounding the last siren marking the end of the demonstration.

The general walked up to Tom and Kaitlyn and congratulated them on a job well done. "You've earned your part here, we'll discuss the other things later." Tom and Kaitlyn hugged each other and as the two of them celebrated their job well done all of the other men came in to show how impressed they were.

Chapter 4

Later that night, after Tom had gone to sleep, Kaitlyn walked to the locker room shower and began to clean up from the days' activities. As she finished up, grabbing a towel and wrapping it around her body, Todd Butcher walked in.

"Glad I caught you Jones."

"Butcher." Kaitlyn acknowledged him as she began to walk to her locker.

"I want to know how you did that on the field today."

"Did what?" Kaitlyn asked without paying much attention to him.

"That tree was falling and you stopped it." Kaitlyn heard him but pretended not to be paying attention.

"What?"

"That tree, you stopped it from falling on us."

She played like he was nuts. "You must have been seeing things Todd, maybe you've got a bit of PTSD."

"Oh I was seeing things. I was seeing things very clearly." He walked up to her, and got right into her face. "I've figured you out." Kaitlyn stepped back a step not quite sure what this guy thought he had figured out or what exactly she should say about it. He continued. "Your partner and you worked well on the field today, almost like you had been partners for years, reading each others' minds…"

"Reading each others…? That's ridiculous." Kaitlyn scoffed nervously.

"No you stopped the tree from falling, I saw it."

"I never touched the tree Todd, in fact even if I was close enough to grab the tree, I wouldn't have been able to stop it from falling." She said as she quickly slid her shorts on. The towel still wrapped around her chest.

"No it was like… like telekinesis, you put your hands up and the tree just stopped falling. I was there, I saw it!"

53

"Todd listen to yourself, that sounds ridiculous, I stopped the tree with my mind, when was your last mental evaluation?" Kaitlyn said as she took her bag of clothes and began to head to some place private to dress. But Todd was getting angry.

"You calling me a liar?" He said as he grabbed her arm and yanked her back in front of him. Kaitlyn wasn't sure what would convince this guy to drop the subject and she could tell he was getting overly aggressive. She knew she needed a higher ranking officer in here to make Butcher stand down so she quickly sent a telepathic SOS to Tom to help her out.

"Tom, I have a situation in the locker room." Tom woke and realized Kaitlyn wasn't lying next to him and quickly slid on his pants and ran out of the cabin.

"I want the truth!" Butcher yelled out as he pushed Kaitlyn backwards into the showers. She nearly slipped on the wet tiles but kept her balance, however Butcher was becoming ever more agitated.

"Butcher stand down! You touch me again and I'll…"

"You'll what? Throw me across the room with your mind?"

"You are nuts! I'm reporting you to the general!" Kaitlyn said as she began to push her way past him, but he grabbed her and began trying to hold her there.

"You're not going anywhere until I get some answers!"

"Let me go!" Kaitlyn yelled back as she fought to remove his hands from her body. But he wouldn't let go, she pushed him away but he grabbed her again. He slapped her, and as she fumbled backwards she slipped on the wet floor and fell on her butt. She started to recuperate, but then he grabbed at the knot on her towel and ripped her up towards him, loosening the knot on the towel. As the towel was yanked off she spun around and fell back to the floor on her hands and knees. Butcher threw the towel to the right and went for her hair.

"Get up!" But he lost his footing on the wet tile himself and fell to the floor as well. His unsteadiness and tight grip on Kaitlyn's hair knocked her face into the floor, making her nose bleed. He then crawled on top of her and rolled her over onto her back. Kaitlyn began to panic, trying everything to get him off of her, her struggle only made him angrier and from on top of her he began trying to grab her wrists and constrain them. Kaitlyn began screaming as Tom ran into the locker room just in time to see Butcher reach for Kaitlyn's throat. Tom leapt for Butcher, tackled him like a line backer and knocked him off of Kaitlyn. Three powerful punches to Butchers face knocked him out then Tom turned towards Kaitlyn who was still lying there on the floor. Her shorts not buttoned, topless, her arms slightly covering her chest as she lay there trying to get her nose to stop bleeding.

Just then three other men ran into the locker room after hearing Kaitlyn's scream. They stopped just in time to see Tom get off of the comatose Butcher and reach for a towel to cover Kaitlyn. He laid the towel over Kaitlyn, blocking her from the others view and then told them to apprehend Butcher and take him to lock-up. Then after the men dragged Butcher out of the building Tom spoke to Kaitlyn.

"Are you all right? What happened?"

"I, I don't know. One minute I was about to dry off the next Butcher came in and started asking me questions."

"What did he want? What did he say to you?"

"He wanted to know how I stopped the tree from falling today."

"The tree?"

"He swears he saw it stop in mid air, but I kept telling him he imagined it."

"What did he say about it?" Tom asked nervously.

"That he's figured me out."

Tom sat back for a second hundreds of worries and concerns filling his head, and then he asked another question. "How did you get on the floor?"

"It was so crazy, he was asking me questions then he was throwing me around."

"Why didn't you fight back?"

"I tried, it all happened so quickly I couldn't keep up with it. I slipped on the wet tile, he slipped…."

"You're stronger than he is why didn't you push past him? Kick him away from you?"

"I tried, but I was in shock. I mean I never expected that from him.. I never expected those questions. I was half naked and felt vulnerable because of it, and all I was thinking about was trying to calm him down and make him forget what he saw."

"Vulnerable? Granted you were feeling compromised but, we trained against that. You shouldn't have felt that way."

"Well I did, I don't know why." Suddenly Tom's face went from concern to disappointment to pure anger. He walked up to her, grabbed her arms in his palms and nearly shook her.

"You listen to me Kaitlyn Jones. You have got to get past that vulnerable place. This isn't high school and you aren't in the choir room any more. You are stronger and more capable than any man out there and you know that. Those emotions make you weak. Those emotions will get you killed. You have got to block those at all cost."

"I know." Kaitlyn stumbled with her voice. Then he pulled her into his arms and held her, apologizing quietly.

"I'm sorry. I didn't mean to yell."

"Don't be. I'm angry with myself. I don't understand what happened. I know I was shocked but I don't understand why I couldn't fight back. I learned how to fight, to defend myself to keep myself from ever getting into that kind of situation, and here I freeze like an ice cube."

"I'm going to break you of that Kaitlyn. I haven't spent all of this time with you, to lose you to some crazed mad man."

The next day Kaitlyn and Tom were to work on more maneuvers but Tom had other plans. Tom walked in the gym the next morning wearing a paper name tag with one word on it, Jed, the name of the guy who had sexually assaulted Kaitlyn in high school.

"Tom…" Kaitlyn said disapprovingly as she noticed the name tag.

"The names Jed."

"Take that off." Kaitlyn demanded pointing towards the name tag.

"Why? It bother you?"

"No. It's just stupid."

"Then get over it. I'm Jed today, and you're going to fight me off or get brought down." He walked up to her, anger in his eyes, a type of anger Kaitlyn had never seen from him before. He backed her into a wall and pinned her there.

"Tom I'm not ready for this."

"The names Jed baby..." He leaned in and invaded her space with his body.

"Tom stop!"

"You can't stop me, you can't fight me. Give into me."

"No!" Kaitlyn yelled as she tried to push him away, but she couldn't find her strength, she knew it was Tom and she knew she had to fight back, it was the assignment, but she couldn't. She had her palm pressed against his chest trying to push him back, but not able to put any strength behind it. She tried to collect all of the strength in her entire body but it felt as if it had all disappeared, she had no strength, at all.

Tom's warm breath soaked her face as he grabbed her upper arms and pinned them to the wall. He pulled them together and held them up over her head with one hand as he roughly rubbed his hand down her breast trying to get her riled up. But even though she was trying to free her hands, yanking on them, he could feel her wrists tugging but there was no strength in it. She was trying to fight back but her strength was gone and she couldn't fight. She felt as weak as a kitten, she tugged to free her wrists but her arms felt like spaghetti. She felt so incredibly vulnerable, she started to cry. "Tom please stop. Please."

He finally let her arms go free and stepped back watching her crumble to the floor crying. He stood there looking at her, speechless. He brought his hand up in front of his face, almost in shame, speechless, then slid it up on top of his head. He had no idea how messed up Kaitlyn had actually been because of that guy. He looked down at the name tag on his chest, then ripped it from his shirt, crumpled it in his hand and threw it to the floor angry at himself for doing that to her. He had hoped to retrieve a spark of anger, to make her want to fight back, to teach her how easy it was to take control of an uncomfortable situation but she hadn't been able to even start. Just the name had set her off.

"Kaitlyn stand up." He spoke again, this time using his demanding majors voice.

"She wiped her tears and slowly began to get up."

"What was going through your mind just now?"

"I'm not sure." She sniffed.

"Be sure. What were you thinking? Why wouldn't you fight back?"

"I tried. I tried but I couldn't. I just couldn't. I lost all will to fight."

"Why?"

"The strength it just left me." Kaitlyn sniffed then continued. "I suddenly felt so helpless, scared and when that happened the strength just disappeared, it was just gone."

"Then get angry. I know you; you are strongest when you are angry. Get angry that a man thinks he can overpower you. Be furious that he thinks nothing more of you than a toy."

"But Tom I…"

"Scream into his face that you are not one to be messed with and then show him! Beat him up! Punch him, slap him, kick him! Fight back! Fight for yourself! Fight for every woman out there who isn't lucky enough to have your strength and agility! And then teach that creep a lesson!"

"Tom I wish I could but I…"

Tom wasn't going to take her weaseling out of this one. He knew her too well to believe she couldn't get through this hurdle. He also knew if she couldn't get past this – today – she'd never get passed it. He needed her to be strong, he needed her to be brave and he needed her to work past this because he needed her in his life. He charged up to her. "Fight back." He pushed her into the wall, her back hit it hard and she shuddered then he yelled again. "Push me back!" She stepped away trying to avoid eye contact. She wasn't ready for this yet, her emotions were still stuck on fear and helplessness. He took her chin into his hand and pointed her face to his. "Disappointment!"

"What?" Kaitlyn asked upset.

"Disappointment! Weakling!" He said hoping name-calling would get her angry enough to fight back.

"I just can't get…" She began but he interrupted her again.

"Pathetic! You can't even stand up for yourself! How can I expect you to defend others?"

"I can! I just can't be…"

"Do you want to be used?"

"No." She said still crying.

"Do you want to be abused?"

"No." She said again, sniffing the tears back.

"You want every man who sees you to think only of you as a toy?"

"No!" She said thinking that was disgusting, thinking he was getting off base.

"Because that's what they'll think!"

"I'm not!"

"Then prove it!"

"Tom I…" She tried to give an explanation again but the time for explanations had past.

"Prove it! Are you someone?"

"Yes!"

"Are you worth listening to? Fighting for?"

"Yes!"

"Then do something about it! Fight back!" He pushed her again, making her angrier.

"Don't push me!" She said gritting her teeth.

"Fight back!" He pushed her again.

"Tom don't!" She yelled again still taking another step backwards but Tom noticed her fists balling up.

"Fight back! Prove to me you are worth being here!" He pushed her again, this time harder. She finally pushed back, but not nearly hard enough to show him her anger. He pushed her again.

"Woosie! Fight back!" He pushed her again, this time very hard; she pushed back with the same strength continuing her rampage.

"Back off!"

"Don't tell me, show me! Fight back!" He pushed her again, knocking her into the wall. She stepped forward but he pushed her into it again. "Fight back!"

Finally, the anger had built, true anger, near fury was boiling up from her chest. Using the wall as leverage she pushed herself away from it, her hands palmed out, ready to push him backwards with all of her might and with full force of her body and the anger in her mind, she sent a thrust of pure energy towards him that rocketed him across the room. Thirty five feet away, he landed on his back and slid another ten feet backwards across the smooth tile floor before slowing to a stop. When Kaitlyn saw him she grew concerned and snapped out of it.

"Tom! Are you all right?" She asked as she ran and kneeled down next to him. He smiled as he sat up.

"Now that's my girl." She hugged him, and helped him back onto his feet.

That afternoon they spent extra time working on this new found weakness of Kaitlyn's. All Tom knew was he refused to allow her to go out there with any ounce of helplessness, ever again.

Over the final weeks of training everyone was given a special ops critique where they were taught many things relating to the spy business that would benefit them before they were given their first assignment. It went fast and furious but what they learned; they knew, would prove to be helpful to them in the future.

"In this class I'll be instructing you on how to use your brain and not your brawn. CWO Rivera announced. By now you all should know that this is not a job but a game. It is a very serious and dangerous game, one you don't get a second try at, one you don't want to lose so I will teach you the tricks

61

to keep you winners. Like when you enter a room, what's the first thing you do? Locate the exits. Catch the side lines, locate everyone in the room, memorize what they look like, what they are wearing, question anything that looks out of place and what doesn't concern you, disregard. It's called SAD, you See it, Assess it and Dismiss it, all of this should take no more than three seconds."

"Three seconds to do all of that?" One of the men spoke up without realizing he was speaking. Rivera kept speaking though.

"You will learn how to do this as easy as breathing, thinking as quick as a heart beat without even the knowledge of doing it. It's a trade craft, one you will get so good at you'll be unstoppable or one that will get you killed on your first mission, it's your choice. You need to be able to get into places without trying, without looking like you wanted to. You'll need to be able to pry pertinent information out of people without lying to them; giving them any information or making them suspect you. You'll need to use the items around you to your advantage. All of those James Bond movies with the lasers in the pen and the remote control cars, we've got them, but you won't need them when I'm through with you. Any questions?"

Before Kaitlyn knew it training was over and assignments were appropriated. Agents were being transferred to new task forces and agencies across the country. Kaitlyn and three other men from their group had been sent to CovSec's main headquarters in the deserts of New Mexico. They were given titles of secret agent lieutenants and given the lowdown on many of the criminal masterminds, terrorists and drug lords CovSec was in charge of following, tracking and taking down in the area. Things were about to get very exciting. Kaitlyn was looking forward to this more than anything but she still thought about what Susan had told her. She knew their secret was safe with her, at least she hoped it was, but Kaitlyn had determined that if Tom ever found out what Susan was really doing, he'd completely freak out.

They had been at the new CovSec headquarters just over a week learning the terrain when Kaitlyn and Tom, Lieutenant Jones and Major M, were given their first assignment. They were looking over the paperwork making preparations when someone spoke rather loud and angrily behind them.

"Jones!"

Kaitlyn spun around to see who called her and when she spotted Jonathan Stangard walking in the door. Immediately seeing his smile she jumped from her chair and ran up to give him a hug. Tom looked up just in time to see Stangard pull Kaitlyn into a long kiss, he stood as Kaitlyn stepped away and shyly turned to Tom.

"Tom this is..."

"I know who this is." He spoke as he walked up and extended his hand out. "Stangard."

"M, how the hell have you been?"

"Keeping my head above water. What brings you out here?"

"New assignment. I'm the new Bridge Agent." He began.

"So we'll be reporting to you?"

"Yup. Quite the turn of events huh?" He chuckled as he noticed Kaitlyn's eyebrows raise. "So I see the demotion to Major came with a couple of perks."

"Perks?" Tom asked.

"Got yourself active duty and got a partner as well. You're one lucky dog!" He smiled as he smacked Tom on the arm. Then he looked at Kaitlyn, "Tom is one moody ol' bear. Has he been riding you hard?"

"In a manner of speaking." Kaitlyn half smiled.

"Well don't let him, that's my job." He said referring back to being head of the secret service and giving her orders of course there was a little innuendo in it as well.

Kaitlyn began to blush. Tom saw the way Stangard was looking at Kaitlyn and figured it out. "So you two..." Tom began but Kaitlyn quickly interrupted,

"Just the once."

"Yeah," Jonathan interjected, "If you mean three times in one night!"

"Jonathan." Kaitlyn scolded her eyes narrowing.

"Just playin' around. So tell me about this mission."

Tom took a deep breath, pushing past the annoyance he was feeling then returned to the paperwork.

As Tom finished going over the mission he handed Stangard the paperwork and clicked his pen closed. Kaitlyn knew they'd need to be working closely with Jonathan and she also knew if there were any hard feelings she needed to get them addressed before the mission began. Collecting her thoughts, she called Tom telepathically.

"Tom..."

"Don't start."

"But you should know..."

"I get it. Just don't kiss him again if you don't mind."

Kaitlyn could feel the discontent in his tone but he was taking it well. She decided not to raise the subject again.

The three of them worked well together. Once Tom got past the awkwardness of Jonathan and Kaitlyn's past the mission went off without a hitch. When they got back to the barracks Stangard invited Tom for a drink and although Tom tried to decline Stangard insisted. "Come on man it'll be like old times."

As Tom and Stangard exited the building they were back to being best buds, Jonathan reminded Tom of some embarrassing moment and the both of them busted out laughing. Kaitlyn was just entering the hallway when she heard them. She smiled when she saw them laughing.

"Jones how about a drink?"

"I don't think so."

"Awe, come on, we were always so serious on the job, let's go out and celebrate!"

Kaitlyn looked at Tom who was not going to help her make this decision. She then decided that maybe she would call it a night. "You two go, catch up. I've got something to do anyway – rain check?"

"Awe Jones, come on!" Stangard insisted but Tom interjected.

"That's cool – guys night out."

Kaitlyn knew by that response, that was the right move. Play it safe, let the guys bond.

Chapter 5

The colonel just got off the phone when he called Kaitlyn into his office the next morning. As she entered the door he wasted no time.

"Jones, good you're here. I need you to run a quick errand   for   me."
"An errand?"

"I'm sending you to El Paso. There is a man there, Joe Johnson. He just got his hands on a piece of equipment that shouldn't be in his possession. It's a national security nightmare so we need to obtain it fast. It should be an easy snatch and grab assignment. According to satellite surveillance he only has two guards working the perimeter, the other movement seems to be maids and cooks. Here is the map to his place, the layout of his home and where the guards are currently posted. Memorize it on your flight up then burn the documents…"

"Back up?"

"You can handle it, besides M and Stangard are in Juarez on a mission."

"Juarez, Mexico? When   did   that   happen?"
"Last night we got a call and they were just getting back to the grounds. You'll be fine, it's a simple snatch and grab."

"Yes sir."

A few hours later Kaitlyn was dropped into enemy territory. She knew her assignment and had memorized the layout. She made her way carefully to her designated entrance point and scoured the area.

She was just making her way over the stone wall towards the back of the perimeter when she was grabbed. She soon realized how large and strong her captive was when she looked up and saw a large hairy ape-like face. He held her from behind, pinning her arms down by her side. His arms were easily 30 inches in girth, he was easily 6 foot 10 and weighed 400 pounds. She struggled with the overgrown ape-like man but he was definitely stronger than she was. He began to drag her inside the office, so Kaitlyn had to act quickly. Using the only free appendages she had she lifted her feet and legs, spread them out like a cat about to get a bath, and firmly secured both feet to either side of the doorway's ledge. The ape-man pushed to get inside with all of his might, but Kaitlyn's strength moved into her legs. 16 inches of pure muscle was locked into fighting position and prime for fighting off the brute of the man trying to push her through the door.

Just then a well dressed man wearing a crimson smoking jacket with jet black hair walked up to her from inside the office, nearly laughing at the two of them as he watched this display. Kaitlyn's legs, holding her from going into his office, were spread out wide and in front of this man's face. He loved the view and even made note to say something about it.

"Ah, Miss Jones, how nice it is to see you, and from this angle…"

"Bite me!"

"I'll take you up on that later."

"Do I know you?" Kaitlyn exclaimed now realizing that he knew her name. Did he know she was coming? Was this a trap?

"No, but I know you. Your reputation precedes you." Joe Johnson exclaimed as he gave the motion for his goon to bring Kaitlyn into the office.

Finally the ape-man gave up on that fowled attempt and pulled Kaitlyn away from the door, turning her and his back to it and starting in backwards. Kaitlyn knew he must have been using the two percent of his left brain to have come up with a full proof plan like this but he just didn't know Kaitlyn that well. In seeing that she was about to go in she again reacted and wrapped both legs, nearly Indian style around a large white pillar and held on tight. Ape-man continued to try to pull her into the office, but the pure power of Kaitlyn's legs held her steady there. Kaitlyn was beginning to get exhausted though. The amount of pressure the man was putting on her chest as he pulled on her felt like he was crushing her rib cage. Kaitlyn felt her grip around the pillar begin to loosen so she tightened her leg muscles. Just then a man came into the room.

"Mr. Johnson, Mr. Manners is here to see you."

"Give me a minute." Johnson said, and then he finally gave the order to put her out.

And with that, big-ol ape-man squeezed every bit of air from Kaitlyn's lungs in the strongest bear hug she had ever received and as she gasped for breath into her nearly collapsed lungs she slowly began to black out. That along with the lack of oxygen now getting to her leg muscles, her entire body went limp and ape-man was finally able to drag her into the building.

About an hour later Kaitlyn was finally coming out of her slumber when she looked around the room. She had been dragged to one of the many bedrooms of the estate. Then she realized why. Johnson had had someone tie her down to the bed. With no room for movement, she had been stretched out and open, her legs and arms pulled to their ability to every end of the bed. She was like a great big X-marks the spot and she couldn't yank her legs or arms free. She yanked at the ropes but they were tied well. They wouldn't give way and there was no chance of breaking the foot and headboard since they were made of thick iron. Kaitlyn tugged as hard as she could and the cast iron yielded just slightly, but not enough to do any good. She knew she was stuck here, she now had to decide what to do next.

Kaitlyn felt vulnerable. Spread out and open, tied down and helpless in the enemy's domain, and unknowing of what their plans were. Kaitlyn scanned the room, searching for anything that could help her out of this predicament, but everything was too far away. There were antique swords hung on the wall, something that would easily slide their way across the ropes to free her, but they were too far away to use. There was a nice large fire roaring in the fireplace, she could grab one of the flaming sticks and burn the ropes away, but it too was too far away. Finally while in mid thought, the door began to open and Mr. Johnson came strolling in the room. He sat down on the edge of the bed and looked at the woman tied there.

"How did you sleep?"

"Fine thanks, but I think it's time to leave now."

"So soon? You just got here. I think you should stay a while."

"Yeah, but I'm expecting the cable man back at my place, he could be there any minute now and you know what happens if you aren't there."

"So why is such a beautiful woman as yourself doing the work of men?" He asked as he once again looked upon the woman in bondage.

"Trying to keep scum bags like you off of the streets."

"I could give you everything you've ever wanted."

"I've already got it thanks."

"Enough with the wit! You won't have your life if you keep this up!"

"You would have killed me already if you were going to you scared rat!"

"I can do whatever I want to you and don't you forget it!"

"I'd like to see you try!"

With that last comment fuming under Johnson's skin he showed her his feelings of true anger. He leaped on top of her body, straddling her hips and gripped hold of her throat securely between his hands. Then he began to squeeze.

"I could kill you right now and no one not even you could stop me!"

"Then do it! What are you waiting for? Chicken!" She choked out which made him squeeze harder for a moment, but then he stopped.

"Ah I see what you want. But you're not going to get it. You can't go anywhere, do anything, you are mine to do with as I please, for as long as I please. And you can't do a thing about it!" He looked at the angry woman below him her eyes showed anger, true hate, but her body; her mind told him she was afraid. She didn't want him to know that, but he could tell, he could almost smell it, like a wolf. He smiled wickedly at her, and then lowered his face to hers to kiss her. She quickly turned her head to the side to avoid it but when she did he whispered into her ear.

"It'll be fun to have you around." Then he got off of her body and stood up next to the bed. "But not right now. Later after my meetings I'll be back, and we'll continue this."

"What meeting? With Mr. Manners?"

"You've got good ears but I don't think you know Mr. Manners and that is a very good thing. You wouldn't want to get your pretty little self involved with a thug like him."

"Oh are you jealous? Think I'll leave you for someone better?"

"Yeah." He laughed as he began out the door, "You'll never leave me."

As Kaitlyn was left alone in the room she felt her heart begin to pound in her chest. She may have bought some time now, but when that meeting was over, she would be out of time and she didn't like that feeling at all.

Kaitlyn knew she was between a rock and a hard place. She knew she couldn't break these ropes and that Johnson would be back soon. She began to worry that she was here alone and there was no one here to help her and it made her shiver. She came in here for a quick snatch and grab assignment and she was the one that was snatched instead. She even began to wonder if the general had set her up since Joe Johnson seemed to know who she was and the fact that she was sent here alone. At the time she had figured the general knew she could handle the task by herself now she was doubting everything. Everything except one trusting name that kept popping into her head, Tom.

Suddenly Kaitlyn remembered where she was, and the last she heard Tom was just across the border. She knew he was with a battalion who had a chopper and she also knew they could be here quickly if she called him. She thought for a moment how any other agent would be doomed, no way of communicating for help, but luckily she and Tom had their telepathic connection. She wasn't sure how he'd explain the call or if he was in the middle of something dangerous himself but she needed some back up.

"Tom, can you hear me?"

"Kaitlyn?"

"I need your help!"

"Why? Where are you?"

"El Paso."

"General, this is Agent M checking in from Juarez."

"Juarez? M! This is perfect! We've got an agent down. Jones has been captured."

"How did this happen sir?"

71

"Apparently really bad intel Major. We are addressing the situation on our end. In the meantime, we need you to take the chopper and secure the situation"

"I'm on my way."

Tom already knew what was going on as the General began explaining the situation. Thankfully Kaitlyn had filled him in. As the chopper shot through the clouds and tree tops Tom informed his men what was going on and what to expect. He knew vaguely what to expect from Kaitlyn's detailed instructions but he worried when she stopped communication. He didn't know what exactly she was dealing with because she wouldn't tell him but he knew she was being detained with no ability to get out and he knew she was in the hands of some really nasty and demented people. He knew of Joe Johnson's history and this was definitely not the kind of people you want to be hanging out with.

About ten minutes after Mr. Johnson left, he sent in a maid to serve Kaitlyn dinner.

"Dinner ma'am." The elderly lady spoke as she walked in the door. The sight of Kaitlyn tied down to the bed nearly caught her off guard, but then she tilted her face to the floor and kept her eyes off.

"I'm not hungry." Kaitlyn growled still angry she was being held captive here. The woman walked in and placed the tray of food down on the side table next to Kaitlyn. She barely looked at Kaitlyn when she gave her rebuttal.

"The Master wishes you eat."

"Oh he does, does he? Well you can tell him to go to…"

"Please Miss, we shan't make the Master angry."

"Oh we shan't?" Kaitlyn expressed sarcastically. Then she realized the woman was just doing her job and that she was afraid as well, she calmed trying to feel out the woman and see if there were a way to take the situation and turn it towards her benefit. "What are we having?"

"Steak and potatoes Miss." The word steak rang in Kaitlyn's ears as she immediately turned her head to see the steak knife just inches from her hands. The old maid continued. "He wanted you to have a meal from your own country."

"Well," Kaitlyn smiled. "Untie me and let me dig in!"

"Dig in Miss?"

"It means start eating."

"Oh." The woman said as she began to cut up the steak into bite size pieces.

"What are you doing?" Kaitlyn asked. "I can cut my own food."

"Not like that you can't." She said as she pointed to the ropes around Kaitlyn's wrists. Kaitlyn wanted to scream but she constrained her anger for the moment.

"Then how about you untie me?"

"I can't Miss, against Master's orders."

"You always do what he says?" Kaitlyn asked snidely.

"Yes Miss. Now open wide." She smiled as she held a bite of food over Kaitlyn's mouth.

"You're going to hand feed me?" Kaitlyn spat angrily.

"Yes Miss, that is what Master wanted."

"I am not going to be hand fed! Untie me damn it! Can't you see I don't want to be here?"

"I'm sorry Miss, if you continue yelling I will have to leave."

"Then leave you worthless ingrate! Leave me lying here helpless! How would you like it if your daughter were in my place or your granddaughter? Would you just leave them too?" Kaitlyn yelled, but the woman quietly got up and walked out of the room. Kaitlyn looked over at the steak knife willing it to come to her, trying to see if she could control the telekinesis she had, but it wouldn't move one bit. She had never been able to control her telekinetic abilities, they just seemed to work when she needed them the most. Of course she needed them now but there was no controlling them. She stretched out her hands towards the knife but it was too far away. She brought her wrists to near bleeding from struggling with the rope so long but finally she gave up. She realized she couldn't reach it.

"Kaitlyn can you hear me?"

"Tom where are you?"

"On our way. How are you doing?"

"Fine for the moment!"

"Are you okay? Are you hurt?"

"Not yet."

Just then the bedroom door opened and Joe Johnson walked back into the room. "Did you miss me, darling?"

"Nope."

"All I could do was think about you lying here waiting for me." As Johnson crawled on top of Kaitlyn's body, licking his proverbial lips, he eyed her up and down, Kaitlyn sent an emotional message to Tom that she wasn't even aware of. Tom was in the middle of securing his weapon when he felt this overwhelming fright and dread loom upon his body and he realized Kaitlyn was in trouble.

"Kaitlyn? What's wrong?"

"Tom! Hurry!" The panic, and fear she sent put a lump in his throat so large he couldn't swallow. Kaitlyn was in serious trouble and he wasn't there to help her.

"Pilot! How much longer?"

"Ten minutes."

"We needed to be there ten minutes ago." As Tom sat there helpless in the chopper he could feel his adrenaline grow as the emotions of absolute terror began to fill him. He knew something bad was about to happen but he had no idea what.

Johnson straddled Kaitlyn's body and looked at the frightened woman below him with a smile.

"I see you didn't eat any of your dinner. Not hungry?"

"Drop dead!"

"So feisty. That is so cute. Especially since I can sense the fear permeating through your skin like a bad perfume."

"That's your cologne."

"Oh you're funny."

"I wasn't trying to be." Kaitlyn said desperate to make him forget what he had come in here for. How on earth had she gotten into this mess? How did she get here... again?

Johnson looked at the steak knife on the side table and then noticed Kaitlyn's bloody wrists. "You poor thing. Look at what you did to your wrists trying to reach for that knife. Let me help you out there." He said as he took the knife in his hand and held it under Kaitlyn's chin. The sharp tip pressed into her throat and although she was terrified she narrowed her eyes and tried desperately to be angry. This was just the kind of situation Tom had trained her for. He had told her to be angry, not scared. That anger was where her strength lie so she tried but she couldn't think. Looking up at the reddening face of Joe Johnson who looked upon her as if he had known her for years her mind went blank. Who was this guy? How did he know her?

As Johnson began to rub his hands forcefully upon Kaitlyn's body, he tore open her shirt. The look on her face showed fire in her eyes, they told him that if she ever got loose she would kill him without thinking twice. However, Johnson knew it was a facade. Feeling Kaitlyn's body tremble below him he knew she was frightened and this seemed to energize him. He laughed as he pulled the knife away from her neck and placed it back on the side table.

"I don't need this do I?"

Kaitlyn glanced at the knife, knowing well that it was the only thing that could undo these ropes if Johnson wasn't going to. Her mind was flustered but as she lay there feeling Johnson reach for her shorts she began to come up with a plan. As he began trying to pull the shorts off of her only to find they wouldn't go far enough down because of the way she was tied up he began to reach for the knife again, this time to cut them off of her. This was Kaitlyn's chance she thought and immediately spoke her mind.

"Well what are you waiting for?"

"What?" Joe Johnson stuttered as he forgot what he was reaching for and looked down into Kaitlyn's face. Suddenly Kaitlyn was smiling and although he at first was caught off guard he knew it had to be a trick. He played along.

"You know if you untie my legs you'll be able to slide my shorts off."

"Right. Like if I untie you, you won't try to escape."

"How can I escape if my arms are still tied to the headboard?"

Curiosity got the better of Joe Johnson right then and he went to untie Kaitlyn's legs.

"Well that ought to do it." He said as he reached for her shorts again.

"Wait!" Kaitlyn panicked.

"Why?" Joe asked as he slid the shorts down. He then climbed back on top of her and secured her legs between his thighs.

Joe was ready to get started as Kaitlyn continued racking her brain. She had to think of something . Maybe if she could just stall him, maybe if she…

"Wait!"

"No more talking."

"No but, if you…" But Johnson wouldn't let her finish. He quickly covered her mouth and entered her body. Kaitlyn could feel her eyes began to swell but she refused to let any tears form. Struggling with her arms still tied by the ropes, thrashing just enough to unsteady him but not enough to slow him down, she realized there was nothing she could do. She just closed her eyes and tried desperately to think of a way to get out of here, anything other than what was happening.

When Johnson became rougher, Kaitlyn tried to ignore, she kept trying to remember her and Tom's first time. Back in high school, before any of this mess started, before her father was killed, before she and Tom began to fight, she remembered the good times. The laughs, the enjoyment, the kisses. Oh the kisses, they were so good, so full of passion. Each time Tom would touch her, just a simple touch of his hand would make her melt and when he kissed her she became putty in his arms. When they began fooling around, the emotions were so high, that it seemed to make the entire world disappear. There would be no one left on the planet except the two of them and there would be no reason to be shy.

When their bodies touched a chemical reaction would happen and before either one of them knew it they were like wild animals, ravaging each other, ripping off each others' clothes and forgetting any of the rules. Kaitlyn remembered all of that passion. Loving every minute of this memory, every minute she found herself enveloped in Tom's arms, and then suddenly it was over.

When Joe Johnson was finished and he began to get off the bed, Kaitlyn was shocked. She had successfully convinced herself she had been making love with Tom and when it was over for a very small second she was disappointed. Immediately growing nauseous at that thought a light went off in her head and although it was against everything she could ever believe in, she spoke her thoughts out loud.

"You can't be done!"

"Shut up!"

"But we were just getting started. It was just getting good."

Johnson's male mind was snared. "What did you say?"

"Don't leave now. Come on, just a little bit more?"

"Are you serious?" Johnson expressed with disbelief.

"Please?" Kaitlyn said so sexily, and looking so determined and sure, so eager, Johnson couldn't hesitate. He slowly, like a zombie walked back to Kaitlyn.

To put the icing on the cake Kaitlyn opened her legs and began gyrating her hips, "Oh just a little bit more."

Her mouth was open in a breathless moan, her eyes relaxed and tired, her face flush with excitement. There was something in Johnson that screamed this is a trap, but the only part of him that was thinking currently could only see the desire of a woman. As he climbed back on top of Kaitlyn, lowering his pants, however this time he was vulnerable. Tired already, being he was out of shape and unable to get his "soldier" to come to attention he reached down to point himself in the right direction, and it was that moment that Kaitlyn made her move.

Wrapping her legs around his torso pinning his right arm down against his body she pulled him upwards where he had to use his free arm to hold himself steady. He began to yell, but Kaitlyn threw him to the side by twisting her hips, startling him. She looked at his free hand trying to help himself out of this and she growled at him,

"Untie my arms!"

"Never!" He yelled back in spite. She squeezed tighter, squeezing most of the air from his lungs.

"Untie my arms!"

He continued to struggle for a moment, defiantly unwilling to set her free, but she continued to squeeze her legs around his chest. Thrashing around in the bed, she spun her hips right and threw his already unsteady body sideways, he lost his balance and she threw him back the other direction. She squeezed his torso with all of her might, he could feel his rib cage begin to collapse. Finally he reached for her right arm and began untying it. When her right arm was free, she reached to her left and tried to untie her other arm herself, but he began to struggle again between her legs almost freeing himself. Kaitlyn couldn't let him go while she was still constrained so she used her free hand and grabbed his throat. He began to struggle, trying to fight with her, but she squeezed him so tightly around his waist his internal organs were beginning to strain.

He punched her in the abdomen with his free arm and although it knocked the breath out of her, she retained her grip around him and continued squeezing, tighter. She knew no matter how much he struggled, how heavy he was, she couldn't release her grip on him or he could get the upper hand again. He again tried to call for help but Kaitlyn knew she couldn't let him do that. She gripped hold of his throat tighter, not able to wrap her hand around his flabby neck, her fingers lost their grip. As he began to pull away, she found her fingers tightening around his windpipe. Puncturing his skin with her fingernails as she clawed at his neck blood splattered everywhere. Punching her with his free hand again, grabbing anything he could with his constrained hand, kicking at the bed sheets with his legs flailing the two of them fought. And right when Kaitlyn was feeling her strength begin to leave her, Johnson pulled his head backward in an attempt to escape which gave Kaitlyn the thrust to rip the trachea right through Joe Johnson's neck.

Blood went splattering everywhere as Johnson's body began shaking violently between Kaitlyn's legs. As blood poured from his neck, oozing all over Kaitlyn's face, she turned her head and released her grip around him, dropping his body to the floor. After hearing the thud of his now dead body land on the floor and feeling the warm blood ooze down her face, Kaitlyn wept. She lay there for a moment feeling her adrenaline pumping, the fear she had been feeling made her shudder, the warm blood that had sprayed all over her face, arm and chest quickly cooling, she found herself beginning to lose it.

She felt nauseous and light headed, and before vomiting, she grabbed the steak knife on the table and sliced the ropes from her other hand. Leaning over the bed now, Kaitlyn threw up, all of those emotions finally escaping her. Still dizzy and now feeling empty, she tumbled to the floor. Now on hands and knees, her eyes closed, the room spinning, Kaitlyn wasn't sure what to do next and then it came to her.

A loud pounding brought her back to reality and she immediately realized that Johnson's guards were trying to get into the room. The door had been locked so they were trying to break it down. She had to act quickly. Pulling her shorts back up, smearing the blood and God knows what else all over her goose pimpled skin, she surveyed the room. Her mind went into overdrive that moment and a feeling of survival swept over her. Knowing she had to get out of there alive to make this all worthwhile she ran over to where the show swords were hanging on the wall, slid them from their scabbards and turned to face the door. With both swords gripped tightly in her blood-soaked hands, two guards burst through the door and into the room.

As they peered into the room, the blood all over the bed, the limp foot peeking out from the other side that surely belonged to Johnson, the woman lunging towards them with two antique Samurai swords in her bloody palms. They immediately went for their guns, but Kaitlyn's speed was prime. The adrenaline pumped through her veins faster than the swords could slice through the first two guards. The slick metal pierced their skin and as if a slow motion movie they both simultaneously grabbed their guts, Kaitlyn yanked the swords out and ran off as they both fell to the floor, dying.

Kaitlyn continued running down the hallway, seeing guardsmen turning the corner, coming after her, but she couldn't stop, she raised a sword into the air and whacked one of the mens' head right off his shoulders. Then as another entered the hallway; she spun in the air and swiped that sword right into his side and through him. As Kaitlyn neared the front door she remembered the equipment she had been sent there to get. She stopped in mid step and turned on a dime and looked around the foyer. She still had no idea where to get it.

Just then another guard came racing around the corner, gun out and cocked but not aimed. Kaitlyn ran up to him and with one of the bloody swords she sliced his hand off, gun falling to the floor. In the same thrust she kicked the guard down to the ground. Then she straddled him to the ground, holding the sword directly under his chin, cutting into his neck. "Where's the office?"

"I don't know." He screamed and cried, flailing and bleeding from the opening where his hand used to be.

"Wrong answer, try again and this time make me happy!"

"It's…it's down the hall to the left."

"Thanks." She growled as she finished the job; no use in letting him suffer. Then she started towards the office. As she charged down the hallway anger in her eyes, nothing but hate and defiance filling her soul, one of the maids came out of the kitchen ten feet in front of her. It was the same maid that had come in to feed her and the hate she felt for the woman was pure. But it wasn't the maid's fault she told herself, and as the maid saw her coming towards her, two bloody swords in her hands, blood all over her body, she began to scream. Kaitlyn yelled out to the woman.

"Run now, because if I catch up to you I will not hesitate to kill you woman!" So without much hesitation the woman ran back into the kitchen and Kaitlyn was sure she kept running right through it.

Finally Kaitlyn made it to the office where she found the equipment. Kaitlyn had just begun to reach for it, when she flashed at another couple of guards entering the room. She spun, swords out like propellers and sliced into the two men. As the first two fell, another two men came at her, she fought them as well. By the time the outer wall exploded and Tom and his men began to enter Kaitlyn was surrounded by a large pile of blood and body parts. She turned to face the sound of the explosion, the sunlight beaming into the dark office would have blinded her but she didn't notice. Swords pointed down and out at an angle she peered at the new challenge ready to attack.

Kaitlyn?" Tom called out but she stood there unmoved ready to attack. Tom motioned his men to hold on going in. "Kaitlyn, drop the swords." He demanded feeling immense anger filling her soul. She continued to stand there. Tom sensed she wasn't hearing him. Toms men all looked in ready to go secure the rest of the building but acknowledged that they'd be walking into a much more dangerous situation that they were prepared for. "Kaitlyn, drop the swords!" Tom demanded again.

Finally, Kaitlyn's eyes met Toms and a moment later she released her grip on the swords and they clanked to the floor. Tom's men ran in and around Kaitlyn towards the hallway to secure the perimeter. Tom approached Kaitlyn.

"Clear!" One man announced as he saw a long hallway pelted with blood and dead bodies the entire stretch down. "Nothing but slaughtered bodies stretching the entire length of the hallway." He announced.

"Damn! What happened here?" One of the men asked of another.

"She did." He said pointing back towards Kaitlyn who was still standing there with the look of death on her face.

"Remind me not to get on her bad side."

Tom went to Kaitlyn; touching her ever so gently upon the side of her neck. She trembled. Terrified about what she had seen, what she had experienced, what she had just done, she shivered as if trying to shake away the images of that moment. His eyes piercing hers as his hand slid over her shoulder and down her arm. Their hands met and he took hers in his, clasping it tightly as a symbol of his strength, as a metaphor to exclaim his undying desire to be there with her and to stay there.

Her heart beat rapidly in her chest, almost as if it were going to beat right through her chest. Her blood ran through her veins wildly, endorphins intoxicating her, sending pulses to her brain that made her head tingle. Was she going to black out? Was all of this too much for her to deal with?

No. She had dealt with things like this before. She paused, had she? Had she really seen anything that came close to this kind of mutilation? Something so gruesome, something so horrific? She was shocked; appalled by the ghastly sight amidst her, surrounding her. Their blood was everywhere, on her. It soaked her. Her clothes were drenched with it, her skin waterlogged, saturated by this warm red ooze that was cooling quick, hardening, thickening, solidifying.

Her stomach churned. It was empty thank God, but it still twisted and clutched within her gut and made her nauseous just the same. And then it hit her, the smell. The repugnant odor of open bodies, of warm carcasses already rotting in the still air. She relieved in the moment as the room darkened, as his body seemed to block from her the only ray of light shining in through the narrow crawlspace. The solace of the darkness was like a respite from the depiction of mortality or that thereof. But the memory of all of this remained. The knowledge of what she had done would stick with her, she knew, but how much of all of this would she truly remember?

It happened so fast, it wasn't even her she thought as she tried desperately to make sense of all of this silently in her head. Did I walk in here on my own? Was I aware of the situation as I pulled my weapon? Did I know there were so many people here, waiting, also prepared and eager to fight? Had I counted them, had I made a mental note of where they all were, what weapons they had? Had I perceived my surroundings? Could I really have distinguished the people from the shadows, the root systems from the weapons?

Tom tried to comfort her, she could tell he was speaking but she couldn't understand him. His lips moved and although she strained to understand him, the weight of what had happened kept her from listening. It was as if she couldn't hear him. Had she lost her senses? It was so dark, and so quiet, and she couldn't feel her own skin, but that was the drying blood, the blood from them all, all of the lives she was forced to extinguish. But she could smell. She could taste the rancid air, the salt in her tears, the iron in the blood. Had she screamed? She tasted blood, was it theirs or her own? Had she been hurt? Was she injured? She decided she should find out. She broke the gaze with his eyes, only to look at his mouth, why couldn't she look away from him? Was he important?

The shock was still strong within her, she could hardly move but she knew she had to find out what was happening now. She knew the fight was over but that there was still more to do so she continued trying to break out of this daze. Slowly she began to hear his words, slowly she began being able to look around. She shivered again and felt his hand squeeze hers, then she felt his other hand on her right arm. She looked at it, her arm was bare and yet covered with a thick coating of blood and as she looked at his hand he slid it down towards her elbow and as he did he wiped away some of the blood. This helped. It was a symbolic cleansing, she needed that.

"Can you hear me?"

She looked back towards his lips and understood what he had said.

"Are you hurt?"

She couldn't determine if she was hurt or not. She was numb, stiff, incapable of moving. Had she answered him?

"Kaitlyn are you okay?" He kept asking her questions, kept speaking her name. His eyes showed such turmoil and fear. There was panic in his voice, trepidation in his touch, apprehension in his posture. Was he afraid of her or for her? "Speak to me. Do you know where you are?"

Of course she knew where she was, the office of Joe Johnson. A dark, dank, smelly hole of a room, that was half full of dead bodies and blood but on what continent, what state, what city? That she couldn't recollect. Had she gone on a mission? Had she been alone?

He reached for his radio and spoke into it. "I've found her but she's non-responsive."

Non-responsive. Had she not said anything to him yet? She was sure she had. She had told him she could hear him, that she didn't think she was hurt, had he not heard her? Was there something wrong with him?

"She's lucid, coherent but she seems confused, there may be head trauma but I can't tell yet."

Did she have head trauma? She wondered this, realizing she needed to find out and finally found the strength to move her other arm. She lifted her hand from her side, it felt heavy. She started to lift it but she let it drop.

"Kaitlyn, I was so worried about you."

She looked into his eyes again as he reached for her face and placed his hand tenderly upon her cheek, cupping his palm under her chin. Just then she heard the radio squawk and a voice on the other side spoke.

"The choppers making a circle it'll be back in a moment. Can she be moved?"

He pulled his hand from her face and reached for his radio again. "Still determining that. Trying to establish alertness. I think there may be emotional and psychological trauma."

"All we want to know is if she is safe and mobile, we'll examine the emotional state of the agent after a safe return."

"Kaitlyn, if you can understand me, we've got to leave. Can you move?"

She closed her eyes trying to regain her composure but as soon as she did images and sounds of what had happened washed over her. The screams and crying, the metal reverberation against other metal and bone, the groaning of the dying and thumping of bodies as they hit the ground. She felt light-headed, as if she were going to pass out so she opened her eyes, but the room began to spin. Her eyes rolled back into her head as the air suddenly staled and became hot. Her face drained of blood and she went pale, and as her body began to collapse, he caught her in his arms. Scooping her against his chest, lifting her legs into one arm, her head resting against his shoulder, he turned and carried her out of the office and into the light of day. The other agents following him, keeping steady eyes out for more enemies, guns drawn and ready for action.

Once in the chopper, still within Tom's arms, Kaitlyn pressed her face into Tom's chest, inhaling his scent. She spoke not one word the entire trip home, she hardly moved, she just held on to him and rested in the security of his arms.

Tom was truly worried about Kaitlyn. He wasn't sure what happened in that place. He had his thoughts, sick thoughts that he prayed silently were just that, thoughts and sick, but he feared by the way she was acting they might not be. He kept his assumptions to himself though; he did however offer her his shoulder for her to lean on, and that seemed to be enough for now.

"We'll be landing in just a moment." The pilot said over the radio of the chopper.

Tom looked down at Kaitlyn and shook his head. They had been in the air for an hour now and she still hadn't spoken about what had happened. Carefully he embraced her in his arms, cradling her, he kissed the top of her head. He had never been this worried about her.

Telepathically he tried to get her to talk. "Can you tell me what happened?"

"No." She said aloud.

"The general will want you to fill out a report when we get there."

"I just want to take a shower." She sighed.

He left it at that. She wasn't going to talk, he couldn't get her to talk, at least not now. Tom could tell she was hiding something that she wasn't all right, but there was nothing he could do about it now. All he could do was offer her support if she wanted it.

She walked straight into a shower stall, didn't even bother getting undressed. She allowed the scalding hot waters to pour down her face, rewetting the blood and cleansing it from her body. And as she felt the waters soak her skin through her clothing she slowly took off her shirt, shorts and shoes. She was in the shower for an hour cleaning herself, her body had turned bright red from the hot water, and then when the hot water ran out her skin turned bright white from the cold. Kaitlyn had been in there for quite some time, the entire time Tom was waiting outside still wondering about what had happened to her. Finally he peeked his head in to check on her to make sure she was all right.

"Kaitlyn? Are you still in here?" He called out to her from the locker room door. But she didn't answer. He heard the water still running and worried she might have fallen; in her current state she easily could have passed out.

"Kaitlyn? You okay? Where are you?" He called as he made his way further into the locker room to the showers. There he saw the water pooled on the floor leading to her stall and he went to it. As he turned the corner he saw Kaitlyn sitting there, leaning against the wall. Her knees pulled up to her chest, her legs crossed in front of her, her arms around her legs, her head resting on her knees, the water pouring on her body.

Tom immediately thought the worst and he kneeled down next to her and raised her head. "Kaitlyn! Wake up!"

"Leave me alone!"

"No! What's going on here?"

"I just needed to sit down."

"In the shower?"

"Tom, please go away."

"No I will not! Not until you tell me what's wrong."

She dropped her head back down to her knees, which only angered him. He cared about her, and was totally concerned and he grew angry because he didn't know how to help her especially if she wouldn't talk to him. He took her hand into his to comfort her, that's when he noticed the bruises, scrapes and cuts around her wrists. The scrapes she had gotten from the ropes that had tied her down, the bruises she had received from Johnson during their struggle. All forms of evidence that had been hidden from him earlier by the blood coating her body. Then he looked down and saw the injuries on her ankles and as much as he hated to think it, he soon began to realize and visualize the truth of what actually had happened.

He quickly leaned over and turned off the water to the shower, then reached out to the towel rack and grabbed a towel to cover Kaitlyn's body. And as he tucked the towel around her body, she began to cry, this time trying to tell him what happened.

"I tried to fight him...I couldn't get away."

"It's alright."

"I couldn't..." She began hyperventilating. "I can't breathe!"

"Take deep breaths, calm down a little."

"I feel sick!"

"Do you want to throw up?" She shook her head no finally able to catch her breath.

"I'm losing it."

"No you're not. You're reacting to a horrible situation, it's normal."

"I should be stronger than this!"

"Everybody has their limits." She looked up into his eyes; his caring warm eyes and found a small smile inside of her. She then closed her eyes and sent him the feelings she had felt and continued to feel moments after the attack. She had started it afterwards because she wasn't ready to share what she had gone through, not yet, but she did send him something to help him understand what had happened in that house, why there was so much carnage, why she had snapped.

Tom felt Kaitlyn's heart pounding, beating so incredibly violently within her chest and he sensed she was giving him information about what had happened. What he felt was truly disturbing. A complete and utter darkness began to grow within her. It started out as a small hole in her heart but it promptly grew, enlarging itself as it absorbed her very being. As it expanded it consumed her soul, it devoured her spirit and incinerated her very essence. It severed her from the world he knew and fused her to an irrational and illogical world of vengeance. It was as if she had been possessed by a demon, unable to control her bodily movements, actions or emotions. Kaitlyn had vanished and what was left in her place was darkness; a rage of such thunderous passion infused itself in her very being. A fury so strong and so deep it proliferated---filled every pore within her until it boiled over in a rush of defiance and vengeance.

With swords in hand she raced into danger, expecting to die and yet expecting to be invincible. She had been so quick so ferocious that none of those men had a chance. She was a powerful force, full of something so dark, so evil it was something that Tom couldn't recognize, it was inside of Kaitlyn but it wasn't the Kaitlyn he had known. He could sense that this force was created out of necessity, that something so bad had happened she had to turn everything she had in her body into rage, like he had trained her to do but at such an immense level that the actual essence of Kaitlyn had left and what was left was pure evil.

When Tom arrived and broke her of that enraged concentration it left her just as fast as it had swept through her body and it happened faster than she could return. That is why she passed out and it is that rage among other things that she was trying to work through there in the shower.

"Tom, I did what I had to."

"I know you did and I understand."

She reached over to give him a hug and as he leaned in to hug her back, to comfort her and make her feel better he slipped on the standing shower water and fell onto her. She began to laugh as he quickly struggled to right himself, and as she laughed he did also. She became nearly hysterical, she couldn't stop laughing. She needed the laughing, it was helping her, healing her, and as Tom continued to laugh with her, feeling things would soon be all right if she could find humor, he sat down next to her and waited for her to recover.

"I think I need a vacation."

"We can arrange that."

Chapter 6

"Is there anything missing from this report agent Jones?" The general asked as he finished reading it.

"No sir."

"So you were taken hostage but escaped and then went on a massive massacre?"

"Yes sir."

"I'm giving you orders to go see the company counselor."

"Sir?"

"Hostage crisis can be very traumatic."

"I don't need counseling."

"I say you do. Some of the other men's reports mentioned your erratic and awkward behavior. We need to make sure our agents needs are taken care of. I can't send you back into the field and have you snap.

"Sir, with all due respect, I don't think I need counseling, I need a vacation."

"Can't do."

"Come on, two weeks?" He looked at her, knowing a vacation would be a good thing but that she needed to work through her PTSD first.

"After at least 5 sessions with the counselor." He challenged.

"One session." She countered. He thought about it for a second then shook his head.

"Two week vacation..." He paused as Kaitlyn started to smile. "But you're taking Agent M with you."

"W-w-what?" Kaitlyn stuttered. Tom walked into the room now, wanting to hear more. The General acknowledged his presence then went back to what he was saying to Kaitlyn.

"We'll send you anywhere you want to go, but you have to take Tom with you."

"Why?" She smiled but was still curious as to why this was working out so well.

"Kaitlyn you know that if you're dealing with post traumatic stress, you can't be alone."

"Yeah, but."

"And Agent M has been trained to deal with these types of situations."

"But I'm…"

"And you know better than to argue with me." The General continued.

"I'm sorry sir."

"Pack up your stuff Jones. Two week leave begins now."

As Kaitlyn walked out of the office, past Tom who was standing there speechless, she looked over at him, grabbed him by the arm and led him out of the office. Once in the hallway walking back to the locker room Kaitlyn spoke to Tom.

"I apologize for acting so weird."

"Hey, I'm used to it." He joked with her, she turned around to play punch him in the arm and he stopped and laughed.

"Mr. Manners?"

"Yes?"

"I have some news for you, about Jones."

"I'm all ears."

Special Agent Kaitlyn Jones was quietly walking down the hallway searching for the stolen equipment when she saw some guards heading her way. She quickly ducked behind a piece of furniture and quietly watched as they ran past her, both men had a large hole in their gut, blood dripping out of it, leaving a trail of blood where they'd been.

She got up from her hiding place and continued to walk down the hall when a guard leaped out from the shadows to stop her. At first he had terrified her but as he began to speak to her she saw a large gaping slice in his side where his intestines were hanging out. She pushed him aside and started to run down the hall. Another guard walked out in front of her but when he turned his head to face her, his head fell right off his neck.

She screamed at that and ran the other way, turning into a room and closing the door behind her. She stopped to catch her breath when she heard a voice behind her.

"Such beautiful legs…" She turned to see Joe Johnson standing there in front of her, his bloody trachea hanging from his neck, blood gushing from it. He walked to her, still talking, she was transfixed on this gruesome site, until finally he reached her and took her wrists into his and yanked them up, trapping her against the wall. Then he leaned in to kiss her. The site, the smell, the fear that filled her made her sweat and panic, and made her lose her breath.

Finally she screamed. She jolted up from her bed, sitting up, looking around the dark room, trying to catch her breath. There was a puddle of sweat on the mattress, and as she looked around the unfamiliar dark room, getting her bearings she began to calm. "It was just a dream." Then she looked at her wrists, even in the dark, the low amount of hazy light that came in from the moon, helped her see what would be scars on her wrists. She remembered what had happened, and she dropped her face into her hands and began to cry.

Knock, knock, knock…. Knock, knock, knock. Through her slumber state Kaitlyn heard mumbles outside the door, key's jangling and finally the door opening.

Tom walked into Kaitlyn's room and looked around. Kaitlyn had insisted on sleeping in her own room last night and as he looked over at the bedroom, the sheets and blankets strewn all on the floor; he realized she hadn't slept well. He continued to look around until he saw her sitting at the dining table, her head resting on her arms on the tabletop. She was still asleep.

"Kaitlyn." Tom called to her to wake her up. But she didn't stir. He grew worried; he walked up to her and shook her shoulder. "Kaitlyn." Her head popped up from the table and she looked at Tom, a kind of fear in her eyes until she realized it was friend and not foe and then the fear dissipated.

"I called you."

"The phone didn't ring."

"I've been knocking for five minutes."

"I didn't hear you."

"Why are you sleeping at the table?"

"Is this twenty questions?" Kaitlyn asked snidely as she stood up from the table and stretched.

"Sorry. I guess I never realized you were such a heavy sleeper."

"It was a tough night. What time is it?"

"Quarter till ten."

"I'll be out in five minutes." Five minutes later Kaitlyn walked out of the bathroom, wet hair, but dressed in a cute flowery dress perfect for the Bahamas. "Ready."

"Wow!" Tom exclaimed as he stood from his chair.

"What?" She smiled showing off the dress.

"You look great!"

"Well, it's not like a secret agent dressed in camouflage gets to wear fun dresses like this too often."

"I didn't think you were a dress person."

"And what is that supposed to mean?"

"Well you've always wore shorts."

95

"So?"

"Well I've never seen you in a dress, so I never thought about you in a dress. But I must say, I like it."

"The look or the dress?"

"You." He answered. She smiled again at that as she grabbed her overnight bag from the bathroom and spoke, "Well, let's get going, the plane won't wait for us."

"She's going to the Bahamas on vacation."

"Thank you for the information, your payment is in the briefcase."

"Last call for flight 109 to the Bahamas." Came the announcement over the loud speaker. Tom and Kaitlyn ran to the doors and slipped on just in time. Tom handed the stewardess the plane tickets and she showed them to their seats, first class.

"And you two let me know if there's anything I can get for you."

"Thank you." Tom and Kaitlyn said simultaneously. They both looked at each other and laughed. Then sat down in their seats and prepared for takeoff.

Hours later the plane landed on the Bahamas airstrip and taxied to the terminal. As the first class passengers started to exit the plane, the stewardess that had greeted Tom and Kaitlyn initially said her farewells.

"Have a nice honeymoon Mr. & Mrs. M."

"Thanks." Tom smiled as Kaitlyn turned around to him as they walked down the gangway.

"Mr. & Mrs. M?"

"Probably just confused." Tom answered, looking away from Kaitlyn's glare.

"Honeymoon?"

"Confused."

"Okay." She said not believing him since his face was roughly hiding a smile.

As they checked into the hotel room, the front counter man spoke out as he handed Tom the keys.

"Enjoy your stay Mr. & Mrs. M." As Kaitlyn and Tom turned to follow the bellboy Kaitlyn took Tom's hand in hers and squeezed it extremely tight. Yet she said with a smile. "Mrs. M?"

"Darn those confused people."

"Yes sir Mr. Manners, they just checked in."

"Good job senor. Gracias."

After Tom and Kaitlyn settled in, they went down for dinner and a show. They ordered the Islands specialty dinner, a couple very fruity alcoholic drinks with all the flourishes and sat back to watch the show. As the night went on Kaitlyn and Tom found themselves wowing, laughing, applauding and even dancing with the rest of the crowd into the wee early morning hours. Finally about two thirty in the morning jet lag began to sink in and Tom and Kaitlyn returned to their room for the night.

Later that night or actually later that morning Kaitlyn had another dream. The throatless Johnson was standing there, pinning her against a wall, as she looked around the room she realized she wasn't standing against a wall but laying on a bed. He had control of her again and even though she saw that her arms and legs were free in her dream she couldn't move them. It was as if a fear factor had taken over and forced her to stay there. Allowing what she allowed to be done to her to happen all over again. She fought him; struggled, screamed even but he began to take advantage of her again.

And as it seemed it couldn't get any worse, she woke up screaming, sitting up in her bed. Tom had been in the other room getting a drink when he heard her screams and ran into her bedroom to check on her. His first reaction was that of shock. The normally strong woman who never let anything bother her was sitting up in bed, covered in sweat and trembling. He went to her, held her in his arms to try to calm her down.

She was trembling and crying in his arms leaving him helpless as to know what to do for her. And what bothered him more was that she was apologizing. That he couldn't take. There was something definitely wrong, what had happened to her was definitely bothering her, terrorizing her in her dreams. He had to try to help.

"What was it about? What happened in your dream?"

"Nothing."

"That's why you're still shaking right?"

"I'll be fine."

"Come on Kaitlyn, tell me what it was about, it may help."

"I can't remember."

"I want to help you. I'm here for you. And I know you remember."

"Tom it's embarrassing."

"What's embarrassing? That you were over powered? Taken hostage? Taken advantage of? It wasn't your fault. There was nothing you could do about it."

"There was!"

"What?"

"I could have fought harder, screamed."

"I know you well enough to know that you gave it your all. And no one would have heard you scream in that palace. What's really bothering you?"

"That's it." She said with slight hesitation.

"I thought you were stronger than that, smarter than that." He said angrily. Kaitlyn pulled out of his arms now and looked at him in shock.

"If you can't show any compassion then I don't need you here!"

"If you can't tell me the truth then I don't need to be here!"

"I did tell you the truth!"

"Bull shit! There is something that you are obviously leaving out, something embarrassing maybe, and all you are doing is hurting yourself by keeping it bottled up and it pisses me off to know that you're doing this to yourself willingly!"

Kaitlyn got out of bed now. She felt she needed to stand, to make herself feel less vulnerable. But Tom's words echoed in her mind, torturing her thoughts, she did this to herself, willingly. She knew he was right. She couldn't tell him about her willing addition to the rape, it was too embarrassing, but it *was* what was bothering her. She looked at him sitting there on the edge of the bed, finally she spoke.

"At first, I was angry. Angry that I got myself into this situation. But even with all the anger in the world, I couldn't break loose from those binds." She stopped to take a deep breath, remembering the incident. "When he touched me I felt sick, like I was going to throw up." She looked up at Tom who was sitting there listening but not making eye contact. He had heard a similar story beginning before and it always made him sick to his stomach, but he had to be here for her now. "I turned my eyes away from him, I pretended it was someone else. And when he went to my…" She stopped talking now, feeling the tears whelping up in her eyes. Tom finally spoke.

"Go on." She looked at him confused like, she didn't want to go on, but he was so certain it would help that she forced herself to continue with the story.

"I was tied to the bed, legs spread, he was going to cut the shorts away from me instead of taking the chance of untying my legs, but I insisted he untie them." Tom grew curious now. Why would a man so intent on doing this, listen to his hostage and untie her legs? But Tom remained silent, letting Kaitlyn continue. "So he untied my legs and slid the shorts off."

"You're skipping something." Tom interrupted.

"I am not!"

"Why would he do something he knows would backfire on him?"

"I don't know!"

"You do! Or you wouldn't be so defensive right now." She took a deep breath knowing he was right.

"He thought I was... that I was enjoying it."

"Why would he think that if you were sick to your stomach, looking away from him, nearly in tears?"

"Tom stop this!"

"Why would he take the chance of risking his life for a woman who doesn't want it?"

"Because..."

"Why Kaitlyn? What do you not want to tell me?"

"Because I told him I wanted it!"

"Mr. Manners am I bothering you?" A young man asked as he peeked his head through the door to the office.

"Always, what do you want?"

"I just wanted to let you know that we are right on schedule."

"Good. Now leave me be."

"Yes sir. Sorry sir."

Chapter 7

Tom was in shock. He sat on the edge of the bed, his mouth covered by his hand when he was finally able to think straight he choked out the words. "But you didn't?"

"Of course I didn't! I needed to be untied so I led him on!"

"So you feel like you *allowed* him to do this to you?"

"I *did* allow him to do this to me!"

"But there was still nothing you could have done! He would have done this whether you said yes or no! You said yes to earn his trust."

"But that's not all."

"What else?"

"He straddled me in such a way that I still couldn't fight back."

"He held your legs together?" She nodded yes. "So how did you escape?"

"I… I can't do this."

"Yes you can. Tell me."

Kaitlyn paused, she had to just spit it out. "I asked him back for more."

"Just so you could escape?"

"I knew if I was able to wrap my legs around his torso I could squeeze him to death, or at least enough to make him pass out. Besides I also needed him to untie my arms or I wouldn't have been able to go anywhere."

"Okay. There's nothing wrong with that."

"But I asked him back! I made something that was awful, that *is* awful out to be something good."

"Kaitlyn you did what you had to, to escape."

"But it gets worse."

"It does?"

"I tortured him!"

"How?"

"I grabbed hold of him and squeezed him. I think I even broke a couple ribs as I did. I tortured him until he untied my hand, then I ripped his throat out of his neck!"

"What do you mean you ripped his throat out of his neck?"

"Just that. I grabbed his trachea between my fingers, squeezed and yanked it right through the skin of his neck!"

"It was self defense." Tom spoke trying to visualize the scene and becoming disgusted.

"It was torture!"

"He deserved it!"

"He didn't deserve *that*!" Kaitlyn yelled.

"He deserved whatever it was you had to do to him to escape!"

"His blood was everywhere. He was trying to gasp for breath but his entire neck region had been destroyed! It was murder!"

"It was self defense!"

"He keeps attacking me in my dreams! It's like his ghost is haunting me!"

"It's your subconscious reacting to a difficult situation." Kaitlyn was shaking her head no.

"And then I went on a murdering spree! I killed everyone in sight!"

"You had to escape. You're trained to do just that!"

"I had the blood of over twenty men on my body Tom!"

"You did what you had to."

Finally Tom stood up and walked up to her. He placed his hands on her shoulders, softly massaging them as he spoke to her.

"Look at me." She hesitated at first, feeling she wasn't worth the attention. "Look into my eyes." She did. "You are a very special, very wonderful, very beautiful woman. You are also extremely smart and strong. You are the best agent I have ever had the pleasure of knowing, and the greatest friend I have ever had. You have been there for me and I'm here for you. I'm not going to judge you or your actions because I know you did what you had to. You have nothing to feel guilty or sorry about, and you did nothing that would be construed of as wrong. And I will tell you this and repeat it and keep up with this for as long as necessary to convince you of this truth."

A tear fell down Kaitlyn's cheek as she heard his words and she finally realized she wasn't going crazy. Their eyes stayed within contact for a long moment, an unspeakable moment and then Tom moved. He inched closer to her, his face came closer, and like two magnets, hers moved towards his. Their eyes closed, their lips puckered and moved closer to each other and finally like the spark that lit the flame, they touched, they kissed. Tom pulled Kaitlyn into his arms, cradling her cold skin in his warm chest and continued the kiss that was growing more passionate. As Tom held Kaitlyn in his arms he found the soft silky material of the gown she was wearing and crumpled it into the palm of his hands. Then as she stayed with him, continuing the kiss that was quickly becoming more than just a kiss, he lifted the nightshirt over her arms and head and then returned to holding her.

He picked her up into his arms and carried her back to the bed. His touch was an excitement. She felt as if she were in a trance, her body eagerly wanted to be held by him, her mind almost blank which was a good thing as far as she was concerned. He continued kissing her lips but he also kissed her nose, her cheeks even her eyelids as he rolled his fingers through her hair in the most loving manner she had ever felt.

Tonight Tom comforted her, loved her and showed her that everything would turn out alright just like he said it would.

As Kaitlyn woke up the next morning to the sound of tropical birds singing and the sight of warm orange sunlight peeking in through the windows she also realized she was laying safe in Tom's arms. His large muscular arms wrapped around her body, cradling her next to his warm body, his face nuzzled in the nape of her neck. She liked it. She didn't move in hopes that he would never let go and she soaked up the feeling of security she felt as his chest raised and fell when he breathed. She slept soundly the rest of the night, maybe because the talk helped her, maybe because she was exhausted. Either way she was happy.

Maybe she had needed this, an act of love and compassion that would bring her through the trauma of the other day. An act that only someone she knew would have been able to fulfill, but thankfully someone she knew well. As he began to stir, yawn just slightly and stretch he let loose his grip around her body leaving the uncovered skin to be brushed by the sensation of cool air. She brought her hand up her arm rubbing it to get the cold sensation to go away then took a deep breath as if it were her first of the morning and slowly rolled over to face him.

As her eyes met his, his were already opened and boring into her soul. They caught each other like a bear to a trap and stayed still there for a moment as she wondered what to say.

"Good morning." He began in the deepest whispered voice he had which sent shivers up her spine.

"Good morning." She repeated, not feeling she gave him the same effect but it was nice nevertheless.

"How did you sleep?" He asked with that same voice, keeping his eyes steadily locked onto hers.

"Wonderfully."

He smiled finally allowing his gaze on her to be disturbed by closing his eyes for a long moment and breathing in the morning air

A moment later he got up out of bed and walked into the bathroom. Kaitlyn ordered breakfast from room service and then slipped on her bathrobe. She then walked out onto the balcony that overlooked the beach and watched the tide come in. Moments later Tom came out to join her. He walked up behind her, wrapped his arms around her torso resting them around her hips and he kissed her neck gently. Then he rested his chin on her shoulder and watched the tide with her for a moment before speaking.

"So, what do you want to do today?"

"I already ordered breakfast."

"Okay, what do you want to do after breakfast?"

"I'm not sure. What do you want to do?"

"I thought we'd go scuba diving this morning."

What? Kaitlyn thought to herself. "Scuba diving?" She questioned.

"Yeah, there's this area I know of in the cliffs. You'd like it."

"Oh I forgot, you've been here, to the Bahamas before."

"Yep. There are many great sites here to see. I want you to see them all."

"I thought I'd take it easy this week, you know?"

"Trust me, you'll like this."

"All right Rodriguez," Mr. Manners began the conversation over the phone. "It's up to you now. You've got twenty thousand now, and thirty due to you when the job is done. You've got pictures of what they look like and you know where they're staying. Follow them, make it look like an accident and get the job done before Friday or I'll have your replacement finish you off!"

105

"Yes sir." Came the evilly skittish reply from the native island bookie that had accepted the job of killing Kaitlyn and Tom.

Thanks to their training as secret agents they didn't need to spend the day learning basic techniques for deep-water scuba diving and shortly before noon, they were on their way under the water heading for the secret place Tom had talked about earlier. Every once in a while he'd look over at Kaitlyn who was keeping up with him perfectly even though the trip was long and tedious, he would smile at her as they swam. He waved at her as they came up to the cave entrance under the water and she followed him into it and through the rocky under water pathways until they reached land. Then as they came up from the water at a rather small hole, Kaitlyn saw what Tom had been talking about. They had come into the back entrance of a cavern that was just as secluded as anything. The light from the water that refracted from the surface shimmered in the cavern illuminating deep green and blue crystals that had formed as the island had been made. Volcanic rock that had been rubbed smooth by the incoming and outgoing tides seemed to make a bed for them on the floor, and as if Kaitlyn had read Tom's mind she figured out why he had brought her here.

As she removed the mask from her wet face, he walked up to her and slipped the tanks from her back. Then he took her wet body into his arms and kissed her. He wanted to be sure it was all right but as she unzipped his wet suit, he got his answer tenfold. They undressed, laid their wet suits on the ground under them and made love in the cavern.

A few hours later, Tom reached over to the bag he had been carrying during their trip and pulled it over between them. Kaitlyn was shocked to see he had packed a lunch for them, she knew he had planned this but he had planned this so well she hadn't had a clue. It impressed her.

"So what is this place?" Kaitlyn asked making conversation.

"Tom's cave."

"No. Really?" Kaitlyn said feeling he was joking.

"It's true, look over there by the water hole. You see there? My initials. It's my cave."

"Well that's kind of cool. When did you do that?"

"About three years ago. I came here for vacation, and you know me, I can't just sit still soaking in the sun, I've got to be busy doing something."

"Yes, I know." She smiled wickedly at him knowing exactly what he meant. They ate and talked a bit more and then suited up for the trip back.

"Hey Tom, are there any other ways in or out of this cavern?"

"Not that I've been able to find, but I do know that this island is nothing but underground tunnels and caves that were created by the lava flow. I'm sure there are many more places like this. Why?"

"Just curious."

"Want to go find some other caverns like this?"

"Maybe, but not right now. There's something else I want to do."

"I haven't seen them for hours. They rented scuba diving equipment over two hours ago and they haven't returned yet." Came the breathy greeting from Rodriguez, the guy hired by Mr. Manners to pop off Kaitlyn and Tom

"So?" Mr. Manners spoke harshly at being disturbed.

"So, there's only enough air in those tanks for an hour each."

"Well good. We couldn't have planned this better ourselves, just make sure they don't return those tanks, if you know what I mean."

"Yes sir."

As Kaitlyn and Tom emerged from the scuba shop after returning their tanks, hand in hand they began discussing what they wanted to do next. The day was beautiful and they had been having the most perfect day when Kaitlyn was struck on the back of her head with the thick grip of a hand-held pistol. As she fell forward reaching for the back of her head, Tom staggered forward catching her. Kneeling on the ground he turned his attention upwards just in time to see a large black boot thrusting violently towards his face. With no time to react the both of them passed out. When they came to they were sitting back to back, hands cuffed behind them in the middle of a jet boat back out in the middle of the ocean.

Tom looked around trying to determine from distant islands where they might be as Kaitlyn too came to and began trying to slip her hands under her and to the front of her body. As soon as her hands were in front of her she leapt to her feet ready to attack the driver, when he threw the boat into reverse which threw Kaitlyn forward and she rolled towards the front of the boat and onto her back. He quickly pulled a gun and pointed it to her. "Get up."

With gun pointed at Kaitlyn, the driver motioned for her to take the wheel. "Let's go. You drive." Then he yanked Tom to his feet and made him stand in the middle of the boat, his arms still cuffed behind his back.

Kaitlyn got to the controls, started up the boat and with a quick glance towards Tom she slowly proceeded forward. As the boat jerked forward Tom nearly lost his footing, Kaitlyn knew she'd have to take it easy for his sake. She was afraid if he fell into the water with his arms constrained behind him that he might drown.

"Where are we going?" Kaitlyn asked.

"Shut up! No talking!" The gunman yelled as he sat on the seat in the back of the boat and overlooked both of them. Then he cocked his gun to show them he meant business and spoke again. "Just drive straight out I'll tell you what you to do when I want you to do it!"

A short while later the kidnapper pointed towards the cliffs edge and Kaitlyn saw a large yacht heading their way. That yacht could have been good or bad news. It could have been someone who could help them or it could have been this guy's back up, which meant either way she would have to attempt something before she reached the yacht. So with a quick look over to Tom who had seen the yacht and apparently came to the same conclusion she spoke.

"How you doing baby?"

"Okay, a little hot." He said using code for do something now, he was ready for a swim.

"Right." Kaitlyn said agreeing with his code as well as sending a bit of code back to him as to which way she was planning on going. And as she finished that sentence the gunman knowing they shouldn't talk stood up from his seat and yelled out.

"No talking! Next person who says a word gets shot!" That was their chance. With the guy standing, after sitting for so long, not having enough time to acquire his sea legs, Kaitlyn had to make her move. Cutting the steering wheel sharply right and giving the boat more gas, the boat nearly capsized. Tom leaned to the left to level out the boat as the gunman fell to the side of the boat's edge, gun slipping from his hands.

Kaitlyn then slammed the boat into reverse making the jolt of speed throw the guy to the front as she leaped from the driver's seat and slid towards the gun. However as the plan seemed to be moving perfectly, the gunman flew forwards unsteady on his feet he hit Tom on the way down and knocked him off the boat.

As Tom sank deeper into the ocean, struggling to slip his cuffed hands from his back to the front and loosing air as he did, there was more struggling happening on the boat. Kaitlyn had grabbed the gun right as the gunman recovered and grabbed for it as well. There was a huge fight for the weapon as the two of them yanked on it, fingers inching towards the trigger but no one really knowing to whom it was pointed at.

Finally Tom slipped his hands around his legs to his front side and he was able to swim to the surface of the water. As he took his first breath since the untimely fall gasping for that sweet fresh air, he heard the struggle going on in the boat. He swam to the boats side and pulled himself aboard and raced up behind the gunman. He then slipped his cuffed hands over the gunman's head and broke his neck. As the gunman dropped so did the ball as the yacht pulled up beside the small jet boat and Kaitlyn and Tom found out it wasn't a friendly encounter. Five men had aimed rifles cocked and pointed at Kaitlyn and Tom's head as the leader of this encounter stepped forward, Mr. Mike Manners himself.

"Come my friends, join me. We have lots to talk about." He said as pleasantly as anything.

"Who are you? What do you want?" Tom asked angry that this was happening here and now.

"The names Manners, I was a close personal friend of the late Joe Johnson, and your girlfriend there and I have some catching up to do about that." During the struggle Kaitlyn had retrieved the handcuff keys from their assailant and was in the process of unlocking her restraints when she heard the man mention Johnson's name.

Sudden surprise, fear and shock filled Kaitlyn as she looked up at the man with her mouth dropped and eyes wide. But before she could even think about what to do next, the boat had already been boarded by three of the five armed goons and they were hurriedly rushing Kaitlyn aboard and tackling down Tom who was still confined by the handcuffs.

Before Kaitlyn knew it she was sitting in a large overstuffed chair in Mike Manners' office and he was lighting up a cigar. She had no idea what they were doing to Tom but she worried he wasn't getting the same type of treatment.

"Do you know why you are here today?"

"Because I de-throated your best friend?"

"Joe told me you had a bit of sarcastic over tones. He enjoyed your spunk, I'll enjoy your blood."

"Ah, you're a bloodsucker huh? Ever try out for a job with the IRS?"

"Silence!" He demanded at the top of his lungs startling Kaitlyn out right. "Your time here will be short, I'll only need you alive long enough to get back the equipment you stole from me. But you are luckier than your friend out there. I don't need him at all, and with that said I'm guessing he's got a few more minutes left on earth. Say your prayers baby, you'll be seeing him soon."

Kaitlyn didn't know what to do. She had no idea what she was up against. Most of the time, she stakes out the place, has a plan set to mind before she even considers entering the enemy's territory. Sure she was trained for just about any situation, but with artillery. She usually has back up, plans of attack, a memorized layout of the territory, now she had nothing!

Kaitlyn frantically looked around the room for an escape. She had no idea what Tom was dealing with right now but she knew there wasn't any time for panicking. Before she could come up with an exact plan though, the boat came to a sudden stop and three armed guards stormed into the office. Kaitlyn willingly went with them in hopes to at least see where Tom was if he was still on board or not but as she walked out of the darkened office she realized the rest of the area was dark as well. They had drove into one of the many caves and docked there.

Kaitlyn walked with the guards off of the boat and onto the rocky undercover shoreline looking frantically for Tom, finally she saw him. The goons had hooked him; handcuffs and all to a large crane and had lifted him off of the ground, and over a large lagoon type area. Kaitlyn couldn't figure out what they were up to. Tom was hanging there by his cuffed wrists, gripping hold of the chains with his hands trying to keep his wrists from dislocating. But he easily could escape if they were to dunk him in the water, the cuffs would slide right off the hook of the crane and he would just swim up to the surface.

But then Kaitlyn realized what their sick minds were up to. They were throwing fresh meat, fish and blood into the water, attracting every shark and meat-eating creature in the sea. They were going to feed him to the sharks! Kaitlyn knew Tom was a terrific swimmer and he was always pretty good at getting out of difficult situations but this may have been a little too much.

"Tom!" Kaitlyn yelled when she saw him. He looked over at her just as one of the armed guards knocked her upside the head with his gun.

"Shut-up!" The guard yelled as the two others pointed their guns at her and forced her back to her feet.

Blood dripped from the side of her head now, where the man struck her and as she looked back over to Tom hanging there like a treat to a snake pit she saw that he too was bleeding, from his wrists. She felt vulnerable all over again. She felt weak and worthless, a feeling she hated. She still continued to rack her brain trying to figure out what to do when Mike Manners walked out of the office and began to speak.

"Lower him to the sharks!"

Chapter 8

Kaitlyn shot a terrified look up to Tom but he still showed the same debonair non-distressed look he always showed. And as the crane began to lower him into the water, he made his move. He swung his legs out from under him like a child on a swing set, showing no pain in his face from the metal cuffs around his wrist. Then he swung backwards, outstretched his legs to the cranes long arm, and kicked off of it, freeing his arms from the hook and flipping in the air out and over to the land, landing with a roll. Then as the stunned guards began to come out of their shocked daze Tom yelled out to Kaitlyn.

"Cave. Ten o' clock."

Kaitlyn looked to her left side and saw a small opening in the rock wall, and without a moment's hesitation she too went into action. Finishing the unlock process on her cuffs, they fell to the ground as she turned towards the guard who had a gun pointed at her and side kicked the gun from his hands and kicked him down to the floor, then she threw the gun to Tom for protection.

"Tom, heads up!"

Tom looked up from his fight just in time to catch the gun, shoot one on coming guard away from him, then, use it on the chain between his wrists. Then when Kaitlyn saw he was safe, she dove into the cave and began to scramble out of there. At first she felt foolish, like she was running away from the fight and she wondered what had gotten into her. She used to be so strong, so eager to get involved in things like this, to fight to the death, preferably others death. But before she could even reconsider going back to help Tom she heard rustling behind her; they were after her. She had no choice now but to keep going. In a tunnel like this, one shot from a gun at close range and there would be nothing left of her except gravy.

She crawled like a professional, keeping up the speed, no matter how many times she scuffed her knees along the sharp jagged rocks. She bumped her head on low hanging rocks from the top of the cave and no matter how many times she hit her head wound and wanted to pass out she knew she couldn't. Finally she came to a fork in the tunnel. Two ways to choose from. Her instinct chose right, that would be heading back out to sea, and out of this mess. Her training made her crawl a little into the left side, leaving a trail of blood from her knees and head. But then she turned back around and turned over into her back in the right tunnel. There she slid on her back far enough into the tunnel to keep the blood from dripping into the entrance of that tunnel. By doing this it would make the goons following her think she went left and they would take the left tunnel, they wouldn't see she went right because she kept her blood trail from that entrance.

She kept in that direction moving just a bit slower now so she could listen for followers. For a long while she heard nothing, but then she heard them start after her again. If they fell for the trick it was only for a few moments. As Kaitlyn began crawling faster along the rigid tunnel she heard the follower coming closer, whoever it was, was coming towards her at full speed ahead. The adrenaline pumped in her body making her crawl faster and faster until she came to a very small hole not much bigger than her finger. There was no way out she was trapped!

Kaitlyn knew there were two options. Fight the on-coming goon in the smallest space on the planet or try to break through the wall. She knew it was relatively thin since there was a hole in it that she could see through, so she chose for that option. She squirmed around in the tunnel, making herself turn around and once her feet were facing the wall, she lined them up, brought them back and sent a powerful kick into the rocks to knock it out. The first time it knocked some of them out but not all, the rest was cracked. One more kick should do it she thought to herself, so she aimed her legs at it again, and in hearing the follower closing in extremely fast she kicked once more, giving it all she had. Finally the opening was big enough to get through and without even checking to see what was on the other side; she jumped through it, feet first.

As she landed on the soft black land she immediately realized how familiar the place looked. And as she quickly scanned the place, seeing a small area of rock missing from the floor and filled with water, then seeing those familiar initials, TM she knew this was Tom's cave and she knew how to escape.

The only problem was, she knew the tunnel leading out to sea was a good two to three minutes under water without an air hole anywhere. That was half-good and half-bad. Good because if she could make it and the others following her most likely couldn't she would have succeeded. Bad because if she couldn't make it either, she would drown. She hesitated for only a moment before she heard the rustling of the followers closing in on the exit of the tunnel.

It was now or never, so without a second thought she ran to the watering hole, laid a hand-touched kiss upon Tom's initials and dove into the cold ocean waters. The sting of the salt water made visibility hard, but Kaitlyn knew if she didn't put up with the sting of the salt, she'd soon feel the sting in her lungs that come from lack of oxygen and that would hurt much more.

She heard the others jump in the water after her, but she knew that if they didn't know the terrain they'll turn back for air or drown chasing her, all she had to do is make it out without drowning herself. She swam harder than she had ever swum before, of course it made it hard on her muscles, the lack of air, but she was determined to survive. She kicked in the water, paddled with her arms and kept a painful stung eye open for any obstacles that may keep her from her destination.

Finally she saw the light of day brightening the water at the end of this tunnel and she knew her swim was nearing its end. But she also knew her air supply was running extremely low and even though she may be able to see the surface there was a possibility she may not make it. She continued kicking, slowly letting out what air she had left to loosen up the tenseness on her lungs, but that made her less buoyant. She kept trying however almost giving into her bodily urges to take a deep breath, until finally like a car pulling into a gas station with only fumes, she made it out of the underwater pit and took a breath of fresh air.

For a moment there she was so relieved she had made it that she forgot all about the others who had been following her. During the entire trip she could hear the echoing of their bodies in the water swimming towards her, but towards the end of her swim she had only enough energy to be concerned with herself. As she inhaled the sweet air into her lungs, basking her face in the sunshine, she was oblivious as to anyone still after her. But just as she wasn't expecting it, a man shot out of the water in front of her and gasped for breath.

The wall of water that shot up and over her made her blind as to whom it was that had just come up, but instinct told her, if it was foe, best eliminate him now, before he tries to eliminate her. She quickly reached over and grabbed the man by the shoulders and used her body weight to push him back under the water.

He struggled with her for a moment, before pulling her under the water as well in a fight for his life. The two bodies struggled, air bubbles blocking their view of each other. Panic began filling Kaitlyn as she realized this man was just as strong as she was and then it happened.

"Kaitlyn – it's me." She heard in her head. Immediately realizing it was Tom who made it and no one else she released her grip upon his head and swam to the surface to take a breath. As he followed and breathed in the fresh cool air they looked at each other and then began to laugh.

"How did you get here?" Kaitlyn began.

"I followed you. Are you alright?"

"I'm fine. So you were the one following me this entire time?"

"Well, I caught your trick at the fork, but the others didn't."

"I thought I was still being chased. You made my heart pound like a jack hammer!"

"You were moving so quickly I couldn't catch up to tell you!" They looked at each other for a moment, speechless; then they began to laugh again. Finally they swam out of the water, onto the land and rested.

"How did you know to tell me about the cave?"

"When the boat pulled in to this cave I recognized where we were." Tom explained.

"But you told me earlier that there were no ways out of Tom's cave."

"There wasn't was there? You had to make an entrance."

"I did but… That was a pretty good move back there. The swinging out and flipping onto the ground. I was impressed." Kaitlyn explained changing the subject.

"You were?"

"Oh yeah, very sexy."

"Well… you know I had to do what I had to do."

"Mm hmm." Kaitlyn hummed as she took her finger and flipped a strand of hair from Tom's eyes. "What do you have to do now?" She asked him as she moved herself directly in front of him, grinning like the Cheshire cat.

"I was thinking about playing doctor."

"Doctor?"

"Yeah, I was going to check over my patient, really good. Kiss all of her wounds and make them better, massaging her every muscle…"

"Sounds good. Who's your patient?"

"Well my waiting room seems kind of empty, so I'll take you if you're up for the challenge." He whispered to her with his deep throaty growl then he leaned in to her, and kissed her passionately on the lips.

Lenny was just walking in the door to an establishment he had been in many times. He waved to the bartender to bring him his usual then sat down at a darkened booth and waited. Behind him he heard a conversation between two men and it intrigued him enough to eaves drop.

"She got away, now she knows your face, her entire organization will be out looking for you."

"I don't care! I want her dead! She killed Joe Johnson, he was a close personal friend of mine and I owe him revenge!"

"The very moment they see your face they'll begin shooting, you must hire someone else to do the job."

"I tried that. They made it past my men. They made it out of there without a scratch. I will find that Agent Jones and I will crush her bones! And anyone who gets in my way will suffer the consequences!"

By now Lenny had heard enough. He knew exactly who these men were talking about and he wanted her dead as much as them. He knew it was risky invading another criminal's privacy but he had to make himself known.

"Excuse me, I didn't mean to over hear your conversation but you mentioned a name that drew my attention. This Agent Jones you just mentioned, would that be Agent Kaitlyn Jones?"

"Yeah, what's it to you?"

"Just that I've wanted her dead a lot longer than you."

"So what?"

"And I've got just the plan to do it too."

"So why haven't you done it yet then?"

"Money. Her damned organization froze my accounts in order to find me, life's been a little rough since then."

"So what? Why should we care?"

"Why, because I heard the word revenge and revenge can be costly, yet I've got the perfect revenge for her all I need is a little financial backing to pull it off."

"Join our table stranger."

"Thank you, the name is Lenny Lane."

"Lenny, this is Mr. Manners."

"Manners, as in the south Hampton Manners?"

"That is just one of my groups, yes."

"Wow, this is truly an honor."

"Go on." He smiled gleefully.

Two weeks later...

"Colonel this is Agent Lane with the IGU, we have an immediate favor to ask of you."

"Who is this again?" The colonel asked not recognizing the name of the organization.

"Agent Lane with the IGU, we're a new organization. I'm sorry for bothering you so late in the day but we are in a real jam. One of our agents was supposed to rendezvous with a particular man we've been tracking for an embezzlement case but she got sick at the last moment. We heard you have a female agent that might fit the description."

"Which agent are you referring to?"

"Agent Kaitlyn Jones, she is part of your organization yes?"

"Yes, she is. What is this rendezvous you mentioned?"

"There is a man, Willie Bronson, he has information regarding a case of ours and we found the easiest way to get it out of him is by setting him up on a blind date."

"A blind date?"

"I know, sounds uncharacteristic of our organization but this man is lonely, he's joined a dating service and we've infiltrated his records and informed him we'd be sending out a woman for him. If no one shows up he'll be wise to us and the mission will be unsuccessful. I know that this is last minute and we'll gratefully pay you for your inconvenience but we need to know if you'll help us now or we'll have to go elsewhere."

"Sure I'll help, but it's already six at night, I don't have time to inform the offices of this matter. To investigate it."

"I know but we're running out of time, Willie's expecting his date at 7pm and if we don't get someone in there, we'll lose our opportunity to get this information. Will you help us?"

"Fine I'll do it, but make sure you fill out and get the proper paper work to my office before 9am tomorrow morning.

"No problem. I'll fax you over the details now. And colonel, thanks again."

"Thank you for considering us first." The colonel said happily as he hung up the phone. He sat there for a moment looking at his phone and thinking "IGU? I must be out of the loop." Then he reached over and pressed his intercom button. "Get Kaitlyn Jones on the phone."

"Yes sir."

Just walking in the door from their trip, Tom dropped their bags to the floor and then plopped down on a nearby chair. Kaitlyn closed the door behind her and then walked into the kitchen.

"Night cap?"

"Anything cold." Tom called from the other room. Kaitlyn pulled out two glasses and began filling them with ice when the phone rang.

"Can you get that?" Kaitlyn called out from the kitchen.

"Let the machine get it."

Kaitlyn smiled but then placed the glasses on the table and walked towards the phone. The machine picked up and a moment later she heard the caller.

"Miss Jones, this is Colonel Daft, I know it is late and that you are probably just getting home but I have another mission for you if you are willing…"

Kaitlyn quickly picked up the phone as Tom rose to his feet and walked over there as well. He listened to the conversation still being recorded as Kaitlyn spoke.

"Tonight?"

"Agent Lane from the IGU department contacted my office a few minutes ago, seems their only female agent took sick and they need to put a substitute in place immediately."

"What's the job?"

Less than an hour later Kaitlyn found herself sitting at a table with a stranger, Willie Bronson, enjoying some fancy French cuisine. Kaitlyn was supposed to play a normal female on a blind date. A simple technicality that gives the date the possibility to ask many personal questions without cause to wonder if she's trying to hit him up for information or learn more than necessary about him. Which indeed was what Kaitlyn's task was to do. Kaitlyn was supposed to find out in any way possible if this guy had any information regarding an embezzlement case and although Kaitlyn usually has more time to prepare for a case and do a little background on her subjects she had little time to prepare and was sent out here blind.

Willie seemed like a nice enough guy, he was a rather large man, plump full of muscles, a large scar on his face that Kaitlyn kept wondering about but she stayed focused on her task. Knowing she needed to find out information about this guy she planned her questions carefully.

"So you're in sales?"

"Actually I'm on the technical side of sales..." He began. Kaitlyn listened carefully for any clues to this case as he continued. "And so the department had to lay off a few of its' employees."

"Really? Doesn't sound like there's that much money in that industry."

"You'd be surprised at how much money there is."

Kaitlyn felt she had just stumbled upon the right conversation and as the check came she knew she had to keep him talking about it. Before long, Kaitlyn found herself sitting in the guys' apartment. He was fixing coffee and everything seemed to be going rather well on the date scene but Kaitlyn had just skimmed the surface on this guy and the missing money and she needed more information. Kaitlyn decided that while he was busy making coffee she'd excuse herself to go to the bathroom in an attempt to check out this guys other rooms. She was just entering the guys bedroom when she found something she was definitely not prepared to find. His bedroom was a shrine to women and carnage; it was a disgusting display of a sick-minded man and a fetish of abuse. Kaitlyn had her incriminating evidence but it was completely different than what she was sent in to find out. Kaitlyn was just about to take her hiatus when she turned around to see her date standing directly next to her.

"Found my bedroom did you? Planning anything special tonight?"

"After seeing this? I think not." Kaitlyn spat as she began to push past the guy and make her exit, but he had other plans. Before Kaitlyn knew it a large fist struck her face and knocked her backwards. Suddenly fighting for her life Kaitlyn began to wish she had just stayed home tonight.

Tom had just finished watching a made for TV movie and was getting ready for bed when he heard something outside. Like a cat on the prowl he padded through his apartment, snatching up his gun as he did and waltzed up to the door ready to attack. After a few moments of hesitation, silence protruded from outside and curiosity got the better of him and he threw open the door. Kaitlyn fell in the door and into Tom's arms. Without a word he scooped Kaitlyn into his arms and carried her inside the apartment, shutting the door with his foot.

Moments later Kaitlyn found herself bundled up in one of Tom's soft thick robes, and she was sitting in front of a roaring fire. Tom had just grabbed his first aid kit and a bowl of hot water and was sitting them down next to Kaitlyn when she basically came to. He dunked a soft washcloth in the water, twisted the excess water out and began dabbing it on a swelled cut next to her eye. Kaitlyn lifted her eyes to meet his and even though she was in pain she found the strength to smile with her eyes. Her hair fell around her heart shaped face and it draped it like soft lace curtains. Shadows and warm orange lights flickered from the fire glowing upon her face, warming her. Tom then noticed that Kaitlyn had been cradling her left arm and he slowly, carefully took it into his hand.

"Can you move your fingers?" It took her a few moments to make them twitch but the pain began making her arm tremble, Tom realized Kaitlyn had fractured her wrist. Without a moment he reached into his first aid kit, pulled out a bundle of bandages and began wrapping her wrist. When he was done he took his finger and slid a lock of hair from in front of her eye allowing her to look up into his eyes again.

"What happened?" He paused taking her unhurt hand into his. Kaitlyn took a deep breath but before she could even contemplate speaking there was a knock at Tom's door. Tom got up to answer it, completely shocked and overwhelmed at who it was.

"Colonel!"

"Tom, I'm sorry to disturb you at home and at this hour but I thought that maybe you could help me. It's about Agent Jones."

"What about her?"

"She's missing. I expected her to check in over two hours ago and..." He paused as Tom stepped aside just enough for the colonel to see Kaitlyn just getting to her feet. Through the darkness he could barely tell who it was but when he realized it was her, he stepped into the house and up to Kaitlyn.

"Where have you been? I expected a report from you hours ago!" Tom however was not going to allow this guy to talk to Kaitlyn that way especially in her current state and even though it was the colonel, he wasn't afraid to speak his thoughts.

"Colonel I'm sure this can wait until the morning. You can see that Kaitlyn is not in any condition right now." Finally the light entered his eyes and he saw Kaitlyn standing there, her wrist bandaged up, her face badly beaten, balancing on one leg, protecting her left ankle. She had been badly beaten and he felt a fool for not noticing a moment earlier.

"I'm sorry Miss Jones." He spoke more delicately. Kaitlyn had her ideas about him but she knew what she had to tell him. Before the colonel turned to leave Kaitlyn spoke her first words of the night.

"Colonel?"

"Yes Agent?"

"He's dead."

At first the colonel was shocked even appalled, he was preparing to scrutinize Kaitlyn for messing up this simple information gathering task and now their suspect was dead? He was about to say just that when he paused realizing why she did it. He simply nodded his understanding and continued walking out the door. Kaitlyn however had her own reservations about the man and once he left she limped over to Tom's computer and switched it on. Tom soon walked up behind her.

"Well I know you're not much of a computer person so tell me what you need."

"You're good at research, would you find for me all of the police posted reports on a man named Willie Bronson?"

"Of course." Tom sat down at the computer logged into the police files and typed in the man's name. "Willie Bronson. Also known as Wicked Willie. He is the main suspect in multiple missing persons cases along with numerous BTK occurrences. He preys on unsuspecting women, lulls them into a state of calm right before he kidnaps them, tortures, rapes, beats and then kills them. Bronson is wanted in fourteen states. He is extremely dangerous." Tom read with astonishment. He turned to see Kaitlyn sitting on the edge of his bed her head in her hands. "You were sent on a blind date with this guy?"

"An embezzlement case is all I was told."

"The Colonel never told you about this guys background?" Kaitlyn shook her head no. "Never gave you any information on this guy?" Again she shook her head no. "Never told you he was dangerous?" Kaitlyn kept shaking her head. "Did he send any back up with you? Did he inform the proper authorities that he was sending an unarmed agent in there?" Again she shook her head no. "Kaitlyn, I find it incredibly hard to believe that no one in our organization knew about this guys history before sending you out to meet him."

"If they knew they never told me."

Tom stared at Kaitlyn for a moment, his eyes shooting left and right as he comprehended this information then he turned back to the computer screen. The words Extremely Dangerous jumped out at him and his mind began racing. Suddenly he stood from his chair. He began pacing across the room, back and forth, each time passing Kaitlyn sitting on the edge of the bed trembling, his blood began to boil. His adrenaline began to pump, a fury began to build up inside of him as the situation began to piece itself together in his mind. His breathing became shallower as his lips pursed together and his teeth began to grind. One hand on his hip the other in the air trying to make sense of all of this. Kaitlyn could see him growing more and more furious, she could see him pacing there like an angry tiger getting ever more agitated by the moment and she realized she had to say something.

"Tom." She called but he kept pacing, "Tom." She called again but he quickly yelled back, "No!" Kaitlyn sat there in silence for a moment, not sure what to think about all of this herself when Tom finally spoke again.

"This is wrong – there's got to be something we're missing. Something you're not telling me."

"I've told you everything."

"The Colonel wouldn't have sent you in there unprepared. There's no reason to put any of his agents in that kind of a..." Tom paused looking at Kaitlyn's battered face and growing more angry. "I trusted that guy with my life! I trusted him with your life!"

"Tom he may not have known either."

"He would have had to have known. Protocol states that a complete background check would have to be done on anyone before sending an agent out into the field. This is easy information to obtain! We weren't even given an alias, they blatantly used his name, they had to have known about this guy's history!"

"Tom we don't know the facts yet."

"I'm going to kill that son of a bitch."

"Tom we should call the general."

"General Harrison here." The slightly groggy man said as he answered the phone at three o clock in the morning.

"General I'm sorry to call you so early this morning but I really needed to talk to you." Tom said quickly.

"Who is this?"

"Agent M sir, calling with Agent Jones."

"What is this about and can it wait until morning?"

"Sir I don't think this can wait. First I'd like to put on the record that I would never consider going over the colonels head unless I felt it was absolutely necessary. But I truly believe if I was to go to the colonel with these particular concerns that I would be risking my own safety."

"I see. Tell me Agent, what are your concerns?"

Chapter 9

Later that morning Kaitlyn limped into the Colonel's office followed by Tom. Both gave their formal greeting before the Colonel jumped right into the situation at hand.

"Agent Jones what the hell happened last night?"

"I was administering the task as communicated to me by you last night sir, when I realized the situation was getting dangerous."

"The guy is dead Agent Jones! This was supposed to be a simple information gathering!"

"If I had been briefed of the severity of the suspects history prior to sending me on this mission I would have been better prepared."

"You were told all you needed to know."

"You sent me in there unarmed. Without back up, without wires or contacts."

"You didn't need it!"

Just then the General walked in, having heard this entire conversation. "It took me two and a half minutes to determine that this mission needed backup…"

General." The Colonel stood and saluted.

"A simple search in the criminal directory pulled up enough pertinent information to know that sending an unarmed agent in there was against all of our policies."

The Colonel stood there in confusion for a moment. "I don't understand."

"The man you sent Agent Jones to meet last night is a known BTK murderer. I don't know how you could have done any research no matter how limited and not have learned that."

The Colonel's mouth dropped open. "What?"

"Colonel Daft I am at a loss here. Can you please explain to me how you can send an unarmed agent out there with out following the very first rule of protocol."

The Colonel sat down.

"Can you show us your written request for an undercover mission?" The Colonel slowly began thumbing through his pile of papers on his desk knowing well he had no information about this mission because the fax hadn't come in this morning.

"Can you show me where the ops department signed off on a mission of this caliber without any pertinent information regarding the situation?"

The Colonel, dropped his head.

"Can you at least explain to me how I should not find you in fault of breaking the most cardinal of rules – of sending one of our best agents into an extremely explosive situation without one ounce of regard for her safety?" The Colonel remained silent.

"Colonel I want answers and I want them now!"

"There was no time for formalities." The Colonel finally spoke. "I was given the order late last night."

"From who?"

"Agent Lane with the IGU."

"IGU? What the hell is the IGU?"

"A new department."

"I authorize all new departments. There is no IGU!"

The Colonel dropped his head into his hands.

"All I was told is their agent was sick, she couldn't make it. It's not rare for other organizations to call us for help."

"And you didn't investigate this new department?"

"There was no time. They needed Jones in place within the hour."

"They asked for me specifically?" Kaitlyn perked up.

"So you just accepted this mission, no paperwork, no one signing off on it, you break every rule just because you had limited time?"

"I'm afraid so sir." The Colonel gulped knowing he had completely screwed up plus feeling overwhelmed with guilt.

Kaitlyn stood there for a moment, gears grinding in her head when she spoke again. "Who was it that you spoke with sir?"

"Agent Lane of the IGU."

Suddenly Kaitlyn fell back into a chair behind her nearly fainting. Tom turned and knelt down in front of her, his right hand on her knee. "Kaitlyn, you alright?"

"I'll get you."

"Excuse me?" The Colonel spoke up knowing he had screwed up but not being prepared for verbal threats either.

"I'll get you, that's the IGU."

Tom shook his head trying to understand Kaitlyn.

"The agency IGU stands for I'll Get You." Kaitlyn explained leaning her head against the back of the chair. The three men remained silent as she continued. "And Agent Lane..." Kaitlyn spoke feeling her stomach begin to churn, "...is Lenny Lane." Kaitlyn finally breathed.

Tom still kneeling in front of her dropped his head. He was so disgusted, so angry about the entire matter he began to feel sick. He slowly stood, head still bowed as the Colonel and the General exchanged glances.

"Colonel, call the operator, have her track down last nights phone call."

Without a word the colonel pressed his intercom and asked for records of last nights incoming calls. The General however was still confused.

"Miss. Jones I'm afraid I'm going to need some explanation.

"Lenny Lane and I go way back – he killed my father.

"I'm sorry but…"

"I'm pretty sure that IGU stands for I'll get you, which are the exact words Lenny said to me last time we ran into each other. He said I'll get you later; you can call it a date." Kaitlyn half laughed at that. "A date, who would have thought he would have been giving me a clue when he set me up for a blind date with a murderer?"

"General, we've got to get this guy if it's the last thing we do!" Tom stated angrily. The colonel then noticed Kaitlyn's arm in a sling and her ankle wrapped in a brace.

"By the way Agent Jones, I meant to ask earlier, how are you feeling?"

"My ankle is sore but operational, my wrist will need a little more time to heal and my face looks worse than it is."

"Well I hope you feel better soon."

"Thank you sir."

"And my most sincere apologies."

As Kaitlyn and Tom walked out of the office the General closed the door to the Colonels office, he needed to have a word with the Colonel about his actions.

"Lenny it didn't work!" Mr. Manner's yelled at the man at the top of his lungs when Lenny walked through the door.

"I know, but it's okay."

"How do you figure? She's still alive? I wanted her dead!"

"Alive yes, but also wounded. And I left enough information with the colonel so she would figure out the assignment was from me."

"You are not impressing me thus far!" Manners growled loudly.

"Ah but you don't know what I have planned next do you?"

"The only thing you should have planned next is a long walk off a short pier wearing cement shoes!"

"Mr. Manners if you'd just give me one more moment of your time, I'll explain phase two of my plan."

"This had better be good Lenny or you'll be dead!"

"Oh it is. Trust me, it is."

Kaitlyn and Tom tracked the phone records to a pay phone on the other side of town. After investigating further they found an abandoned warehouse not far away that had many shipments in the last few weeks, something an abandoned warehouse shouldn't be getting. They began to stakeout the place from a building down the street and they finally spotted Lenny through their binoculars.

"There he is! Let's get him." Kaitlyn said as she reached for her gun.

"No wait." Tom said as he placed his hand also on her gun keeping her from pulling it out. We need to do this by the book. We'll inform the general, put together a team and come back tomorrow morning, we'll catch them completely off guard."

"But Tom, we can take him."

"We have no idea how many men he's got in there, we can't run in there half cocked, that kind of thing will get us killed."

"You sound like the chief of police in San Diego. However he said you never went by the book, so why start now?"

"Because sadly he was right. Now come on. Well come back first thing tomorrow morning."

Kaitlyn begrudgingly left the scene although she knew she could take him out without trying. Little did they know their stakeout was not secret. Lenny had been watching

Kaitlyn and Tom all day and had heard their plans fully. Lenny had them exactly where he wanted them.

When they reported back to headquarters, the general called in a team to inform them of the project. They made their plans and were completely set up for a morning take down when the general dismissed them to go get a good nights' rest.

"We'll begin operation take down first thing in the morning. Now everyone get a good nights' sleep. Report back here at 4am sharp. Dismissed."

As they all left the generals office, while they were walking home, Kaitlyn turned to Tom and began talking.

"Come on Tom, I know we can take them down ourselves. Let's just go, get it done and come back heroes tonight? Lenny's group will be sound asleep, there's no better time."

"Yes there is a better time. Tomorrow morning when we'll have a full team of men backing us up. Look I know you are chomping at the bit to get this man but you'll just have to wait."

"Tom he killed my father. He's a murderer. It's killing me to know that he's out there putting together some despicable plan and all we're doing is going to bed."

"Kaitlyn I know it's difficult but you just have to trust me. Do you trust me?"

"Of course Tom, it's just…"

"Then trust what I'm saying. Going there tonight is not a good idea."

"Fine." Kaitlyn said reluctantly. Then she looked into Tom's eyes. "I know you're just looking out for me."

About 1AM Kaitlyn woke up. She looked to the side of her to see Tom, sound asleep. She slowly slid out of bed and into the other room. There she quietly got dressed and sneaked out. Kaitlyn then jumped into a nearby car and drove away. Tom may have said the words, us going there tonight is not a good idea, but he never said you going there tonight is. Kaitlyn knew he'd be angry that she disobeyed orders but she just had to do this. If she could single-handedly kill the man who murdered her father she'd feel like she lived up to her father's expectations and revenged his death. She had wanted to do this for years and now was her chance.

When she pulled into the empty parking lot of the building across the street, she cut her lights and engine so as to not alert Lenny's men she was there. She then got out of the car and began making her way across the field to the far south side of the warehouse. She crouched down behind a nearby bush and watched as a guard paced back and forth in front of the door and she knew it was now or never. As she prepared herself for the ultimate take down she knew, this was for her father.

"She's right outside." Called a man sitting in front of numerous security screens.

Little did Kaitlyn know but she had been watched from the very beginning. Not only did they know she was there, they also knew she was alone. Lenny laughed with glee at the prospect that he was one up on the infamous Kaitlyn Jones and as he gave the order to go retrieve his prize he rubbed his hands together in expectation. He peered over at his prize piece, an hourglass shaped torture device that he had been infatuated with creating since his last run in with Kaitlyn and now it was ready to use.

Kaitlyn was outside, about to make her move. She had a silencer on her gun, she had a plan in her head that kept changing by the minute. The will for revenge in her made her feel untouchable. She had envisioned killing Lane so many times tonight she didn't even care how it went down, she just knew it would. Every method seemed to work; so as she went in, she felt her plan was fool-proof. As she aimed her gun and began to squeeze the trigger a curl of her lips began as a sense of pride filled her.

Suddenly she was struck – looking down at her chest she saw a tranquilizer dart sticking out and as she pulled it looking up towards the shooter on the roof, pointing her gun towards him and taking aim, her vision became blurry and she passed out.

Kaitlyn was lying down inside of an oblong and uncomfortable metal device when she slowly woke up. Her back was in the most uncomfortable position imaginable and screaming for her immediate attention and the blood seemed to have all rushed to her head. She was bent in half backwards, some rather sharp point lifting the crease of her back higher than her legs and head. She opened her eyes to look around and saw that the fitting around her torso was rather lose. Not able to figure out what was going on, but knowing well where she was, she realized that it seemed easy to get out of this device, so she began to pull herself free. However as she did this, she realized that the device opening was too small to get her pelvis through. Just then, her captors came out of the office to greet her and as they spoke to her, the device she was in began to move.

"Agent Jones how good it is to see you up and about. About to die that is." Lenny laughed as he watched the device do a 90 degree rotation with Kaitlyn holding on tight, she scrambled about the device as she realized her legs were dangling free through the underside and her torso dangled free from the top, but as the device came to a full upright position and stopped, Kaitlyn realized what the man meant. The weight of her body, her legs pulling her down with the force of gravity, Kaitlyn soon began to feel the strain and the pain to her rib cage and vital organs. As she tried to escape by pulling herself up through the opening, her pelvis caught the bottom of the crease and pulled her back downwards again. She realized through her straining that the hourglass shaped device was impossible to break free from.

"Like our new creation Miss Jones? It was a dream I had shortly after our last meeting, my machine shop guys made it for me just so I could torture you with it. Wasn't that nice of them?"

"Delightful." Kaitlyn growled as she quickly realized she needed to hold herself up with her hands to keep from sliding through the hole. Problem was, it was designed just for her, the side walls too short for her to extend her arms and lock her elbows, too tall for her to use her forearms. She was now straining her upper arm muscles just to hold herself in an upright unlocked position and her arms were already beginning to shake under the pressure. Plus her sprained wrist, which had almost finished healing, was beginning to hurt again. Her entire body began to tremble. She was strong but not strong enough to hold herself up like this for an extended period of time, this she knew but she wasn't prepared to let Lenny know it.

She watched as one of Lenny's men walked up to give him an update. She was busily studying their lip movement trying to determine what they were saying when the sweat on her palms made her hand slip, losing her grip on the edge of the hourglass and she fell into the crevice of the device. Her rib cage stopped her fall, the crevice too small for her to fall through, one rib cracked under the pressure of the fall. The pain of the broken bone made Kaitlyn cry out.

"Oh look at this." Smiled Lenny as he pointed his attention back up to Kaitlyn who was scrambling to keep the weight of her body from bearing down more upon her broken rib. She reached for the top edge and pulled herself back up, slower now than before, the pain of the broken rib searing through her body. Using every bit of upper body strength she had to pull herself up away from the funnel her hips then caught hold of the underside of the funnel thus making her lose her grip and she fell into the funnel again.

A second fall onto her already cracked ribcage, she heard another crack, this time it seemed that everyone heard it crack and the shear pain of the break drew the tears from Kaitlyn's eyes and she screamed out in pain. The very breath from her body left her, and the pain kept her from having the strength to inhale for a couple of very long moments.

"Kaitlyn darling, you're looking a bit uncomfortable."

"Screw you!" Kaitlyn yelled loudly gasping for breath.

"What language, and I was going to lay you back down again. Maybe a little longer in my new piece of equipment, will do the body good."

As they turned and left the room the sweat began to pour from Kaitlyn's brow. She pulled herself back up to relieve the pressure on her ribs being careful as to not pull too far. The edges of the device were sharp and they cut into the palms of her hands and blood began to drip down the sides of it as she held herself up in that half pull up. Her arms began wobbling from the pressure, the pain of this extended exercise searing through her as the broken ribs added to her already bruised up body. Kaitlyn knew she wouldn't last like this for very long and she knew she wouldn't be strong enough to die in silence, so with a very difficult clearing of her mind she sent a telepathic S.O.S. to Tom.

"Tom, help."

"Kaitlyn what's wrong? Where are you?" Tom woke quickly looking to his side to see Kaitlyn wasn't next to him

"Torture, pain." She breathed, each word coming slower than the last.

"Where are you?"

"Warehouse."

"You went after Lenny? Alone!"

"Punish later."

"I can be there in twenty minutes."

"I'll be dead in twenty minutes."

"I'm on my way!"

"I'm blacking out."

"Stay awake. I'm on my way!"

"Too much. I can't…"

"Keep talking to me." Tom said telepathically as he lifted his radio to his mouth and began barking orders. "Agent down, South Warehouse, Carter Street, immediate back up required!" "Kaitlyn are you still with me?"

"Tom, hurry."

"Kaitlyn tell me about security."

Kaitlyn looked around the room, salty sweat filling her tear filled eyes as she looked over the edge at the three men in the room. One keeping his eyes on Kaitlyn, stroking his gun like a phallic symbol. The other one talking to Lenny who every once in a while peeked through his window out at Kaitlyn, curious to see if Kaitlyn was getting tired yet. Kaitlyn passed those images to Tom, knowing that the mental communication was all that was keeping her from passing out from the pain and exhaustion. The sweat began pouring down her arms, her palms were sweating and bleeding, the ledge was getting slippery again, the trembling of her muscles made her lose her grip continuously. It was beginning to be too much to handle, she slipped down into the funnel and that final drop cracked a second row of ribs, one piercing her left lung and the shock from the pain made her pass out.

"Kaitlyn. Kaitlyn?" Tom called but silence filled his head. He knew that his presence was needed and he was still ten minutes away. The pedal was to the medal, the car soared down the road at high speed, tires squealed as he turned the corner onto Carter Street and towards the warehouse. By now he didn't care if Lenny's gang heard him coming, Kaitlyn was his top priority. Besides, he also knew that the helicopter was on its way.

"She's down." Lenny said as he leapt from his chair. He pressed a button on a remote then rushed out of his office. The remote triggered a small platform to begin to rise directly underneath the hourglass lifting Kaitlyn upwards by her legs. Her knees were like jelly but as the motion made her stir she slowly opened her eyes and feeling the platform continue to rise under her, her leg muscles began to resume operations in holding her up.

As the platform stopped Kaitlyn strengthened the muscles in her legs which were bent at nearly a forty-five degree angle and used them to lift her rib cage from the device crevice. Starting to straighten her legs however she realized when her pelvis hit the crevice she couldn't do that. Just like her arms couldn't straighten and lock into place at the top of the device, her legs couldn't straighten and lock at the bottom. Knees bent, thigh muscles at maximum capacity, pain from her broken ribs and punctured lung still burning her veins, fractured wrist throbbing, headache from the tranquilizer; Kaitlyn knew she was a mess.

"So what do you think of my contraption now?" Lenny asked as he made his way across the warehouse to her.

Kaitlyn felt nauseous, the pain was searing through her veins like poison, burning her muscles. Her breathing was shallow, each time she inhaled the cracked rib pierced her left lung further, sending even more pain down her spine and throughout her body. Her fingers tingled and grateful for the relief from the hourglass, weak from the exposure and fading in and out of consciousness from the pain and lack of oxygen to her body she still had enough about her to know to keep her mouth shut. He wanted her dead and the very fact that he hadn't done it yet was a good sign.

"Would you like me to let you out of there?"

"I can't…" Kaitlyn began to say breathe but began coughing instead. The motion of the diaphragm collapsed her right lung temporarily and made her lose her breath. Tears were streaming down her face and although she was awake she was silently praying for piece from this.

"Tom."

"Kaitlyn you're awake!"

"Where are you?" She asked with such fear in her telepathic voice that Tom knew without a doubt that she was in serious trouble.

"I'm almost there."

"Come in through the far south door. Two guards standing there, can catch them both off guard, Lenny is…"

"Kaitlyn?"

Lenny had just walked up to Kaitlyn, he had rolled a ladder over to the side of the hourglass contraption and had just approached the top of it, standing next to Kaitlyn, he leaned over and rested his elbows alongside the edge of the contraption. He looked into the contraption at the fading Kaitlyn and smiled sympathetically.

"Are you okay?"

"The pain is…"

"I know baby, I know."

"If I could just…"

"A break? I will let you out babe, you know I will." He egged on.

"Please, the pain is just…"

"I can imagine. I'll let you out. Right now if you want, all I need is for you to tell me what I want to hear."

"What do you…" Kaitlyn breathed still trying to keep her composure but forgetting her true duty through her anguishing body.

"I can make all of your pain go away, just tell me you want me to end your pain and I will."

Kaitlyn looked up into Lenny's eyes, eyes that she had seen angry, eyes of hate, eyes of the man who had killed her father but at this particular moment she saw compassion and caring. She didn't see the man behind the eyes, just the man who would be able to end her suffering. Her judgment was becoming impaired.

"You would let me out of here?"

"I would. I promise." Lenny said with such determination that Kaitlyn truly believed he was here to help her. Although Lenny's plan was much more merciless and corrupt. Kaitlyn Jones had been a thorn in his side for years, stopping all of his plans, but she had also been intriguing to him. He couldn't quite explain the thrill he got when he saw her struggle, he enjoyed toying with her. He'd love nothing more than to torture Kaitlyn for an indefinite amount of time but Lenny was becoming well known throughout the underworld and he knew that killing Kaitlyn Jones, would seal his name in gold. However, he didn't want to just kill her. He wanted her to beg for death, to beg him to kill her, and she was just about there. "Just tell me you want your pain to end, and I'll make it happen."

Kaitlyn was so weak and in so much pain she wasn't thinking straight. She just wanted to be able to breathe normally again, to be rid of this pain and she was just about to say the words Lenny was waiting to hear when Tom came back into her head.

"Kaitlyn I'm here."

"Tom?" Kaitlyn said aloud, catching Lenny off guard. Lenny grew curious, he looked to his two sidemen standing around like bumps on a log and barked orders at them.

"You two! Search the grounds! I think we're expecting company."

The two men scrambled towards the door and although Kaitlyn was very much out of it, she knew Tom would soon be found. She closed her eyes and tried to telepathically contact and warn Tom.

"Tom they're looking for you."

But Tom had already seen them coming and without missing a step he drove into the warehouse full speed ahead, knocking the two guards over the roof of the car and to the side. Exiting the car, gun drawn and aimed at Lenny's head he noticed Kaitlyn.

"Open that thing up!"

"Sorry, can't do." Lenny smiled innocently. Then he sent a quick glance to something behind Tom. As Tom turned he saw two men behind him, guns being drawn. Without hesitation, Tom took a shot at one then dodged the bullet for the other. Bullets began flying as Lenny started to make his exodus. Rolling to the left side of the car avoiding stray bullets Tom was shot by a dart that he quickly smacked off of himself and returned fire at the shooter.

Going over the numbers in his head, how many men Kaitlyn reported there were, how many were down, adrenaline keeping him focused on the sounds of bullets whizzing by his ears yet the tranquilizer beginning to take effect, Tom realized he needed to stay aware until the helicopter arrived. Shooting left to gain cover as he maneuvered into a new position he glanced over at the contraption in the center of the room and saw Kaitlin passed out inside. Taking aim at the padlock in the center he fired, watching the bullet pierce the casing then ricochet off of the iron contraption.

That shot gave the others his position and as he knew he needed to move three shots were fired, dodging them, one bullet grazed his shoulder. Falling backwards but regaining his footing he scrambled to a nearby shelving system and reloaded.

The metal reverberation on the device being shot vibrated frantically and jolted Kaitlyn awake and as she pressed on the walls to secure her footing the device swung open like a book and she fell out. Landing on her feet, sharp pain shot through her nerves and forced her muscles to become like jellyfish, she collapsed to the floor like a puddle of gelatin, the cold cement almost feeling soft as she struck it with her head.

Knowing that there was a gun battle happening Kaitlyn looked up to see if she could help, if her position was secure, if Tom was okay but as she did her head began pounding harder and as a bright light shone in through the warehouse windows and the noise of an approaching helicopter startled the men, Kaitlyn's head dropped back to the ground. Smoke bombs were blasted in through the windows and all of the men ducked for cover. The Calvary had arrived and just in time.

As Tom's men ransacked the warehouse grabbing fleeing goons, Tom slowly regained his balance and helped to knock out one of the fleeing men. Once the job was under control, Tom went over to Kaitlyn to see how she was. Passed out on the floor, the fall had done her in the rest of the way. Tom kneeled down next to her, his shoulder bleeding, the tranquilizer taking effect. "Kaitlyn." He spoke as he looked into her face. She opened her eyes for just a moment, a moment long enough to see that Tom was here and that they'd be safe now.

Chapter 10

Two months had passed and no one had heard anything of Lenny Lane. Lenny had escaped out the side door when Tom showed up, knowing well that the jig was up. He didn't care much about his men getting caught; he knew well that he could hire more goons next time. But the repercussions of what he had succeeded in doing had lasting effects.

Kaitlyn had been laid up in the clinic for nearly two weeks before released for bed rest only for the next six. Her ribs had almost healed completely by now and she was looking forward to returning back to duty. Tom made a point to come by and see her when he could. It made her happy to see him but the fiasco with Lenny had taken its toll on their relationship. The day after as they both lay in the clinic receiving medical attention Tom laid in on her. He had pulled the I-told-you-so card, if she would have waited until the morning, when there was back up, neither one of them would have gotten hurt and the likely hood that they would have captured Lenny would have been greater. As it was she had completely screwed up. She alone destroyed weeks worth of planning, wasted thousands of dollars and man hours on a mission to go in there early, half cocked and without back-up. If anything she had succeeded in allowing Lenny to go free which to him was as close to treason as you could get.

Kaitlyn tried to explain her reasoning, of course it made more sense to her the night before than it did now but she couldn't apologize enough for failing him and the department. The guilt hurt about as much if not more than the torture chamber she had been in and knowing she was the one who put Tom in harm's way grated on her more than anything else. He had always looked out for her, always bent over backwards to make sure she didn't get hurt and here, she disobeyed orders and nearly got herself and him killed. She kept thinking about what would have happened if he would have been killed and she could barely stand the thought of it, of losing him, and now, it was as if she had. He didn't trust her anymore. As the weeks passed, he calmed, but she could tell, no matter how big his smile, there was something missing. It was in these moments she realized things had changed.

Looking forward to today, getting back to work all she could think about was finding Lenny. Vowing revenge on him, she wanted nothing more than to rid the world of this scum, however each time she mentioned his name, Tom tried to change the subject. She figured he was just tired of hearing about it, but all it did was make her want to find this man even more. Sitting in the boardroom with the rest of the organization for their morning meeting, Kaitlyn carefully worded her objective in her head. Tom sat next to her and was smiling at her when the General walked into the room.

"Let the meeting start, who's got the floor first?"

One of the other agents began speaking of a mission in South Africa and everyone seemed to open their books and follow along. Then another Agent began his comments. Shortly later, Tom announced Kaitlyn's return and the general spoke to her.

"Agent Jones, how are you feeling?"

"Fine. Ready to get back to work sir."

"Good, we've got a project for you in Georgia."

"Georgia sir?"

"Problem Agent?"

"It's just I was hoping to get back to finding Lenny Lane."

"Agent that case has been closed for the time being. We believe your efforts will be best served on a different project."

"Closed? How could you close that case? He's still out there?"

"We've got another task force on the lookout for him but he hasn't shown up on the radars thus far."

"General sir, begging your pardon, but I really want to be assigned to that case."

"Jones, it is done and over with. Now, anyone else got information for me?" The general quickly changed the subject then began to look around the room. Kaitlyn however was not done with it; she hadn't even gotten started yet.

"General you are making a big mistake..." Kaitlyn exclaimed as she stood from her chair.

"Agent Jones if you do not drop this you will be the one making the mistake." He growled back angrily. Tom stood and placed his hand on her shoulder trying to get her to shut-up but she paid no attention.

"I'm sorry general but I believe..."

"I don't care what you believe Jones! You entered unknown territory without back up. Without notifying anyone of your situation. You put Agent M in danger, almost got him killed! It cost the organization tons of manpower and expense in flying a helicopter in to save your ass and you're lucky you're still a part of this organization after a botched assignment like that. So if I were you, I'd sit down and shut up before I write you up on formal charges of treason! Do I make myself clear?"

Kaitlyn was shocked, she hadn't expected that. "Yes sir." She said low as she slowly sat back down. A feeling of complete stupidity overwhelmed her. Everyone was looking at her and she felt so foolish and embarrassed she almost wanted to hide under the table. She looked over at Tom, but as soon as she did, he turned his eyes away from her. Suddenly she realized why he kept trying to change the subject every time she brought up Lenny's name, he was trying to warn her. Unsuccessfully.

After the meeting Kaitlyn disappeared. Tom went about his day as usual and as evening approached he decided to go take a shower, get the grime off of his body before dinner. He was in the shower when Kaitlyn stopped by his apartment. Spending the day soul searching she realized finally the true error in her ways. Before she had known she screwed up and she could have lost Tom because of it, but it had never occurred to her just how many people she let down with that one thoughtless act. She had known Tom was upset but she figured he'd get over it, she figured the brass were upset but by now it would have been forgotten. She had spent so much time planning how she'd get back at Lenny she spent very little time being remorseful of her own actions or even apologizing and now it seemed like it was too late. Feeling like she was losing control she felt she needed to see Tom, to talk to him and to figure this thing out.

However as she opened the door, hearing him in the shower and then walking into the bathroom and seeing him there, a new thought came to her. Suddenly like a flash of heat burning her body, she realized how much she wanted him. Removing her clothes, she quietly walked up behind him. Startling him by rubbing her cool hands over his hot wet flesh she began rubbing her body up against his. A feeling of vulnerability swept over Tom as Kaitlyn began kissing his shoulders and neck. He stood there, taking her in, eyes closed as he felt her body desiring him. He turned to face her, to accept her and she kissed him on the lips, grabbing hold of him tightly. Allowing her to touch him, to massage his body, he was completely accepting of her love. His body burst with the sensation of what she was doing to him and he moaned his want for her.

The warm waters of the shower dripped down over their bodies heating them up. Tom knew he wanted her, and he was going for it, he began kissing her neck, moving down to her supple breasts cupping them in his hands as the waters rushed by them. Kaitlyn wrapped her left leg around him, pulling his torso closer to hers, giving him that in that he wanted and he was eager to take. Pressed against the shower wall, he embraced her. Filling her with every bit of himself. Wanting nothing more than to make them one now and forever when he paused. Suddenly he realized the true reason why she was here. She wasn't here for him, she wasn't coming to him because of her love, because she wanted to express her love to him, she was here because she needed to feel better about herself. She needed to feel like she wasn't a screw up, like she could still be in control and as he realized this, he began to hurt.

He was holding her against the wall, when he paused. She loved his touch and everything he ever did to her and when he paused she soaked it in, grabbing him and pulling him deeper inside of her. He stood there for only a moment, as he, unbeknown to her, reached for the water faucet and prepared to turn the hot water off. As Kaitlyn kissed him, waiting for him to continue this passion upon her body he pulled away from her, grabbed his towel and left her standing there. She opened her eyes to see him walking away.

Confused, she looked at him, he just walked out of the room, never even looking back at her and then suddenly she felt the water quickly turn cold. She frantically turned the knobs to turn off the water, realizing as she did this that Tom turned the hot water off on purpose. Frantically grabbing for a towel, she wrapped it around her body and ran after him. As she entered the bedroom she noticed he had already slid his pants on, still wet and sticking to his body, droplets of water glistening off his abs, she became even more confused, her emotions high. He had never been shy around her, she had seen him naked many times, but now it was like he didn't want her to see him.

"What's wrong?"

"I'm tired of this!" He said angrily as he turned to face her.

"Tired of what?"

"This!"

"What? Having sex?"

"You're using me!"

"I've never used you!" She exclaimed with confusion.

"You've always used me! You use me to help yourself feel better and I'm tired of it!"

"I have never done that!" She said with absolute shock not knowing where this was coming from.

"I know you. I know the truth, I know you better than you know yourself. It's all a lie.

"What's a lie? I love you. I want you. What's wrong with that?"

"Kaitlyn you're never around."

"I'm right here." She said a tear forming in her eye.

"Your body is here, but your mind is still in the boardroom." Tom said referring to the meeting this morning.

Kaitlyn had been truly embarrassed there and although she didn't show her embarrassment, Tom could tell she was hurt and he felt it. As Kaitlyn came to him in the shower he could sense that she needed to be in control, to feel better about herself and this was the only reason why she came to him today. She had been absent from him many times during these months until she needed him and then all of a sudden she was there for him and with him. He was getting tired of the charade, tired of this story and he was ready to put a stop to it. Kaitlyn was confused; she didn't know what to say when Tom said it for her. With nothing but compassion and love he exhaled.

"Kaitlyn I love you. You know I'd do anything for you, but I'm getting hurt in the process. I'm standing here giving myself and my heart to you and you decide when you want it and when you're going to throw it back in my face..."

"Tom I don't..."

"I can't continue this way." He said as he grabbed a shirt and his keys. "You mean everything to me and I feel like I mean absolutely nothing to you."

"Tom that's not..."

"Kaitlyn I want you to think about this. I don't want to be just some man you go to at night. I want more and you know it." And as he walked away, leaving his apartment and closing the door behind him Kaitlyn just stood there, the towel still wrapped around her cold wet body. Not quite understanding what had just happened she began to realize what he said was true. And as she stood there shivering, she knew she had yet again screwed up.

Tom had given Kaitlyn some space, two weeks worth of space and as much as she had wanted to go talk to him she was embarrassed too and grateful she had been given that assignment in Georgia. Of course, even though the assignment kept her busy it in no way kept her mind off of him. Maybe, she thought, if I contact him telepathically, but he was also on assignment, what if I contacted him at the wrong time, caught him off guard, made him drop his attention at the task at hand and get hurt? She couldn't call him.

When her assignment finished and she returned to the base she found it harder than ever to stay focused. She kept bumping into Tom, in the hallway, at the mess hall, in the exercise room. When he looked at her she could see in his eyes he wanted to say something to her but then he wouldn't.

She knew she needed to make the first move but what could she say? She was so embarrassed. He had been so right about her.

That evening when she walked into the weight room and saw him laying there doing bench presses she almost turned to leave but instead, mustered up her courage and walked up to him. Standing at the foot of the machine she spoke.

"I'm sorry."

Tom pressed the weight upwards then looked down at her. Without skipping a beat he started to bring it back down and spoke. "Spot me."

Kaitlyn went and stood behind his head spotting the weight as she again decided to speak.

"You were right."

Tom stayed silent as he continued with his lifts.

"You've always known that working my mind required a physical release and you seemed easier and more fun than fifty miles on the treadmill."

Tom's arms trembled just slightly as he pressed the large weight upwards again but he still brought it back down.

"I didn't mean to use you. I just wanted to be with you... I still do."

Tom pressed upwards again, this time his arms trembled more and he couldn't press it up to the rest. He started to stammer when Kaitlyn grabbed it with her right arm and helped lift it to the rest. Tom sat up and wiped the sweat from his hands with a hand towel. Kaitlyn walked around the bar to squat down next to him.

"Can you forgive me?"

"Always."

"Kaitlyn can you hear me?" Came the female voice of Susan into Kaitlyn's subconscious. Kaitlyn opened one eye and looked at her nightstand to see that her alarm clock showed 3:42 am. Kaitlyn could have strangled Susan.

"Susan it's not even 4am are you in trouble?"

"Not really, I'm working on this project and I need your help."

"What kind of project?"

"You remember what I told you I was going to get into a while back?"

"The ESP training, yes."

"Well I'm head of the department and..."

Kaitlyn sat up in bed and rubbed her eyes, rolled a hand through her hair and stopped Susan, "You're head of the department?"

"Yes I am now, but to the point I've been doing research on those who show the slightest Extra Sensory Perception abilities and have made great strides in the industry..."

"There's an industry?"

"Well it's not as strong as you'd think, that's why I need your help."

"I told you I don't want anyone to know about my abilities."

"No one will find out I just need to run some scans of your brain and..."

"Scans of my brain?"

"Kaitlyn please stop interrupting me. I can keep your name anonymous, would you come down here, I can show you easier than explaining it this way.

"I guess, when do you need me?"

"Preferably before the others get here at seven."

Kaitlyn groaned as she slid her legs over the edge of the bed. "This better be good. I'll be there in twenty."

"Thanks Kaitlyn you're the best!"

Twenty minutes later Kaitlyn walked in the building sipping on a to go cup of coffee. Susan met her at the door and led her up the stairs and down the hall to her office. There were colorful images of brains plastered on her wall, charts and graphs and two large piles of paperwork on her desk. Kaitlyn peered at the top page and noticed Susan had already begun to fill it out, Subject's name was anonymous, Incredible ESP capabilities." Susan reached for the paperwork and a clipboard, grabbed a set of keys off the wall and had Kaitlyn follow her the rest of the way down the hall.

"Are you wearing anything metal?" Kaitlyn removed her belt. Then Susan opened a large thick door and they both stepped inside a very white room with a large machine. There was a flat white counter like bed that slid into a large round opening like an MRI.

"An MRI?"

"Actually to be exact an fMRI, stands for functional Magnetic Resonance Imaging. It's actually designed to evaluate the brain anatomy. It peels away the secrets of emotion and exposes the thought process more clearly than anything else out there on the market."

"Sounds harrowing."

"It's perfectly safe." Susan said as she motioned for Kaitlyn to get in.

"You're serious?"

"I didn't bring you down here to guess at flash cards." Susan gripped as she started the machine and the rhythmic hum of its mechanics began to fill the room."

They started out with a basic scan to get a baseline of her medial brain usage and then when that was done, Susan began recording as she and Kaitlyn began a telepathic conversation. The colors in the frontal lobe began exploding with bright reds and oranges, hues designated to show major brain activity. The data the machine collected rushed in and started to slow the massive machine down.

When Kaitlyn emerged from the machine Susan was eager with excitement. "Look at these results! It is amazing!"

Kaitlyn wandered over to see the vibrant rainbow of colors that illuminated her brain scans. As she watched, Susan began jotting down notes.

"This is amazing. Kaitlyn look here, you see there are two brain regions that we were focusing our study on; the amygdala and the posterior cingulate cortex which is associated with the emotional learning and decision making. I expected to see the higher levels of activity in the frontal polar cortex section mainly due to the speculation that the anterior prefrontal cortex is mostly used for empathic and cognitive processes for understanding the supernatural but not for using it. But your brain scans actually show a greater usage of the brain in varied areas not just the frontal lobe.

This is amazing because it means that for telepathy the brain not only constructs the thought but sends it to varied areas that in essence work in conjunction to send out the thought like a radio signal. This is excellent information! It will help scientists determine why the majority of the human population does not have ESP abilities and how to change that in soldiers."

"So that's what you are doing? Trying to figure out how to get soldiers to use telepathy?"

"Telepathy, telekinesis, ESP, any type of Extra Sensory Perception would benefit the active duty soldier. Imagine if someone was caught by the enemy, they could contact base camp, notify them of their whereabouts, give detailed descriptions of the layout all without the need for radios. We wouldn't need to worry about bugs or tacking devices being found, we'd have an enhanced advantage over the enemy. It'd be awesome!"

Kaitlyn nodded her approval knowing all too well how beneficial telepathy in the field truly is.

"You and Tom communicate that way right?"

Kaitlyn looked at Susan dumbfound. She knew Susan knew she just hadn't acknowledged the fact that Susan would not only put two and two together but be experimenting and embellishing upon this particular situation. All of a sudden this stopped being about a science experiment and hit really close to home. Until this very moment, Kaitlyn hadn't really considered the dangers of this knowledge being in Susan's hands. Susan was working towards actually creating truly scientific ways of enhancing others with this ability and even though Kaitlyn was anonymous now, how much longer until the brass demanded to know whom this telepathic anonymous person was. They'd have to have security access so that limits the appointees to those as active parts of CovSec stations. And the real-world implications of this particular knowledge coming out into focus made Kaitlyn for the first time in her life feel what Tom had feared for his entire life. Suddenly Kaitlyn began to wonder just how much longer she'd be able to keep this news from Tom.

Later that afternoon, Tom was called into the colonel's office. Five other men met him there. The colonel sat down at his desk and began to speak.

"I've got a job. There's an organization in Vegas that… well I can't go into details yet, but it requires I send a man in for an indefinite amount of time. This is a high security undercover assignment, and one that will put that man out of touch with anyone here for an extended duration. It's a very dangerous assignment, one that should not be taken lightly, but it is necessary to get the intel we require. I'm telling you five men this because I am considering each of you for the position." The colonel paused to let it all sink in then continued. "Now I want you to think about this fully before accepting. It is a dangerous mission, one you might not come back from, one that will keep you out of touch for a long time. I would understand if you decided to decline this offer Agents, but I needed to make you all aware of it. The first man to come back with an answer will be chosen. Now, you five are excused. Go think about this, but do not discuss this mission with anyone else."

That night Tom invited Kaitlyn to dinner at his place. There were lit candles on the table, an aroma of pie coming from the kitchen and as Tom stepped out of the kitchen popping open a bottle of wine, in front of a nicely placed meal Kaitlyn spoke up curiously.

"What's the wine for? Are we celebrating something?"

"I just wanted this to be a nice dinner. I love you."

Kaitlyn smiled. "I love you too Tom." Tom looked into her eyes for a moment he could feel it in her tone that the words were something routine to that phrase, he knew he should work on this situation more, talk about it further, analyze it more in depth, but there wasn't time. He needed to know where they were in this relationship, if there was going to be a true future or if this was it and although he knew in his heart that this wasn't fair to Kaitlyn he mustered up his courage, took a deep breath and then came out with it.

"Kaitlyn will you marry me?"

Kaitlyn had just taken a bite of food when her mouth dropped open. She looked up into Tom's eyes studying his expression, attempting to determine if what she heard was actually what came out of his mouth. He just sat there watching her. Do I have time to analyze this, Kaitlyn wondered, should I go through the pros and cons, but he's waiting for an answer, I can see his brow furling, he's waiting for an answer, is he serious?

"Excuse me?" Kaitlyn finally mustered through her full mouth and then quickly chewed and swallowed.

"I asked you if you would marry me."

Kaitlyn looked at him curiously again, he was serious. He was proposing. He couldn't be, she rationalized, this was a test or something. She was preparing to dismiss it when Tom spoke again.

"I know this isn't what you imagined it would be, if in fact you ever imagined a proposal from me, but I am asking you and I would like to know if you would accept."

Kaitlyn was stunned. This wasn't an on-your-knee, ring-in-hand romantic music playing in the background and a crowd of expectant people awaiting a joyous answer, this was something completely different. This was a needed request, like he needed an answer for some reason and Kaitlyn was truly confused. He had been so angry at her not too long ago, he had accused her of using him, they were working their way through it but she was certain they weren't at the marriage proposal point in their relationship. They had such demanding and dangerous jobs, such confusing and erratic schedules, why now would he choose to go this route?

"You're serious." Kaitlyn spoke, nearly starting to stand from the table. Maybe if she stood she'd be able to focus, maybe if she stood she could determine his rationality. Tom stood too and walked to her, taking her hand into his.

"I love you Kaitlyn. I always have, I know there are things about this job that are going to get in the way, I know that the timing will never quite be right but I want to know if you feel the same way. I want to know if this is it or if we are destined for more."

Kaitlyn wasn't sure what to say. She needed time, she needed to rationalize this, she needed to kiss him. She embraced him, rolled her fingers through his thick brown hair, pulled him close to her and seduced his senses. They made love that night with such passion they couldn't speak but when it was over, and Kaitlyn lay on Tom's chest caressing her fingers in small loops on his chest, just wanting to soak in the moment, Tom broke the silence.

"So... will you marry me?"

Kaitlyn was completely caught off guard she had bought time but time was up already and now he expected an answer. Why was she having such a hard time saying yes? She did want to marry him but she hadn't thought about it for so long. She was happy with the way things were. She looked up into his eyes weakly wishing this could be easier. Tom however looked more serious now than he ever had before and this almost frightened Kaitlyn. She loved him, there was no doubt about that, but their relationship had been so bumpy, it almost seemed wrong to try to form it into something more so soon.

"Will you? Yes or no." He spoke again waiting desperately for an answer.

"Tom, I can't just give you an answer." Kaitlyn shifted restlessly in the sheets.

"Why not?"

"I need time to think about it." She said finally raising up from bed to stand.

"Kaitlyn..." Tom sighed acquiring her attention. "You've had almost ten years now. When will you know?" Kaitlyn was dumbfounded.

"What?" Ten years, she thought to herself, had they known each other for ten years?

"You've known of my love for an entire decade, today is the ten year anniversary of the day I pronounced my love to you telepathically at the Macs when we were in high school." Kaitlyn was shocked. Ten years, he had remembered that day, what had happened, sure it was a turning point for the both of them, but to remember that day, ten years later, she was shocked.

"It's time for an answer." He pestered on. He felt as if he were spreading himself out in front of a runaway train and it was up to Kaitlyn to decide if he was about to get hit or if she could hit the brake in time. He wanted so much to show her with words, with actions, with everything necessary how much he loved her, but he also knew if she wasn't accepting that all of this was a waste of time.

"Tom I..." Kaitlyn began but didn't have the chance to finish.

"Kaitlyn I can't wait any longer. I need to know. I need an answer. I can't keep doing this, falling in love with you and being left alone."

"Tom this is not an easy decision, remember last time?"

"Yes I do, and yes it is. Either yes or no. But let me tell you right now if your answer is no, then that's it."

"What?" Kaitlyn stuttered the words felt like a slap in the face.

"I can't keep doing this. If you can't say yes, then I can't be around you any longer. We'll be over, for good."

"Tom, don't say that. Don't say that."

"Kaitlyn? Yes or no?"

"I can't, I mean, you're not..." Kaitlyn stuttered trying to find the words, but Tom knew she was just trying to let him down easy. Tom was already out of bed and had slid his pants back on.

"Fine." He said as he turned to leave, Kaitlyn called after him.

"Tom don't go. Don't leave things like this."

"It's your decision Kaitlyn. What'll it be?" He asked his back still to her, his hand on the door handle. Kaitlyn didn't speak, she couldn't make a decision, "I'll expect you to be gone when I return." With that, he opened the door and left. Kaitlyn fell to the floor, and cried. She had lost the only true love in her life because she couldn't make a decision.

As Tom left he knew this was goodbye. His heart couldn't take another rejection. He couldn't keep putting himself on the line and allowing himself to fall off. As he walked away he felt sad, but he also felt an incredible burden had been lifted from his shoulders. For ten long years he had been waiting and now he knew however sad it was, that his wait was over and that it had all been in vain but now he could move on with his life.

"Colonel, I'll take the job."

The next morning as Kaitlyn reported for duty at CovSec. Headquarters the General walked up to her.

"I've received top orders to send a small team down to the coast of Guymas to retrieve the black-box from a recent plane crash."

"Guymas as in Mexico, Gulf of California?"

"That is correct." The mission is a simple snatch and grab, should take less than 6 hours. Problem is we must act fast, there are other organizations that want to get their hands on the box as well."

Kaitlyn listened to the details of the job and then immediately expected the general to be bringing Tom aboard. She worried about how they would work together after last night but she looked forward to doing a mission with him because maybe after the mission they could talk. Just then Jonathan walked in the door.

"Sorry I'm late general, I've just received the details of the mission."

"Good. You leave in ten." The general voiced as he dismissed the pair and took a phone call.

Kaitlyn and Stangard walked out of the office and as Jonathan was about to speak, Kaitlyn interrupted him. "Not that I don't look forward to working with you Jonathan but I usually get paired with Tom."

"Yeah I know, but he's off on some big mystery job so it's just the two of us for a while."

"Mystery job? I didn't hear of any..."

"Yeah, it's hush, hush but word around the base it's a one-man undercover mission and it's a long-range assignment. I was shocked when he decided to take it myself."

Kaitlyn didn't understand. Had he known about this assignment last night. Is this the reason he proposed? Was her non-answer his reason for accepting the job? Why would he do this?

As Stangard and Jones were on the flight heading to Guymas, Kaitlyn attempted to contact Tom telepathically.

"Tom what are you doing? Why did you take that assignment?" Tom wouldn't answer. "Tom I know you can hear me, are you in the middle of something?" She waited a moment. "Tom talk to me, what's going on? Why didn't you talk to me about this?" Kaitlyn sighed. "So you're just not going to answer me? This was a selfish thing to do. I can't believe you can be so selfish."

"Selfish?" Tom came back abruptly. "You're the one who couldn't commit."

"You put me on the spot with expectations of grandeur and then take off like a child throwing a temper tantrum when you don't get the answer you want!"

"I'm not going to fight with you Kaitlyn. I already told you it was over."

"You gave me an ultimatum. I could sense you weren't being overly sincere about your proposal, that there was something else on your mind forcing the issue and look I was right! You used my hesitance to influence your decision on this job instead of proposing to me properly with love in your heart." Kaitlyn waited for a response. "Tom?" She waited a moment, nothing again. "See, you know I'm right so you're now not talking to me. I can't believe you would take this job. I don't know a fraction of the details but what I do know is it is an incredibly stupid move... going undercover, with no back-up. Even I've learned that's suicidal. I never knew you to be suicidal Tom."

"I'm not suicidal. I can do this."

"Like I could take down Lenny on my own?" Kaitlyn spat back sarcastically, there was silence for a moment, then she spoke again. "Tom."

"What?" He barked.

"Be careful."

Tom closed his eyes and dropped his head. He knew that he wouldn't have any other contact with anyone from CovSec for an indefinite amount of time and even though he knew he could talk to Kaitlyn, he knew he shouldn't. He needed his emotions intact, strong, he couldn't show any outward vulnerabilities. "I will."

Kaitlyn knew this was it. She could sense things ending, drawing to a close and she began to worry. She knew Tom wouldn't contact her again, not until the job was over and she could feel it in her soul that it would be a very long time. His words echoed in her skull for a few moments, lulling her until her meditation was interrupted by Stangard.

"We're almost there, you ready?"

Kaitlyn opened her eyes and looked at him with a smile. "Always."

Kaitlyn and Stangard dove into the dark waters of the Gulf of California about 10 clicks off the coast of Guymas and started their decent towards the location of the plane crash. When Stangard spotted the debris he motioned for Kaitlyn who also noticed it and they dived down closer. The wreckage had been scattered about the ocean floor, there was part of a wing and about one hundred feet south was one of the plane's seats. They kept on their search until they came across the head of the plane which was still primarily intact.

Kaitlyn motioned for Stangard to take the external while she went in, the waters were hazy and dark so they both flipped on their flashlights for better visibility. As Kaitlyn noticed something, a blinking yellow light, dimly illuminate from under the captains chair she turned to Stangard to motion him over when she saw two men in black scuba gear swiftly make their way towards Stangard.

Trying to get his attention with her flashlight but seeing that his attention was focused away from her she began swimming towards him, still oblivious of her or the two additional scuba divers quickly making their way towards him, Kaitlyn sent a telepathic "Stangard behind you." in hopes that he would turn. He did, just as one of the divers pulled a knife and lunged it towards Stangard. Dodging the attack and grabbing the assassins wrist, he knocked the knife from the man's hand and began a full-on attack as the second attacker closed in.

Kaitlyn was just making her way towards the second attacker when she was jolted to a stop feeling the tug of someone behind her ripping at her tank she spun her head and caught a glimpse of a knife slicing her air hose. Immediately realizing the danger she was in, she spun a kick towards the man knocking him away from her tank. Quickly determining the air hose was leaking and her air would be depleting faster than necessary, she attacked the man and began an assault to take him down first. As the attacks continued and the waters splashed violently around them knocking up sand, dirt and debris the visual clarity of the water deteriorated and soon all was dark. Kaitlyn didn't know if Stangard was holding his own against the two that went after him and she couldn't see the one who was clawing and punching at her. What she did know was the air in her mask was becoming warm and she knew her oxygen was nearly out.

Closing her eyes, she heard the muffled underwater sounds of distant fighting, of air bubbles and of the violent cracking of water as her own attacker went in for a full-on assault, sensing his plan, hearing the distance close and knowing with her peripheral senses where his limbs were heading, Kaitlyn struck, grabbed his arms as they neared, spun the man backwards, grabbed his neck and broke it. The sound of his spine shattering under her pressure lulled by the sound of the air tanks ceasing their steady breathing sound. Kaitlyn, unlatched the buckles holding the scuba tank to the dead man's body and quickly exchanged his good tank for her failed one, swiped the mouthpiece from his mouth and took her first fresh breath of air in over a minute. Then she turned to check on Stangard.

Swimming as fast as she could through the dark mucky waters, she swam into a warm stream of red which quickly cleared the vision to see one man's dead body spiraling down towards the ocean floor and cleared the visibility to see Stangard stab the second attacker in the gut and release his grip on the man who also began his decent towards the ocean floor. Stangard then wiped his knife and replaced it back in the sheath just in time to look up and see Kaitlyn coming towards him. He quickly gave a thumbs up and they proceeded towards the plane.

When the two emerged from the ocean waters, the black-box safe in their possession, they removed their masks and took a deep breath of fresh air. Stangard radioed for the chopper and the two took off. Once on board the plane Stangard couldn't take his eyes off of Kaitlyn. Kaitlyn had a feeling that if he had indeed heard her telepathic warning he'd have questions and his staring at her may have been his way of trying to decide if he was crazy or not. Kaitlyn attempted to disregard his curious staring, instead wringing out the excess water from her long hair. She had just flipped her hair back when Stangard moved closer to her. Leaning in to her right ear he whispered.

"Are you in the brain study?"

Kaitlyn stared at him carefully and curiously for a moment when it hit her, Susan.

As the chopper landed at CovSec headquarters Kaitlyn immediately excused herself and sent a telepathic contact to Susan to meet her, ten minutes later Susan walked into the locker room and up to Kaitlyn who was just finishing up with her shower. As Kaitlyn threw a towel around her wet hair she turned to Susan and smiled.

"So, what have you been up to lately?"

Susan smiled curiously then realized Kaitlyn knew something. She stepped to the side just slightly and smiled brightly as she spoke carefully. "I've started a really informative study using the information I've gathered and have begun conducting trials on individuals."

"Trials, on what exactly?"

Susan took a deep relaxing breath and looked Kaitlyn directly in the eyes, "On telepathic ability."

Once Susan and Kaitlyn were outside and making their way to the educational building Susan began explaining her research and what she had found out.

"Your brain scans were what opened the doors to this possibility. Once I was able to determine what area of the brain controlled it and what areas to isolate the imaging onto, I began conducting trials on myself."

"Susan who knows about your ability?"

"Nobody. I've conducted them all in secret and under an alias, I know how you feel about being found out, but get this. I was able to determine that the same area of the brain that detects telepathic signals, the anterior prefrontal cortex, can be trained and basically talked into receiving those signals."

Susan, I'm getting a headache, can you just tell me what you've been doing?"

I've been doing trials, I have found four men that show great probability of having the ability of telepathy, all they need to do is learn how to use it."

"You've what?" Kaitlyn asked feeling nauseous.

"Now don't freak out. I've tested over a hundred men, almost all of them heard nothing, these four men that I've asked on board just think they are in some silly ESP program, none of them really realize yet that they could possibly be telepathic. I've told them we have a radio signal that I play that the ear cannot detect but that the fMRI images show some color variances at that particular time and that they may be detecting the signal."

"A radio signal?"

"Actually it's a telepathic message from me, but nobody knows that."

"Susan! Oh my god!"

"Kaitlyn calm down." Susan turned and placed her hands on Kaitlyn's shoulders. "All they hear is a digital sound of SOS via Morse code." Susan sent Kaitlyn the sound. She listened then raised an eyebrow.

"Everyone here knows that code, out of the four men's scans who detected it only one man spoke up and told me what he heard. Only one man out of over a hundred told me he heard the SOS."

"Stangard." Kaitlyn spoke low.

Susan's eyebrows raised, "How would you know that?"

Kaitlyn half smiled half smirked, of all of the people in all of the world that she would come across, of all of the people that Susan had tested of all of the possibilities how on earth had Jonathan gotten mixed up in this?

Susan realized Kaitlyn knew something and her curiosity was growing. "I told Stangard and the other three

167

men that I had the highest expectations for, that I wanted them for extended studies. I've run extensive tests on them, and we've been working towards isolating the exact variances... Stangard heard you didn't he?"

"We were in the water, I couldn't get his attention, without even thinking I warned him as I would warn Tom and he turned in time to block an attack. After, all he asked was if I was in the brain study."

"What did you tell him?" Susan asked realizing that Kaitlyn may have given her own self away.

"I looked at him like he was nuts, I said nothing."

"You're going to have to, he's going to have questions."

"How can I? What can I say?"

"You could admit that you are in my study as well."

"We are talking about telling him that we all have the ability of telepathy, we can't take the chance of him telling others."

"Kaitlyn I understand your hesitance but it's going to come out sooner or later and it truly is a blessing. You saved his life today!"

"Who else is going to find out about this?"

"I don't have to tell anyone."

"What if he tells someone?"

"We should get to him first."

Chapter 11

"Hello? Is anybody here?" He asked as he looked around the darkened lab curiously.

"Agent Stangard, thank you for coming." Susan spoke as she entered the room. She flicked on the light then closed the door behind her. "Please take a seat."

Stangard was about to sit when he noticed the light on the camera blinking. "Is someone in the other room?"

"Jonathan," Susan motioned for him to sit again as she sat down and continued speaking, following, Jonathan too sat down. "How was your day?"

"Fine." He spoke as he looked around the room, he had a feeling someone was watching through the two-way mirror and he was hesitant about the situation.

"I just wanted to follow up on the results of last week's trials." Susan spoke calming.

"You know it's interesting you'd call me in today, a funny thing happened."

"Oh really?" Susan chimed curiously, expecting him to tell her about the telepathic call.

"Well I was thinking about when you mentioned that there were four men in the trial..."

"That is correct."

"Any gender biases?"

"How do you mean?"

"Any of those men actually women?"

"Why would you ask me that?"

"Just curious is all." He spoke, his attention still focused on the mirror.

"You know I can't talk about the others, this is a highly classified top secret trial, you signed a confidentiality contract."

"Yeah I know..." Stangard paused finally looking at Susan sitting across from him. "Hey you mind refreshing my memory about this trial again?"

"What is it you want to know agent?"

"What are you expecting to get from all of this?"

"I'm afraid I can't divulge the particulars..."

Stangard looked at Susan and smiled, "of course." Susan was just about to go on with her next question when Jonathan quickly stood, grabbed his chair and slammed it forcefully through the mirror, shattering it. Susan jumped to her feet as the glass shards fell to the ground and Jonathan peered in at the woman behind the glass, her arm up to block her face from the glass and then brought down towards her weapon when he spoke.

"Jones!"

Kaitlyn looked at him, her eyes glued on him, trying to judge what his next move was going to be when he spoke, "I want to know what's going on – now!"

"I don't believe you!" Stangard yelled.

"That's your mind trying to dismiss the impossible, you believe me or you wouldn't still be standing here." Kaitlyn yelled back.

Stangard started to walk towards the door but then turned back towards Kaitlyn, "This is ridiculous! There's no way that..."

"That you would have signed up for ESP trials? Oh wait you did. That you came here tonight wondering about the ocean today?"

"It is impossible!"

"Stangard you saw the results of the MRI, you heard the sound."

"It was an audible recording, my hearing is just keener."

"It wasn't really an audible recording." Susan spoke quickly, Jonathan turned to face her when she continued telepathically this time so he could see her mouth not move, "It was a telepathic sound that I sent."

Jonathan's mouth dropped open. "How did you do that?"

"If you can hear me then you can send a message as well."

"Where's the recorder? What are you trying to pull?" He asked as he went to her and began patting her down. Kaitlyn went up to him afraid he was getting too aggressive. "Jonathan it's not a trick, it's telepathy."

"It is not!" He swirled around and knocked Kaitlyn backwards. "You're trying to make me sound crazy."

Kaitlyn caught her balance and with him looking at her she sent a message to him, "You're not crazy, it's telepathy."

"I did hear you today!"

"Jonathan I need you to sit down, we need to discuss..."

"Tell me telepathically."

Kaitlyn and he locked eyes for the longest moment, Kaitlyn's heart was racing, she had no idea how any of this would play out, there was no way to determine how exactly he was taking this or if he would be able to keep his mouth shut. Finally Kaitlyn knew what she needed to say, thinking back to their history at the secret service, thinking back to their friendship and then thinking back to that one night they shared so long ago, she closed her mouth tight and spoke cautiously, "Jonathan do you trust me?"

His lips parted just slightly as he comprehended the situation and then finally loosening his gaze upon Kaitlyn he noticed a chair to his right peripheral vision, and reached for it to sit down. Once he was sitting down, he exhaled deeply, inhaled and then exhaled again returning his sight to Kaitlyn, then spoke. "I'm listening."

The audio of the Vegas strip were distant sounds as the warehouse door closed and the darkness turned to dim light. The driver made his way around to the back passenger door of the black limo and opened the door and he watched as the rotund man in dark silk pin stripe suit stepped out of the car followed by two slender showgirls. He watched as one girl wrapped her white feather boa around her shoulder and the other flicked her bouncy strawberry blonde hair over her shoulder and then both took the rotund mans arms and walked casually into the back of the casino. He watched as they led the way down the back service hallways and up to the freight elevator and then entered the elevator as one of the staff keyed in the penthouse floor and swiped his employer card for access.

When the doors of the elevator opened to a lush and extravagant hallway, exterior of dark red cherry wood panels, gold chandelier accents and red velvet curtains lined down the hallway exposing the bright colorful lights of the Vegas strip below he watched and followed as the door to the penthouse opened to a party already in play and the attendant recognizing the man approaching quickly spoke his introduction. "Good evening Mr. Devers." Four goons led the way as Devers entered, a gorgeous girl on each arm and various other ladies chimed up with enthusiasm as he entered.

A waiter came rushing up with a tray of champagne and he graciously took one followed by his two ladies. He followed as they made their way through the large lavish room, through adorned patrons and party-goers to the backroom where the doors were opened to expose a high rollers poker game already in progress. As the man entered and the doors closed behind him he looked around at the lavish surroundings.

Floor to ceiling panoramic windows expose the city, pool and spa on the deck full of gorgeous bikini clad ladies, five 42" plasma televisions on, at least a hundred people, orgies in both bedrooms, he looked around the room carefully. Walking over to the bar the bartender offered him a drink but he declined, he looked down at one of the coasters and read the name of the hotel, the Palms, then looked up as a beautiful woman approached him, "I'm Candy, want a taste?"

Kaitlyn woke to the sound of the telephone ringing and glanced towards her clock, it was two in the morning, and her eyes were sore from being woken. She reached for the phone and groaned a hello.

"Kaitlyn I can't sleep."

"Jonathan? It's two in the..."

"I know but I can't sleep, can I come over?"

Kaitlyn sighed, "Sure I guess."

"Thanks." He hung up the phone and a moment later Kaitlyn heard a knock at her door. She rose from bed, wrapped on her robe and then slowly opened the door. Jonathan stood there with a half smile on his face. "You said I could come over."

Kaitlyn exhaled, then opened the door for him. He walked in, and immediately began talking.

"I can't get this out of my head. It's absolutely amazing." He spoke as he watched Kaitlyn walk into the kitchen. He followed. "I mean, I never thought that this could be real but I had always hoped, I mean..." He paused as he watched Kaitlyn grab the coffee pot and begin filling it with water. "When did you find out you could do this?"

"This isn't about me Jonathan."

"But it is. You can't have one without another. I mean you have to have someone to talk to right? Why aren't you more excited about this?"

Kaitlyn poured the water in and pressed the power button then looked up to Jonathan. His eyes were wide open, he was completely wired. He was excited and curious. She looked at him and feigned a smile, "What do you want to know?"

Over the next few weeks Kaitlyn, Susan and Jonathan practiced their telepathy together. Susan continued her trials on the other three men but neither of them showed the ability like Jonathan had so more and more of her time was focused on him and turning the trials onto a new direction. It had taken Jonathan the first two weeks to hone his skill and Susan tracked his progress on the fMRI and was able to determine Stangards gradual progression and strengthening of his usage. His own mental limitations stood basically from his inherent disbelief and gradually subsided the more use he got, the more messages he heard. Susan knew from previous scans which regions of the brain needed to be sparked for his ability to transmit messages back but she believed he was coming close to that and as his progress advanced so did her desire to capture the entire advancement.

"I can't do it." Stangard gripped throwing his head into his hands.

"Sure you can," Susan countered telepathically. "Tell me you can't do it telepathically."

Jonathan tried again, his head pounding, why couldn't he do it? Why hadn't he figured out how to do it? Susan could see his head was hurting, she didn't understand why he was having such a hard time, she had picked it up quickly with Kaitlyn, how had Kaitlyn done it?

"Jonathan look at me." Susan spoke. "Look at me." Jonathan looked up at her. "Look at me sitting here, remember me sitting here as you close your eyes. Close your eyes and now visualize me sitting here. Visualize my face, listen to my voice, visualize my voice as you listen to my words." Susan watched as he closed his eyes and dropped his head, then she switched to telepathy. "Can you hear me? Nod your head." He nodded. "Now with your mouth closed answer me, can you hear me?" Susan waited a moment listening carefully until she heard something. It sounded faint and as if it had been from a speeding train, there and then gone, fading off violently quick. "Answer me again, can you hear me?" She waited, nothing, "Visualize me, visualize my face and then answer me, can you hear me?" The sound came again but it was faint and quick and hardly audible. "Be more clear with your response, answer me directly, can you hear me?"

A few moments passed and still nothing – this had to work. "Jonathan think about me, imagine my face, see my eyes with your head, visualize my mouth moving and then answer me as if you were visualizing your mouth moving.

"I can hear you." It was faint and distant but he kept repeating it. "I can hear you, I can hear you." Each time he repeated it, it got louder and louder. "I can hear you. I can hear you."

Finally, Susan spoke. "I can hear you too."

Jonathan's eyes shot open and looked at her. "You heard me?"

She smiled yes. He jumped to his feet, arms in the air in excitement. "This is awesome!"

"Tell me telepathically."

Jonathan looked at Susan, his eyes peered in on hers and he thought with everything he had in him, "This is awesome."

"It is, isn't it?" Susan spoke with a large smile on her face. Jonathan pulled her into his arms and hugged her. "This is so amazing!"

Watching Kaitlyn emerge from the fitness room he stood off in the shadows down the pathway and began watching her, visualizing her. She had been working out hard, he could tell, she was quite sweaty, a towel dangling from around her shoulders and neck. Watching her, thinking about her, thinking about their history, her face, her body, he spoke telepathically, hoping she could hear him. "Turn to your left." He waited and received no response. He tried again," Turn to your left." She kept walking, he began to panic, he wanted her to hear him so much his heart began to race, "Turn to your left!" Kaitlyn slowed and turned to her left, spotting him she smiled. He smiled too, excited, exhilarated, he began walking towards her as she began to walk towards him, "You heard me?" He asked telepathically, she smiled brightly and answered him back,

"Yes I can."

"This is great, we should celebrate." He spoke in thought,

"What do you want to do?" she answered back telepathically as they came within distance of each other. He pulled her into a hug and kissed her passionately on the lips. He embraced her tightly, just like the last day at the White House when he embraced her for the first time and they made love.

Kaitlyn felt her heart flutter, but didn't feel the passion she had once felt. Still reeling over Tom leaving and needing to be coy about her slight depression since no one, especially Jonathan actually knew the truth, she allowed the kiss to end then slowly pulled away. Needing to change the conversation Kaitlyn spoke aloud.

"So Susan got you functioning. I'll bet you are excited."

"It is absolutely amazing, once we narrowed down the exact details I needed to do to accomplish it the only thing I could think of was telling you about it."

Kaitlyn smiled shyly. "So do you want to practice?"

Jonathan pulled her into his arms again and spoke telepathically, "I don't need to practice this." He said referring to the desire to make love to her but Kaitlyn knew what he wanted and although a slight desire was there, she wasn't prepared to go the distance. Pulling back again she spoke back telepathically, "but you do need practice on this." She thought as she sent him an image of his upcoming physical exam.

"How did you do that?" He spoke aloud once receiving the image.

"Practice." She smiled as she took his hand and led him towards the practice field. She knew there would be other agents there so Jonathan's focus would stay clear but she also knew that by changing the subject and giving him something else to focus on she was only buying time.

As the weeks progressed, Susan studied Jonathan's progress as Kaitlyn and he practiced not only telepathy, clear focus and determination but also on the greater benefits of telepathy in a partnership. Susan joined them for some of the tasks, her physical capabilities assisting in their training as Susan setup hurdles and it was up to Kaitlyn and Jonathan to clear them without radio contact. Kaitlyn played it similar to the way she and Tom used to practice but she was adamant about keeping the partnership strictly platonic. She liked Jonathan a lot but she wasn't prepared to take it to the next level especially not knowing where or how Tom was.

Each night however, Kaitlyn was side-tracked by on-going dreams. Like the first that started weeks ago, she was the eyes of someone as they went through their evenings activities. Mostly parties, prostitution, illegal gambling, there was drug dealing, large quantities of money exchanging hands, weapons sales. Kaitlyn didn't know where the images were coming from or why she was receiving them. There were never any faces, never any details that could assist her, there was never really anything worth being concerned about. If it would have been one of her flashes she would have seen danger, she would have felt the need for action, to do something to assist someone, or help in some way but the dreams only left her exhausted and confused. Why was she getting all of this information? What was the reason?

Susan had thoroughly enjoyed spending time with Kaitlyn and Jonathan training. She had always enjoyed the physical aspects of the training she had received from Kaitlyn. Granted what Kaitlyn had taught her in the past was primarily for defense but she had embellished upon that knowledge and it grew into something all-together different. From the desire to make her defense training more difficult making the benefits of escape more profound, to landing herself in a career of creating harder training techniques, Susan had slowly trans-morphed her desire for fighting to the more educational and scientific aspects of it. She didn't mind it, in fact she excelled at it which back in high school she never would have imagined, but she felt she was coming to the end of her capabilities.

She had discovered the how and why's of telepathy, she had determined how to locate one with the ability as well as train them on how to use it. She knew her knowledge and experience on the matter would take her places but she also knew it would only be beneficial if the other scientists and teachers were telepaths themselves. The trick and downfall of telepathy is to be someone with the ability of telepathy and not only know it and know how to use it but know someone else with the same capability, otherwise you are nothing.

She knew that if she exposed herself as one with the ability and exposed the fact that to find others with the ability you had to contact them through the ability, she would never be able to get out of this. She remembered Kaitlyn expressing Tom's worry about being found out, of becoming the science experiment, and she realized she would emphatically become the experiment if she allowed her findings to come out. She either needed to announce that her experiment failed and move on or she needed to find someone else with the ability who'd be willing to take over. She also knew that the only three people in the world she knew with the ability would never want that position and since the numbers were so incredibly low she decided she needed to finish up with her investigation, write her report and thank the brass for the financial backing for experimentation and apologize for not being able to reveal anything new or helpful.

Susan also knew that upon finalizing this task she'd need to begin a new project, either with the defense arts or in an entirely new direction and the joy and thrill she experienced working with Kaitlyn and Jonathan these past weeks was peeking her interest in a new direction all together.

One evening Kaitlyn had decided to call off practice early. She was exhausted. From waking in the morning after an evening of these exhaustive dreams, to completing her regular duties in eight hour shifts to extra-curricular activities in the training field with Jonathan and Susan; Kaitlyn was becoming burnt-out. The telepathic communication had a tendency of exercising her intellectual muscles but left a feeling of inadequacy in the rest of her more physical muscles. In the past, she had released her tensions in the gym. With punching bags, treadmill, exercise bike. She'd literally exhaust herself just to relieve that tension only to start the entire process again the very next morning.

When it had been just her and Tom they limited their communication to ease her extenuating situation, but more often than not she was able to release it much quicker and easier with Tom in a more intimate physical release. She loved Tom, never considered it using him but recently he had come to view it as such. Enjoying nothing more than simply being with him she began to realize she had used him as a crutch. His anger and ambivalence of being with her every time she desired him she hadn't been able to understand. She knew he loved her just as much as she loved him but for years it had simply not occurred to her why she needed to be with him so much.

When he pulled away from her that day in the shower, she was hurt and her feelings inhibited her ability to hear the words he was actually saying. He had exclaimed that she was using him, using his body for sex and at the time her desire for him was so strong she couldn't make sense of it. Now with his being gone, the desire for that physical contact growing, Kaitlyn began to realize where Tom had been coming from.

In recent days Jonathan's desire to communicate via telepathy was near constant. He found this gift absolutely amazing and apparently it was only Kaitlyn who felt the need for physical release when using it. Whether it be from her extreme past and the true nature of her gift and where it came from or if she was just plain different didn't matter. Kaitlyn found herself at the gym exercising more and more, excusing herself more regularly and working twice as hard as usual.

Jonathan however, had his own thoughts and feelings on the matter. His excitement about this ability, his eagerness to practice and use this gift, only confused him as to why Kaitlyn wasn't as excited as he was. It had only partially occurred to him that she had more experience with the ability, knew more ways to use it and embellish upon it. In the past weeks Jonathan hadn't even come close to figuring out how to send images in thought. The night Kaitlyn showed him that image it enthralled his senses and although he desired to know how she did that, he desired something else much more.

Thinking about Kaitlyn to concentrate on his telepathy signals only made him more infatuated with her. Memories of their last romantic night, even though quite some time past, were drawn into more recent recollections. Working with Kaitlyn again brought about feelings he had only subsided but never quite relinquished and with all of the possibilities they now had dangling in front of them, Jonathan was more than eager to take their relationship to the next level.

So that evening, when Kaitlyn excused herself early and returned back to her room to change into her workout clothes, Jonathan followed. And as Kaitlyn proceeded into her closet to locate her clothes, Jonathan entered her room and closed the door. Preparing his emotions, controlling his feeling and focusing on the beautiful silhouette of the woman standing in front of him, he sent a telepathic message to Kaitlyn as he pulled her back first into his arms and embraced her body within his.

"Make love to me."

Kaitlyn's body, pressed against his, his arms engulfing her torso, rubbing her breasts, down her arms, to her pelvis, she embraced the passion. He moved his body with hers, dancing his physical message as he slid his hand down her pants and pressed his hand on to her, thrusting two fingers inside of her all the while pulling her so close to him they were almost one. The motion of his fingers pulsing in and out of her, the touch of his manhood throbbing against her buttocks, the desire he filled her with all the while invading her mind with telepathic messages of desire, "Make love to me. I want you so much." all filled Kaitlyn with a warm rush of emotion and physical desire she couldn't quite ignore.

Near orgasm and yet so far away from complete satisfaction, Kaitlyn too began gyrating her hips to the pulsing of his fingers. Her lips swelled as she leaned her head back against his chest, enjoying the senses he was filling her with, enjoying what he was doing to her and desiring more. He spoke again telepathically, "Make love to me." and with that Kaitlyn's body would only allow her one spoken word, "Yes."

Jonathan turned her around to face him, pulled her into a long passionate kiss and undressed her, taking her, thrusting himself into her depths so far she finally felt the release her body had so longed for.

They were just entering the warehouse office when Mr. Devers recognized a friend and addressed him by name. "Samuel, I haven't seen you in what two years?"

"Two and a half." The man spoke as he poured a brandy sniffer half full and handed it to Devers. "You're looking like you are doing well for yourself. Armani suit, Louis Vuitton tie..."

"Actually the tie is Bill Blass."

"Four personal guards each carrying two 9mm Glock semi-automatic pistols."

"Seventeen round detachable box with two additional clips to pull on, but we aren't here to talk about my guards guns we're here to talk about the shipment I have coming for you." Devers steered the conversation back to business as he paused to take a sip of brandy. "I've got ten thousand Barrett M107 bolt-action sniper rifles arriving at the end of the week and I hear you'd like to place an order."

"I would." Samuel spoke as he placed his brandy on the table next to him and motioned for one of his men to advance forward. The man stepped forward, angled a briefcase he had been carrying towards Devers and popped it open exposing a large quantity of banded one hundred dollar bills. "Three hundred thousand now and the remaining three hundred thousand on delivery."

Devers motioned for one of his men to take possession of the briefcase which he did, then spoke. "I will be in touch." As he stood and began his farewell.

As Devers and his men left the office another one of Samuels' men was making his way up the stairs. As the man neared visual proximity, he was recognized by whomever Kaitlyn was dreaming about. His attention focused in on the man carefully, a recollection process began in his head followed by a searing sensation of rage. Whether it was Kaitlyn's own rage or whoevers eyes she was peering through she didn't know, all she knew was she had caught her first glimpse of Lenny Lane in quite some time and if she would have been there that moment the man would have died miserably. Unfortunately, he walked past her visual perception and up to the office as her rage woke her from her dream.

Bolting up from bed, ready to attack she looked around her room. Disappointment swept over her as she realized she wasn't going to be able to kill Lane and even more disappointment flooded over her when she realized she didn't know what warehouse they had just been in. She knew if it would have been a flash she would have known where they were. She knew if Tom had just contacted her she would knew how to find him, what she didn't know was from whom or where these imagery and dreams were coming from and what to do with what little knowledge she was receiving from them.

Deciding now that these dreams were definitely coming to her for a reason she realized she should write down as many details as she could and begin studying up on what she did know. If the dreams were coming from the same person then all of the combined details would help her determine what she needed to know if in fact she needed to put together some sort of operation in the near future. She looked around the room for a pen and paper when she noticed hers and Jonathan's clothes strewn across the floor, then she turned to see Jonathan fast asleep in her bed.

Remembering the events of the evening she was happy that he came to her, satisfied, but she couldn't quite place her feelings on the emotions the night would eventually lead to. Jonathan was obviously attracted to her, as she was with he, unfortunately she was certain his attraction was much deeper and spiritual then hers since it seemed to her that what she desired most and what she received ten-fold was of a more physical nature than she's sure he ultimately intended.

As she reached for a robe off the back of her bedroom door and wrapped it around her body she took one last glance at the sleeping man in her bed and wondered. Could she do this? Could she allow herself to accept his passion even though she had none to give?

Chapter 12

It had been two days. Kaitlyn spent every free moment she could find noting every detail of the dreams she had been having. As she started piecing together each evenings details she was able to pinpoint favorite areas on a map of Las Vegas, Nevada. She knew about the evening parties at the Palm, illegal fights at an abandoned warehouse just off of the strip, the fact that it took a limo driver twelve minutes with two stops to get from their favorite strip club to Dever's offices where she had seen Lenny. She knew there was a large shipment of illegal weapons coming in and she knew that where ever this guy that she had been following conducted his business was in a very decrepit apartment building where the entire top floor was opened to his drug packaging business. She also knew every street corner this guys personal prostitutes stood to sell his drugs and their bodies. The only thing Kaitlyn didn't know was why she had received all of this information.

Her apartment dining room was covered in maps with push pins, satellite images of the area, buildings, roads and terrain, hand written notes of details and situations that if asked she totally couldn't explain and next to that was a calendar, a large wall calendar with situations detailed times and dates past and future. She was almost ready – but for what?

Exhausted she fell asleep at the dining room table, head on her crossed arms she closed her eyes and was almost immediately transported to Vegas where she started by watching an illegal fighting match currently in progress.

She watched as the guy in red sent a punch to the guy in black and blood cascade from his mouth, then she began looking around the room. Men and women all cheering, placing bets, drinking, the crowd was large, the attire was evening wear, scanning the room she quickly put together possible dangers, exit routes and familiar faces. Right then the most familiar face stood out from the crowd, Lenny was standing in the VIP section left and someone had just come in from the back door and approached him. The man leaned over, said something into Lane's ear and then turned to point towards her direction. When they turned Kaitlyn not only got a clear visual on Lenny Lane but on Mike Manners. Just then the crowd leapt to their feet to cheer and the focus was turned back to the ring to see the ref holding up the left arm of the guy in the red shorts and the bell rang.

When Kaitlyn woke she was certain she wanted to go in there now but she still needed to get more intel. Who's eyes was she seeing all of this through, was all of this information accurate? If she went in there would she be interfering with another governments operations? She needed to know more.

That evening she went out to the gym to work off some of the pent up aggressions she had been feeling. Along with these dreams came an angry desire, a desire to stop this guy, take down the entire organization but being forced to wait, wait for the right moment and it was driving her crazy. From the moment she saw Lenny Lane walking up those stairs she was ready to run in there and kill the man in the most violent way she could muster, but her training had kicked in and she knew she had to have a plan.

She was busily taking out those aggressions on the gyms backroom punching bag when Jonathan walked in the room.

"I've been looking for you everywhere! Where have you been?"

"Putting together schematics for a mission."

"Do I know about it?"

"No."

"Am I a part of it?"

"Not sure."

"How can you not be sure, didn't the brass tell you?"

"Not from the brass." Kaitlyn continued punching on the bag.

Jonathan walked up to the other side of the bag and grabbed it to hold it steady, Kaitlyn continued on it. "Then who is it from?"

Kaitlyn stopped punching and looked up at him. Could she tell him? Could she trust him? "It's a side project."

"Tell me about it."

Kaitlyn thought about it for a moment, she might need the help, she hasn't been able to put together a plan that she could do alone no matter what the tactic she came up with. She took a deep breath, "I've been having these dreams..."

"Oh kinky." Jonathan interrupted. Kaitlyn turned to leave. "Wait – I'm sorry." Kaitlyn stopped, her back still to him.

"I'm receiving details about a crime organization, incredibly detailed information that in many cases I have been able to confirm through satellite imagery."

"Okay, what does this have to do with your dreams?"

"I'm getting the information through dreams."

Jonathan started to scoff but then realized that if telepathy was real why couldn't this be? "Tell me more."

"I can do better than that, come back to my place, I can show you."

"I knew you had been missing me." Jonathan coolly chimed in a sexual innuendo. Kaitlyn looked at him and smiled. Yes, some physical release with him would be nice and might come after, but right now she needed to share some of these details with someone because there was almost too much to deal with alone.

When Kaitlyn opened her apartment door Jonathan walked in and immediately saw the mess of papers, maps, pictures and calendar dates. He had been here just two evenings prior and the place didn't look like this. All of a sudden he realized what Kaitlyn was saying was true, not innuendo, not a reason to get him back to her place.

"You've been busy." He spoke as he went in and began determining what all he was seeing, piecing the information together the way agents are supposed to do in preparation of an assignment. "This is Vegas."

"Yes it is." Kaitlyn spoke feeling like it was obvious but forgetting that she hadn't mentioned it before. "Problem with that?"

"Yes and no... you know Tom's there."

"Hmm?" Kaitlyn questioned feeling caught off guard by that response.

"That's where Agent M has been stationed all of this time. How have you been getting this information again? Has he been in contact with you? I thought that had been strictly prohibited, for safety reasons."

"He hasn't contacted me." Kaitlyn quickly volunteered.

"He was your partner it makes sense he'd be reporting to you but this would put him in a lot of danger."

"He hasn't contacted me." Kaitlyn insisted.

"Look you don't have to lie to me, I don't care but..."

"Jonathan damn-it I haven't talked to him since he left!"

Jonathan stood there for a moment. "Dreams?"

Kaitlyn sat down on the edge of the dining room table and sighed. "You don't have to believe me but I get dreams and sometimes even flashes that warn me of things before they happen. These dreams have been different, like they are coming from someone else' eyes and they seem to be only in the informational gathering process. If Tom was sending them to me he doesn't know it."

"How would Tom send them... wait is he telepathic too? Is it a requirement to be your partner?" Jonathan was intrigued, Kaitlyn on the other hand was becoming uneasy. "Is he? That would be so cool!" Jonathan continued, "How long have you known about him? Does Susan know?" Just then Jonathan contacted Susan telepathically. "Did you know Tom was a telepath?"

"Of course. When did you find out?" Susan answered before thinking.

"Just now..."

"Hey where are you?" She interrupted quickly.

"Kaitlyn's apartment."

Realizing Kaitlyn must have spilled the beans and she wasn't responsible she wanted to know more, "Tell Kaitlyn I'll be right there."

"Susan's on her way over." Jonathan announced aloud. Kaitlyn looked up at him curiously, shook her head and spoke.

"You just talked to Susan?"

"Well yeah, she's your best friend right?"

"Why would you have...? Wait, how did you know that?"

"Secret Service background evaluation remember? You were roommates after high school."

"You've known this whole time?" Kaitlyn was stunned.

"It was my job."

"What else do you know about me that I didn't know you knew?"

"You name it. I know where you grew up, how your mother and father died..."

"Lenny Lane!" Kaitlyn interjected, "He was there!"

"Yeah story is he was the one who killed your father."

"No, I mean yeah he is but he was in the dream, this building right here." Kaitlyn pointed on the map.

"You know Lane's whereabouts?"

"Jonathan I'm going to need help on this."

Just then Susan knocked, tested the door knob and walked in. "Hey guys what have I missed?"

"Susan? You just walk in?" Kaitlyn scoffed placing focus on privacy issues.

"I knocked." Susan smiled

"You don't know what you could have been walking into." Kaitlyn scolded.

"Yeah we could have been naked in bed." Jonathan added.

"In your dreams." Susan laughed

"Speaking of dreams Susan, I've been having them." Kaitlyn spoke up changing the subject.

"Like before in high school?"

"They aren't flashes, they're different but I feel I'm getting them for a reason."

"So what's the low down?"

"Drug lord, prostitution, illegal fighting, illegal weapons, and Lenny Lane and Mike Manners are involved.

"Holy crap it's like a convention!"

"Maybe it is," Jonathan interjected. "Las Vegas is known as the convention capital of the world."

Just then Kaitlyn began receiving a flash, she saw the drug lord receive a text message, "Undercover agent in your unit." then a picture came in on his phone, it was Tom. The man closed his phone, looked over at Tom standing there also looking around the room, it was Toms eyes she had been looking through. Then she noticed Manner's pointing towards Tom just as the crowd leapt to their feet to cheer." Kaitlyn jolted out of the flash.

"I can confirm it, the information is accurate and it's coming from Tom."

He's been in contact with you all of this time?" Susan questioned.

"I don't think he realized, we didn't leave things on a talking basis."

"So Tom's a telepath too, why didn't either of you tell me? Tom and I go way back."

"Jonathan, Tom doesn't..." But just then Kaitlyn was startled into another flash. Flashed forward to Tom out back of the Palms resort in the loading dock, four men beating him up, two holding him back as another punched him, he kicked the one back and the other came in.

Using his upper body strength he pulled the two holding his arms forward then knocked them away. He was gaining control of the situation, he kicked the third guy back and sent a punch at the forth as the two before regained their balance and came back at him. Turning towards a crate in the alley, Tom grabbed it and thrashed it in the head of one man as another tackled him to the ground. With a quick jolt of his elbow backwards, he knocked that guy back and leapt to his feet ready for the next however as he kicked back, the next guy came at him with a knife. Stabbing him in his gut, the jolt made Kaitlyn scream out "Tom!" and although eyes-wide and aware the flash continued to grasp a hold of Kaitlyn's attention as one of the goons punched Tom in the jaw and he went down.

As Tom's face jerked right and he lost balance and fell to the ground, Kaitlyn did too and as she came out of the flash in time to catch her fall, she looked up at Susan in panic. "Tom's in trouble!"

"What can I do?"

"We've got to help him, his cover is blown and he was just stabbed in a back loading dock at the Palms."

Susan turned to the wall and began taking it all in. "Tom's in Vegas?"

"Yes."

"Whoa," Jonathan interjected completely confused now, "are you sure you want Susan to know this? It's supposed to be an undercover op."

"Susan's safe, I trust her."

"Awe thanks Kaitlyn." Susan remarked then pointed to one of the buildings, "You mentioned the loading docks at the Palms?"

"That's right, he was just stabbed."

"I'm on it."

"What are you going to do?"

"I have friends at the Palm... We'll need to get Tom to safety if he's still there and you'll need to get in when we arrive. You have here the Palms Penthouse B?"

"Yes."

"I'll make a couple calls."

"Whoa! Wait a second ladies, what are we talking about here?"

"We're talking about rescuing Tom, stopping a huge weapons deal, and killing Lenny Lane and Mike Manners." Kaitlyn barked.

"How do you know all of this is real? How do you know Tom's been stabbed?"

"Jonathan," Susan spoke, "If Kaitlyn says it is – then it is." Susan grabbed a map from the table and her cell phone, she dialed a number then spoke. "Mark I need to call in a favor... yeah I know... I need you to check on a situation in loading dock B. Thanks."

Ready for this mission, no questions asked, Jonathan grabbed his phone and dialed a number while speaking to Kaitlyn "If we're going to do this then we'll need back-up and we'll need to keep this out of CovSec hands. There is no way we can explain any of this and get the support we need" He waited for an answer then spoke to the person on the other line, "Todd it's Stangard how you doing? Good to hear."

Kaitlyn wondered if he was talking to Todd Pickens one of the secret service men they worked with at the white house. Jonathan continued, "We've got a situation I may need your help with... Good, see if Sam Roberts and Greg Gold are available as well... Thanks."

As Jonathan hung up Kaitlyn knew without a doubt that those were three men she had trusted with her life while secret service and she was grateful to have them on board. Just then Susan spoke again, "Damn! Can you pull up surveillance for a warehouse off of sixth street then? Thanks" Susan covered the phone and announced "I've got surveillance being taken from the area, we'll have a tail on the vehicle that Tom was in momentarily.

"Tom wasn't in a vehicle..." Kaitlyn spoke confused.

"Security cameras caught the stabbing, then the four men dragged him into the back of a Limo and took off."

"Oh God!" Kaitlyn's eyes widened.

"Do you think they're going to dump the body?" Jonathan asked.

"There is no body, Tom's not dead." Kaitlyn interjected quickly.

"How do you know..."

"Trust me Jonathan," Susan spoke with such conviction there was no questioning it, "If Kaitlyn says he isn't dead then he definitely is not dead!"

Kaitlyn smiled at that then spoke again, "Tom's been inside this organization for weeks, he knows everything about them, they're going to want to know what he knows before they get rid of him.

"They're going to torture him?" Susan spoke with fear.

"It's what I would do." Kaitlyn then looked at Jonathan, "You willing to do this? I know you are taking a lot on faith here and I'd understand any reluctance."

"I've followed you into all sorts of missions, I trust you completely." Jonathan smiled although Kaitlyn could tell this whole thing was a bit weird to him. Then she looked at Susan, "I don't want to put you in any unnecessary danger."

"Me neither. I may have the training but I took a lab position for a reason, my adrenaline doesn't need the smacks that yours does, I'll get you in, put you in touch with my connections and I can take care of myself from there, you and your team do what you need to.

"Thanks Susan." Kaitlyn smiled realizing they were about to go on the most important mission yet. The mission to save Tom's life."

Tom's arms were in chains hooked to the ceiling of some rusty warehouse somewhere. It was dark, dank, there was the sound of dripping water. As he came to he saw his stab wound which wasn't deep or life threatening had been patched up and although not bleeding now had continued for a while after the patch until it scabbed over. He looked around the room and wondered what had happened, he had seen Lenny Lane at the fight but hadn't expected Lenny to know who he was. Now Mike Manners was a different story but as soon as he saw the man he made maneuvers to secure his identity. He had been certain he hadn't been made and yet here he was, captive in some warehouse awaiting what he only expected to be torture for information until his death. If ever there was a time to implement his telepathic abilities and call Kaitlyn for help this would have been it but to Tom, this was just another day and he was not going to go down that road again. He knew where he stood.... maybe when he had a better idea of the situation.

194

As Tom spent the next few minutes yanking and tugging at the chains trying to determine how loose they were and if he could break free, his 'drug boss', the four guards who captured him, Lenny Lane and Mike Manners were in the next room over yelling at one another. Blame was definitely going around as to whom could let an undercover agent into the organization and so close to the 'boss' but how much could he know, how much had he shared and who was this Jones Lenny kept speaking about.

"This is great, she'll be coming here for sure." Lenny pined quietly as he stood by the window on proverbial lookout.

"I don't understand you man," Manners spoke up to Lenny, "If any of the stories I've heard are true, then why on Earth would you want her to come here?"

Lenny looked at the man curiously and smiled, "Because it is time. I have been following this woman for so long, have come so close to destroying her so many times, it's my turn, I look forward to crushing her and now, now I think I have finally come up with the best plan yet."

"And what is that?"

"Him." Lenny spoke pointing his attention out towards the warehouse where Tom was currently being held captive. "From what you've told me of your happenings with the two of them, where he is, she won't be far behind. But enough about that, this is my own little side job, what have they decided upon?" Lenny spoke now focusing on Devers and his men on the other side of the room.

"We should just kill him now."

"We should find out what he knows."

"We should torture him until we find out how he's been communicating and to whom."

Devers finally lifted a hand to stop the men from speaking and smiled, "I'll have that taken care of soon. I am having a professional torturer come in this afternoon. We'll know what he knows soon enough."

Chapter 13

"Jones, good to see you again Todd spoke as he handed her and Jonathan ear buds and checked the circuits.

"How did you and Greg get here so quickly?"

"We were already here scoping out the SCI show for Bush."

"SCI?" Kaitlyn questioned.

"Safari Club International. They hold a huge convention here every year and 41 enjoys a quick cart ride through before it opens to the public."

"We were going to fly out this afternoon but when we got the call from Stangard we both wanted to help." Greg added.

"Thank you." Kaitlyn spoke as Stangard walked up and began giving them the low down on what was happening. Kaitlyn then stepped outside the parked van and pressed up against the side. She hadn't had a flash or any dreams from Tom since late last night and so she didn't have any further intelligence on the situation. She knew that now that they were here it would be nice to know a little bit more so she closed her eyes and opened her mind to anything she could receive. For quite a few moments there was nothing, blackness but then, wham, it came to her like a burning hot poker in the thigh. She struggled to keep from screaming as her vision brightened as if Tom's eyes were opening and she began visualizing the scene before him.

"Who's your contact?" The man demanded as he turned and threw the iron poker back into the flames. Tom refused to speak. The man asked the question again as he reached for a bottle of vodka and poured a glass. He sniffed it as he waiting for a response but when none came he doused it on Tom's open wounds and he screamed out in pain.

Kaitlyn began to wonder how long this had been going on, whether it had just started when Tom's eyes scanned the room. He looked to the east side of the warehouse and towards a closed door that he knew led down the hall to the office and suddenly Kaitlyn knew that too, then he peered left to the west side and towards a very dirty window with very little sunlight shining through. He leaned his head down just a bit more and focused his attention through the broken bottom corner to see another rusty sheet metal warehouse across the way and a few letters of a sign 'D TR" Kaitlyn was trying to determine what the rest of the words were when her attention was smacked away from the window and returned as the sensation of a metal pipe being struck against Tom's back nearly knocked her off of her feet.

Stangard was just coming out of the van when he saw Kaitlyn stumble and caught her, quickly glancing to see if she were being attacked. Her eyes opened and she looked up at him, "The torturing has begun." As she pulled from his arms he was confused for just a moment, still highly curious as to how she was sensing all of this, he followed her back inside the van as she began speaking to Todd.

"Do you have satellite surveillance on the warehouse district yet?"

"We do, we were just about to see if there had been any traffic going to it."

"Pull that up on computer B, I need this computer to zoom in as far as you can on the East side of the fourth warehouse." Todd tapped at the keyboard as Kaitlyn watched it zoom in while Greg continued scanning the feed on computer B. "There, zoom in there." Kaitlyn spoke as she pointed to something leaning up against the opposite warehouse. Todd zoomed in further and as soon as Kaitlyn could read the old hotel sign "World Trade Center" that had been stored here after the building was demolished years ago. Kaitlyn now knew exactly where everyone was. "That's where he is. Pan out just a bit." Todd panned out then began the sequence to turn on heat signatures. Before it could come up Kaitlyn pointed it all out. "Tom is being held there in the main portion of the warehouse, over there is a hallway that leads to an office sectional, Devers, Manners and Lane are all there right now along with four goons, we need to get our team there."

As she finished speaking Stangard looked on just as the heat signatures focused in on two in the warehouse and at least seven in the front of the building. Jonathan wondered if Todd and Greg would wonder about that but they said nothing as Greg hopped into the front driver's seat and drove the van down the street and near the opposite warehouse. When they were close enough, Todd, Jonathan and Kaitlyn leapt out from the back of the van, guns drawn and began making their way towards their designated entry points. Kaitlyn wanted the back as Jonathan took the front, Todd on the west side entered in through the side door. Greg however had resumed his spot behind the computer terminals, radio communication active and ready to announce if there were any changes.

"We're down two bodies in the office, I can't account for their whereabouts."

"Knowing that two people were either dead or had left the building was beneficial but not knowing which was going to make things difficult. Timing their entrances in sync the three of them entered the warehouse at the same time, Jonathan started up the stairs and Todd came down the hallway, checking rooms as he proceeded inwards. Kaitlyn on the other hand entered the back warehouse quietly. She knew from her vision that Tom and his torturer were just beyond the crates in front of her and she needed the element of surprise if she intended on saving Tom before the other guy killed him.

Peeking around the corner to verify the scene she saw Tom hanging by his chained wrists in the middle of the warehouse. His shirt had been stripped from him, his back was bloody, he was dirty and his head was down. Kaitlyn realized he was unconscious again. Crates piled high in various locations would supply the cover she needed to get close enough to determine the best escape route. The one thing Kaitlyn did not see was the torturer. Tom was out cold, bruised and bloody, she knew well what kind of pain he had experienced and she wanted nothing more than to go to him and release him, but she knew the area was not secure. She had to find out where everyone was and she had to figure out how to release Tom from his chains. She was studying the area deciphering a plan when she saw the torturer return with another red-hot poker.

As he neared Tom's body Kaitlyn had to react, she couldn't stand idly by and watch this, she pulled her gun from its holster aimed and shot. The bullet went through the man's right hand and his left shoulder. Dropping the poker to the ground with a clang and being knocked to the ground himself, Kaitlyn started to make her way cautiously to the scene. Gun aimed, ready to fire, she checked the surrounding area, feeling confident they were alone. A nagging feeling in her kept insisting there was still more danger but not seeing anything and not knowing how long she had to release Tom, she went to him, replaced the gun to its holster and began full-strength at the chains, pulling them apart.

Kaitlyn had always had the strength of six men, with an average lifting weight of three hundred pounds, she made the chains pull apart like cold taffy. However right as she was making headway she was shocked, struck on the back with a stun gun, the electricity shot through her like lightning and her body convulsed to the floor. Turning to see the prod coming at her again she reacted as quick as her body could allow at the moment and kicked the guys left shin, knocking him backwards. Collecting herself, she leapt to her feet right as the man came at her again, knocking the prod away with her forearm, it left the man's hands and flew across the room, then the fight was on. As a large fist came towards her face and a reactionary block ensued Kaitlyn recognized the attacker as Lenny and the fury filled her veins.

Blocking the first punch, sending the next and blocking a kick, Kaitlyn found herself fighting her long-time nemesis once again and she knew her mind needed to be focused or she'd allow him to escape again. As they fought Kaitlyn was able to determine that he had had much practice since the last time they fought. He blocked every punch she sent, she blocked every punch he sent. When she spun a kick towards his face he dodged it and retaliated with a low kick that she leapt over. Besides the initial cattle prod jolt Lenny hadn't laid a hand on her and she hadn't laid a single punch on him. Either they were both off their game or so on their game they were just wasting time. Kaitlyn knew she had to do something to break the monotony, with a spinning high kick and then twisting to her knees, she slid a dagger from her boot and came back up at Lenny dagger forward. Lenny leapt back to miss the blade as a smile spread across his face. Unable to contemplate at the moment why he was smiling, Kaitlyn quickly realized as she was struck in the center of the back and thrown forward into Lenny's arms.

Pain searing up her spine, Kaitlyn caught a glance of her attacker with her peripheral vision and the splintered bat he was holding. Grabbing and constraining her arms, Lenny held on for dear life as Kaitlyn attempted to regain control of the situation. There was no time to wonder why she hadn't gotten a flash of the oncoming assailant as he was coming towards her again, Mike Manners himself, with bat in hand, raised for another swing.

Kicking upwards with all of her might she struck Mike in the arm as Lenny lost grip of her wrists. Falling now to the floor on an already pulverized back that she was certain might have a slipped disk, Kaitlyn mustered up her strength to continue the fight. Lenny and Mike were at the top of their game as they reached for Kaitlyn and she knew she couldn't let them capture her, quickly rolling to the left three turns and stopping on her front, she pushed up with her arms and knees to get to her feet and block off their grabby attack.

Her back was in sad shape, the pain searing up her spine made her head throb and the stinging where she was struck continued even though she was certain the adrenaline should have enabled her to ignore it. As the two men neared again, Kaitlyn reached for her gun and yanked it from her holster, with milliseconds to aim and fire, she missed as Lenny kicked it from her hands in a spin-kick even Tom would have been proud of. As she watched her gun fly from her hand and her right wrist become clutched in Lenny's hands Kaitlyn wondered what was happening. Why was this pain keeping her from fighting?

As Lenny spun her back to his chest and wrapped his left arm around her, covering her mouth, Kaitlyn began thrashing trying to break free but even she could see her feeble attempts looked more like a fish out of water than an agent fighting for their life. Glancing over at Tom who was still unconscious, and then noticing a syringe in Lenny's hand, Kaitlyn had to do the next best thing, she sent a telepathic SOS to Jonathan whom she hoped wasn't as preoccupied as she was.

"Devers and his men have been apprehended" Jonathan reported through his radio back to Todd in the van as Greg rounded up the cuffed men and began leading them out of the building. Jonathan was just about to join them when he heard Kaitlyn's telepathic call and ran that direction. As Jonathan raced down the hall and towards the main warehouse room, he saw Kaitlyn knock a syringe from Lane's hand through the window and then he burst through it surprising the two men enough for Kaitlyn to break free.

As she fell to her knees on the floor, another burst of pain shot up her spine into her head making her nauseous. As her head began to pound but the adrenaline kept coming she pushed herself to her feet again only to find her knees give out. Jonathan had already taken a shot at Manners and another one at Lane who were now on the defensive in a full-blown gun battle. The sound of the shooting woke Tom to the commotion and as he came to he yanked at the chains realizing many of the links had been stretched and opened. Freeing himself before a stray bullet came at him, the chains rattled as he fell to the floor acquiring the attention of the once passed out torturer who was now angrier than before. Reaching for his gun, Tom knew he had to react quicker than the torturer, spotting the stun baton, he lunged towards it, clasped it in his hands and pierced it onto the chest of the torturer sending five thousand volts of constant electric current jolting through his body. Vibrating screams of a high pitched frequency echoed through the warehouse grabbing Lenny's attention as Mike took another shot at Jonathan.

Dodging his way to a better position, Lenny Lane aimed ready to take the kill-shot at Tom who's back was to him. Relishing in this moment for a moment too long, his attention was struck back to reality when he felt his body jolt sideways and then go numb. Quickly looking to assess the situation all he saw was the bright yellow cab of the warehouse forklift pressing against his shoulder then the warm ooze of blood dripping down his legs. As Kaitlyn looked over the control levers in the cab of the fork lift she saw that she had succeeded in impaling Lane with the forklift tine and pinning his body permanently to one of the large wooden crates.

The commotion grabbed Toms attention from the now silent yet still convulsing torturer whose flesh was smoking and sizzling from the stun baton but whom was most certainly dead by now. Jonathan was able to take the kill shot at Manners who fell to the ground and Jonathan yelled out "clear" to announce he was good. Tom yelled out "clear" as Kaitlyn too yelled out "clear" She then took a step to exit the forklift but fell out instead.

Tom and Jonathan both ran to her as she again tried to get up on her feet but her legs were too wobbly to support her. As she began to fall again, Tom caught her. Looking into her eyes curiously, Kaitlyn felt the situation was secure and with adrenaline releasing her into a more appropriate calm she spoke in barely a whisper, "I don't feel so good." As she closed her eyes, Tom felt a warm fluid soak his hands as he held Kaitlyn up and when he moved his hand to see what was wet Jonathan saw the blood oozing from the center of her back.

"She's been shot!" He yelled as Tom quickly laid her down on her belly to assess the damage on her back. Ripping her shirt open the two saw quite a horrific sight. A large black bruise encompassed the majority of her back centered around a large gaping flesh wound so deep they could see her spinal column. As Jonathan immediately got on the phone to call for an ambulance, realizing this was much worse than a bullet hole, Tom looked closer at the wound and knowing what he did about wounds of this nature a small voice in the back of his head started to ask the question – how did she keep going on when any other person would have surely been paralyzed?

"Ambulance is on its way." Jonathan announced as four uniformed police officers entered the warehouse.

"Is everyone okay in here?"

"Three dead, 5 in custody, one of ours has been injured."

"Your men outside got us up to speed, are you in need of medical attention?"

"She's been hurt bad." Tom spoke almost afraid of what he was looking at.

Jonathan ripped his shirt off, scrunched it up and placed it over Kaitlyn's wound to compress the bleeding.

"Not too hard, I think there has been major spinal damage." Tom spoke as Jonathan's pressure lessened so much he released his grip on the shirt.

Tom grabbed the shirt and applied pressure realizing Stangard was too shocked to perform.

One of the officers radioed in for immediate medical assistance as the other approached noticing how bloody Tom was as well. "Are you hurt?"

Tom's eyes left Kaitlyn's back for a moment as he looked at the cauterized flesh wound on his side, the stab wound that missed internal organs and was scabbed up and the multiple lacerations on his chest and arms. He hadn't even felt them after he saw Kaitlyn. He shook his head, "I'm fine."

"Is she still alive?" Jonathan asked almost panicking as he stood three feet away looking down at her still body.

"She's still breathing." Tom spoke, still applying mild pressure to her wound, his other hand placed delicately under the side of her face keeping tabs on her breathing and pulse. "I think at this point it best that she stay still."

Moments later sirens of the approaching ambulance blared in the internal walls of the warehouse and two paramedics ran into the area. Tom wanted to give them space but he couldn't find the will to move, he wanted to stay there with Kaitlyn. The first paramedic, removed the blood soaked shirt to take a better look at the wound then reported back to the second paramedic. "Looks like we've got at least two ruptured disks and major compression to the spinal column. Do either of you know what happened?" Jonathan shook his head as Tom began to but stopped. He paused for a moment then spoke.

"She was struck on the back by a baseball bat."

The second paramedic looked around and saw the fractured weapon on the ground. "That's a Louisville slugger."

"We've had some major swelling, spinal fluid seepage, she's lost a lot of blood. We need to stabilize the vertebral column, control the hemorrhaging and alleviate the compression on the cord to prep her for immediate surgery."

"Is she going to be paralyzed?" Jonathan asked.

"That depends on how much damage has been done and how good the surgeon is."

The other paramedic was wheeling a gurney in as Todd walked in to assess the damage. Seeing Kaitlyn on the ground face down, back bloody he feared the worse.

"I need four ccs of methylprednisolone sodium succinate." The first paramedic spoke to the second.

"What's that?" Jonathan asked.

"A corticosteroid. It's used to reduce inflammation in the injured area and help to prevent further damage to cellular membranes that can cause nerve death. Sparing nerves from further damage and death is crucial

"Death? Is she going to die?" Jonathan asked only hearing key words of the conversation.

"Nerve death Stangard." Tom barked angrily.

"Please sir, just let us do our job." The second paramedic pleaded.

As Jonathan stepped back and the paramedics began prepping Kaitlyn's body for transport. Tom continued to sit there on the ground though. He didn't know what he could do, he didn't know what to say, he didn't know how to act. Kaitlyn had been severely injured while rescuing him and he didn't know what to think about that.

"Sir we need to immobilize her for transport." The paramedic said encouraging Tom to give them space. They brought in the gurney and a plank, carefully keeping her straight.

"If she was in such bad shape how was she able to keep fighting?" Jonathan asked just trying to keep up with the situation.

"She was going into spinal shock." The first paramedic spoke as he secured Kaitlyn to the gurney. "Sometimes the effects of the damage take time to manipulate the body. The adrenaline from the fight must have kept her going."

"She must have been in such pain." Jonathan spoke without thinking. Those words were like a bullet to Tom's heart.

Tom stood there in silence watching, guilt and remorse swept over him. Kaitlyn however, unconscious yet aware and scared entered Tom's head only if to escape her present circumstances but also to ease his pain, this at least, she knew she could accomplish.

"Stop it! Stop feeling guilty McKinney, suck it up."

"Kaitlyn this happened because of me."

"Nonsense. This happened because I wasn't aware of where Manners position was and was too focused on my own personal demons in regards to Lane. This had nothing to do with you."

"You were here to save me, that much I know."

"Granted, but this could have happened to anyone."

"Which reminds me, how did you know where I was? I was under the impression that CovSec sent me in solo, I didn't realize they were keeping tabs on me."

"They weren't. They don't even know about this rescue mission."

"What? Why not?"

"There was no time for protocol, permission or authorization. To get approval for this assignment would have to have come from the top. Especially with the insiders knowledge you were acquiring. You had been made and the last I saw, stabbed and left for dead."

"I don't understand, how did you know that then?"

"You told me, gave me constant updates."

"Kaitlyn, I didn't."

"We're talking telepathically, you've been on the receiving end of the benefits of my flashes and dreams for years and you're asking me how did I know?" Kaitlyn wanted to smack him upside his head.

"I studied and trained on mental blocks for years. I kept you out of my head successfully for five years!"

"You're acting like I spied on you!"

"Well didn't you?"

"I didn't even know the information was coming from you until last night."

"That's bull shit! I left without a word and you decided to spy on me in spite!"

"My God are you full of yourself! I can't control my dreams and you damn well know that! You're lucky I have them though or you'd be dead right now!

"I should be dead! I was made and too weak to escape. You shouldn't have come!"

"Are you pissed because I saved you?"

"I'm pissed because you were damaged saving me!"

"Tom! Snap out of it!" Jonathan spoke standing over Tom who was sitting on the ground with his head in his hands. Jonathan looked over his shoulder as the paramedics loaded Kaitlyn into the ambulance as Tom looked up at him and realized no matter how nice it was alone with Kaitlyn in his head he needed to figure out how to be there for her now more than ever. The two men ran up to the ambulance.

"Sorry guys, no room in here."

"Where are you taking her?"

"Southern Hills."

Jonathan radioed to Greg in the van to request a ride and the two hopped in the back of the van as Todd hopped in the front passenger seat. Moments later, they sped away following the ambulance. Jonathan then sent a telepathic update to Susan to let her know what happened.

"Oh my gosh, is she okay?"

"Don't know, they're taking her to Southern Hills."

"I'll meet ya'll there... how bad is it?"

"It doesn't look good." Jonathan acknowledged.

"Tom?" Susan asked needing an update on him.

"Beaten and bruised but otherwise fine."

Susan opened a telepathic channel with Tom as she ran through the hotel lobby to the front to catch a cab. "Glad to hear you're safe. How's the stab wound?"

"Susan?" Tom was caught off guard.

"Yeah, I'm hailing a cab now, I'm meeting you two at the hospital."

"How do you know all of this?"

"Jonathan just filled me in."

"I'm sitting right next to him, he didn't make a phone call."

"He's telepathic too Tom, catch up."

"What? When did that happen?"

"Oh right, you've been gone. Sorry – blonde moment. Yeah I discovered his ability a few weeks ago, Kaitlyn and I have been working with him since."

"Is there anyone who doesn't have the ability?"

"How bad is the damage?"

Jonathan nudged Tom's shoulder to get his attention as he spoke, "Hey you talking to Susan?"

Tom looked up at him with the weirdest, how-dare-you-interrupt-me – can-you-seriously-be-a-telepath – how-do-you-know-I-am, look on his face. Jonathan caught the confusion and anger immediately and spoke quick with his palms up "Don't shoot the messenger."

Tom tried desperately to grasp all of this; his head pounding as he knew his recent wounds and the stress of all of this was beginning to tear him up. "One conversation at a time." He spoke aloud to Jonathan as he returned a telepathic message to Susan "Just meet us in the emergency waiting room."

"Tom I have an idea."

"Just meet us there."

"Tom!"

Tom looked over at Todd and Greg in the front seat and then back to Jonathan with a puzzled look.

"Oh, they're secret service." Jonathan spoke up to get their attention, "Guys, you haven't met Agent M yet."

Todd looked back and said hi as Greg, who was currently driving spoke a good to meet ya'.

"Glad we were available to assist." Todd spoke to Tom then turned his attention to Stangard, "What do you know?"

"Man it's bad, I saw her spine and it didn't look like the models."

"Crap. How did it happen? I've seen her take down entire rooms."

"I was watching on thermal man – she was struck from behind, didn't even see it coming." Greg added as he signaled a left turn. "Hold on guys." He spoke as he turned the wheel and the van jolted right as Greg's high speed turn lifted the left wheels from the ground.

Tom wanted to get sick. Todd's words 'I've seen her take down entire rooms' struck his nerve. He knew Lenny was a raw nerve for Kaitlyn, he was glad she had finally killed the man. At least that phase of her life was finally over – and then that thought struck a nerve. Her life was not over, she would survive this – but how much damage had she done? Would she be paralyzed? He knew Jonathan asked that same question, he heard the paramedics response but it meant nothing to him. Kaitlyn was strong, the strength of six men. She had telepathy, telekinesis, she was special. Born from traumatic and extraordinary circumstances, he felt she could do anything if she put her mind to it. Could she make it through this though?

The van came to an abrupt stop in front of the hospital and Stangard and Tom both rolled forward, immediately recovered and then hopped out of the van. As they exited, Tom ran inside as Greg spoke out to Stangard "We can't stay man, our plane's waiting."

"I get it, president's waiting, thanks for the assist guys, I owe you big."

"Wouldn't have used our down time for anything else man." Todd spoke.

"Yeah, it's not like there's anything to do in Vegas." Greg added.

Jonathan half laughed, then shut the back door to the van. As he ran into the waiting room he saw Susan and Tom discussing something, he ran up to catch what he was missing.

"Mind over matter Tom, and with her mind, her abilities, her strength – which comes from her mind – you can help guide her towards recuperation while in surgery!"

"Susan mental communication is not going to..."

"Tom listen to me! I know how you two escape into each others' mind, my God have I heard the stories about the sex!" Susan spoke and for a fraction of a second wanted to feel what that was like but then returned to the conversation at hand while seeing the look on Toms face of embarrassment. "The training you two did, telepathy and physical assertion have put you in the absolute perfect position to try this."

At that moment Tom would have freaked out using the word telepathy out loud and in public and as Stangard looked around the room realizing they were attracting attention, he motioned for the two of them to take the conversation to more private places.

Tom started to walk out of the room while keeping visual awareness on the nurses station as Susan followed and continued her conversation telepathically. "They've got her in MRI now, they'll have her prepped for surgery within the hour. When they get in there, when they administer the anesthesia she's going to go down, there will be no communication with her for eight to ten hours at least and those are the most important hours of this entire procedure!"

Tom was listening, confused as to what he could do, knowing that all he could do was wait and pray, Susan sounded as though she had a better plan. He continued listening, trying desperately to open his mind to the possibility of telepathic assistance from outside the operating room, but not clear on what good it would do.

"Tom I have done extensive research on the brain. I have mapped the cortical responses of physical manipulation with mental capabilities. I have studied Kaitlyn's thought processes thoroughly and I honestly believe that I can walk you through saving her."

"How?" Tom spoke aloud desperate to understand.

"You need to enter her mind completely. You need to shut down out here, go in there completely, find her and train her."

"Train her to do what?"

Jonathan walked up listening again to their conversation, also wanting to know how he could help.

"Strength training. Just like those afternoons in the high school gym when you two worked together. You took her from weak and scared to strong and capable. You taught her fight, Karate, Tai Kwan Do, Jujitsu, Kickboxing, Aikido."

"Right?"

"Aikido is your key. Having harmony with your life force; Zin-art."

"Wait," Jonathan interrupted, "You knew Kaitlyn in high school?" But Susan continued, ignoring him.

"If you know Aikido then you probably know Tai Chi?"

"Yeah, we did that summer of..."

"Doesn't matter when, what matters is that you two know it. Tai Chi uses one's internal energies and channels ones internal power. Physical and cognitive exercise to develop emotional, mental and spiritual clarity. By increasing the communication between the body and mind it reduces the stress and creates calmness and confidence that she is going to be in desperate need of. By becoming aware of where the tension is and relaxing it mentally, she'll be able to allow the physicians influence to cultivate the proper techniques required to heal her properly."

Jonathan interrupted again but this time for both he and Tom's benefit. "Slow down Susan, you're trying to say that all this will be to relax her – wouldn't the anesthesia do that?

"Yes and no. This technique the physician is going to do is going to be very stressful to her body. Recovery is going to take months and she's probably going to need additional surgeries. What I am suggesting is for her to go into rehabilitation while under the knife. To begin the healing and strengthening process prior to immediately so she'll have the most benefits possible. The focus is more on the mental and energetic levels rather than the physical level. Basically, what

I am saying is keep her fighting and her mental energies will advance the healing process and shorten recovery time."

Just then the surgeon walked up to meet them and discuss the surgery he was about to perform. "I've taken a look at the MRI, she's received a massive spinal compression that has dislocated various vertebrae, those included being the 2nd through 5th thoracic, the 4th was fractured. Two spinal nerves have been severed and she's had seepage of cerebrospinal fluid from a tear in the dura membrane."

"Doctor what all is involved?" Tom asked hearing this and wanting to freak out.

"We're looking at needing to remove all bone fragments that may be pressing against the cord and that severed the nerves, reconstructing the fourth thoracic, reconnecting the nerves and relocating the second and fifth vertebrae. This kind of reconstructive, remodeling and peripheral nerve surgery can easily last eight to twelve hours."

"What happens if she's left paralyzed?" Jonathan asked.

"We don't like to speculate but there are additional procedures we can take including but not limited to advanced orthopedic procedures combining embryonic cell cultures. Once the reconstructive process is complete we'll be able to determine what kind of permanent damage has been done. Until then all you can do is wait."

As the surgeon walked away to prepare for surgery, Tom, Susan and Jonathan just stood there silent for a moment. They each were numb, not even sure how to comprehend all that was said, then the panic began to build.

"What do I need to do?" Tom asked.

"I want to help." Jonathan interjected.

"No offense Jonathan but we don't need a testosterone battle going on inside Kaitlyn's head."

"I don't understand." Jonathan spoke innocently.

"Think about it for a moment." Susan spoke annoyed at how dense men could be.

He and Tom both stood silently for a moment when Jonathan spoke aloud to Tom without making eye contact, "You two were a thing?"

"Guess that means you two are?" Tom spoke putting two and two together.

There was a bitter silence for a moment as the two men comprehended the truth. Finally Tom spoke, "He should do it." Jonathan looked at him as he continued. "Kaitlyn and I are over, she's with him now."

"Right." Jonathan agreed aloud. Susan rolled her eyes.

"No offense to your ego Jonathan but Tom's gotta' do it." Tom began to protest but Susan explained. "Tom, you and Kaitlyn are connected in ways that I can't even begin to fathom. The telepathic connection between you two is..." She paused shaking her head remembering back to their history. "She knew you weren't dead. Knew it. She felt your presence in this world even with all of your mental blockades and control. You tried to hide and she found you! Your car went off a cliff and she saved you! Whether you want to believe it or not, the connection you two have is genuinely substantial. She called you soul mates... and only her soul mate can bring her through this."

Chapter 14

Aware of her situation, Kaitlyn tried desperately to stay calm as she was wheeled down the hall to the operating room. Face down on the gurney, her head on a specially designed head rest with a hole for her face to look through. Her arms and legs were already constrained to the table and as she watched the floor, enter the operating room and shoes covered in blue disposable shoe covers approach the gurney, she knew she didn't have much time. Everyone was prepped for surgery. She saw the anesthesiologist approach with his tank and clear mask and she truly began to panic. Her blood pressure spiked and a nearby nurse announced it.

"Ms. Jones, this is going to help you to calm down." He spoke as he placed the mask over her nose and mouth and strapped the elastic around the head rest and her head. "Now breathe deeply. Count backwards from one hundred."

Kaitlyn began to count but she was scared. Terrified. She was about to undergo major back surgery. She hadn't gotten to talk to Tom, hadn't put any affairs in order, hadn't even had the time during all of this rushing around to even think about what was going to happen to her. But here she was, moments from this and her blood pressure was still high. The attending nurse was checking her vitals and reporting to the doctor. The anesthesiologist, cranked up the dosage. What if I stay awake? Kaitlyn wondered, panic intensified.

"Hey you." Tom spoke. Kaitlyn turned inward to her head and saw Tom standing there. She ran up to him, wrapped her arms around his neck and hugged him.

"I am so glad you are here. I was so scared."

"Where else would I be at a time like this?" He spoke.

Kaitlyn looked around, it was dark, there was a light from above shining down on the two of them but they were completely surrounded by darkness. Even the ground they were standing on was black even with the light shining down on them. "Where are we?"

"In your head."

"I've never seen it like this."

"You haven't supplied us a scene. Why don't you take us somewhere, someplace nice."

Kaitlyn thought about it for a moment then smiled. Moments later a scene appeared around them. The two of them stood in front of a swing set on a beautifully green pasture. Spring flowers were blooming, there was a light breeze blowing, the sun was starting to set and there was the most gorgeous pink and purple skyline Tom had ever seen. "Where are we?"

Kaitlyn took his hand and led him over to a granite podium. He walked up and noticed the plaque and read it aloud.

"In loving memory of Harold Jones. A good man who gave even after his passing. May his memory live on in the hearts of every citizen who ever had their lives touched by him." Tom looked at Kaitlyn quizzically. "The town put this up for your father." Kaitlyn smiled.

The two of them then walked over to the swing set and sat down. Swinging slowly back and forth Tom spoke. "I should apologize to you."

"Why?"

"I left without an explanation, I left without saying goodbye."

"You were angry, it happens."

"It's no excuse. I could have been killed and there are things I never said to you."

"Like what?

217

Tom sighed, stopped swinging, clasped hold of the chain on Kaitlyn's swing and stopped her from swinging. He took her hands into his and began to speak.

"You are the most important person in my life. I have loved you longer than you know."

"You mean it didn't start at the Mac?" Kaitlyn smiled.

"It didn't even start the day you found my car." Kaitlyn was intrigued, Tom continued. "Nonetheless, there is something I want to tell you."

"Go on."

Tom took a deep breath and looked into Kaitlyn's eyes. They locked onto each other for a moment, intense looks saying it all, but then the look was distracted when Kaitlyn screamed.

"What's wrong?" Tom leapt to his feet in panic, catching Kaitlyn from falling backwards.

"The pain! Oh God the pain!"

Tom realized by keeping her mind active the anesthesia wasn't going to block her from feeling the surgery. Kaitlyn was going to feel everything the surgeons did to her and this terrified him. Wondering for a moment if this was the right thing to do he realized he was here and it had to work, there was no other option at the moment.

"You have to focus on me Kaitlyn. Ignore the pain, focus on me, look at me." Tom spoke gripping her chin in his hand and directing her face to his.

"I'm so scared!" Kaitlyn cried out in panic.

Tom helped her to her feet, keeping her attention directed on him, he spoke. "Focus on me, you are capable of ignoring what is happening to you."

Just then Kaitlyn felt a surging pain radiate from the center of her back that knocked her knees out from under her. She screamed as she tried to reach for the pain with her right hand. Tom quickly grabbed her hands and pulled them forward and lifted her to her feet again.

"Ignore the pain."

Kaitlyn felt the surgeon placing a cold metal clamp on either side of her spine, spreading her muscles and ribcage just slightly. The pain was so intense Kaitlyn was certain she'd go insane.

"Tom help me!"

"Look into my eyes. Kaitlyn! Look into my eyes! I'm here for a reason."

"I hoped there was a plan." Kaitlyn tried to joke but wasn't feeling the funny.

"Your back surgery has started, you are under the knife. I'm here to help you get through it."

"Wow if only everyone had that ability."

"Listen, Susan has this idea that seems plausible."

"Don't let her blonde hair and high school memories distract you, she's become quite a scientist." Kaitlyn added hearing the disbelief in Tom's voice.

"I'm getting that. Tom smiled knowingly. "Do you remember when we trained in high school?"

The scene around them immediately changed to the high school gym and to their left Tom saw himself grab Kaitlyn by the forearms and pull her into a passionate kiss. He released his grip of her forearms and she rolled her fingers through his hair. He wrapped his hands around her torso and lifted her into the air just slightly. Enough for her to wrap her legs around his hips and hold on tight. He slowly rubbed his hands up her back spreading his fingers out so his hands could touch every inch of her skin.

The kiss became more intense, emotions and feelings flowed through them. Wanting him more than she had ever wanted anything in her entire life, she was powerless to stop it, unwilling to allow such an intense emotional climax end without feeling everything it had to offer her. Tom held her tight, stumbling for only a second as he bumped her back against the wall for support. Still kissing, she began pulling his shirt from inside his pants with her fingernails. As she lifted his shirt just slightly, uncovering his muscular abs, she tickled his sides with her fingertips, sending more shivers through his body, making him want her even more. He let go of her for just a second to rip his shirt over his head and throw it to the floor, but she held tight with her throbbing thighs gripped securely around his hips. As he came back to her he grabbed her arms by the wrist and thrust them against the wall so he could have full attention of her body as he kissed her around her collarbone, tickling her with his tongue.

As the shivers spread through her body, she moaned and felt his hands slide down her side and begin untucking her shirt. Kaitlyn started undoing his belt buckle and she could feel that he wanted her just as much as she wanted him. She was ready for anything, but then again, when wasn't she? Unfortunately the both of them knew what happened next in this memory, fortunately, Kaitlyn now had the ability to control the situation in her mind and as the image of the two of them faded, continuing their passion; Kaitlyn looked back into Tom's eyes and smiled.

"Want to pick up where they left off?"

He wanted to, now more than ever, but he knew they needed something different at the moment. Seeing the gym scene still surrounding them, he looked over at the mats and spoke. "Do you remember how we used to practice?"

Kaitlyn walked over to the mats and took her fighting stance. Tom approached, took his stance then threw a punch at her. She blocked it and sent one back. Training was what they did best, well, outside of the bedroom. Kaitlyn smiled a bit at that but kept focus on the situation at hand. They warmed up, then Tom paused. Do you remember Tai Chi?"

"Could I ever forget?"

Tom and Kaitlyn stood side by side, simultaneously inhaling deeply and raising their arms skyward. With a slow exhale through the mouth they brought their arms down bending at the torso and touching the floor with their fingers. As they inhaled and began to come back up Kaitlyn's back twinged with pain and she coughed and started to fall forward, Tom turned and caught her in his arms and she stood upright again.

"Tom what's going on?"

"Susan's idea is to work on your mental strengthening while we're here which should enhance your body's ability to heal, strengthening your muscles, nerves and yes your spine too."

"I don't get it."

"I didn't either at first but basically, the brain is what controls all of your bodily systems. Your brain tells your heart to pump, your legs to move and your immune system to take action against a cold. So why can't it learn from our training how to heal the damage in your spine?"

"Isn't that what the surgeon is doing?"

"The surgeon is putting you back together again..."

"...and all the kings horses and all the kings men..."

"You will go back together again and you will begin advanced rehabilitation and you will get better."

"So why do we need to train here and now?"

"What else have you got to do?"

"I could think of a few things." Kaitlyn pondered allowing visions of an afternoon in his bedroom appear around them. Tom knew Kaitlyn well, better than she knew herself at times and he knew this was her way to keep her mind off of her fears. He also knew if he allowed her to ignore the reality of the situation he wouldn't be helping her.

"Arms up." Kaitlyn looked at him, scowled then raised her arms. "Chin lifts." A metal bar appeared bolted to a brick

221

wall and Kaitlyn clutched her fists around it and began pulling herself upwards. "Count them out."

"Two, three..." Tom watched as Kaitlyn lifted herself then shook his head sadly.

"Scoot over." He said as he reached for the bars and joined her. In unison, they counted out their pullups. He didn't want to be her superior, he wanted to be her partner.

"How do you think it's going in there?" Jonathan asked of Susan as they sat next to the couch Tom was asleep on. Susan looked at Tom sleeping, a couple of beads of sweat forming on his forehead, then she looked at the clock on the wall.

"It's only been an hour."

"I know but I hate this part, the waiting."

"I understand but there's nothing more we can do."

Jonathan stood and began to pace across the room. Susan watched him for a few minutes then turned her gaze back to Tom. She could see he was happy, even though there wasn't a large grin on his face she could tell that he was at peace.

When Tom left those few weeks ago, Kaitlyn came to Susan in tears. She knew that their relationship was turbulent but she also knew that their relationship was destined to be. Whether she was a romantic or not, she felt she could write a harlequin love story about the two of them that would teach others the truth behind destiny. Susan wondered why she hadn't met that kind of love in her life yet. She had had boyfriends but nothing like that and she found herself feel a twinge of jealousy. Why can't someone love her?

"You have to open yourself up to it."

Susan turned to Jonathan who was standing next to her. She looked into his eyes for a moment then shyly looked away. Embarrassed that he had heard her thought she tried to decipher his response. "I'm more open to it than she is."

"Actually, you're not."

Susan turned back to him almost angrily. "What do you know about it?"

"I know that you never imagine or fantasize, you never give off any endorphins, you never have an inviting look on your face, never show it with any bodily movements."

"I portray myself professionally, I can't walk around like a call girl."

"Even when you are off duty you never really let go of your professionalism. But I understand why."

"Oh really? Tell me Jonathan, why don't I?"

"Stereotypes. You see yourself as the blonde cheerleader still."

"I'll have you know I had more fun back then."

"And that's the stereotype. You want so desperately to be taken seriously that you have pushed that fun girl into a prison so dark she can't escape."

"That was deep." Susan cooed with annoyance.

"If I would have thought you would have been accepting of my advances, I would have made them a long time ago."

Susan looked at him curiously. "Really?"

Jonathan smiled and kneeled down next to her. "If the opportunity would have been present, I would have knocked."

"Would have?"

Jonathan looked up at the clock and Susan realized he was still infatuated with Kaitlyn. He was not the kind of man to stray and even though the situation with Kaitlyn was speculative and the history with Tom was intense, Jonathan was going to wait and see how this turned out. He liked Susan, but he wasn't going to be the man who moves on while his girlfriend was fighting for her life in surgery. That was just tacky.

"Whew, what's next?" Kaitlyn asked as she and Tom caught their breath after their exercises.

"Gymnastics."

Kaitlyn looked at Tom curiously. She loved the tumbles, the parallel bars and even the pummel horse, but she was in the middle of back surgery.

"I'm in your head. You don't think I can hear your thoughts?"

"Well that's not fair."

"Let's start with Pommel Horse Drills."

Kaitlyn brought up the scene with a gymnasts Pommel horse and walked over to the center handles and lifted herself up.

"Start out with front support swings. Straddle the handles, then kick you left leg up sideways, bring your right leg in and swing sideways to the right side. Keep it up for at least twenty swings."

"Kaitlyn was performing the technique flawlessly when another twinge rose up her spine. Constraining her grip on the bars she stopped, landing on her feet and holding her upper body up just enough to keep the weight off of her feet.

"It's only in your body, it's not in your head."

"That's backwards."

"It's the truth, we're in your head. Your brain is performing the technique and your body wants to send it signals that you can't. Your brain needs to tell your body that it is the boss and you can. It will help your body heal. Now take a deep breath, send a signal back to your body that you are going to continue and give me twenty more."

"What you aren't going to join me?" Kaitlyn asked as she brought up another pummel horse in her vision. Tom smirked, walked up to the horse, placed his hands on the bars and lifted himself in the air.

"Just remember, I'm not as good at this as you are."

"Hey, you're in my head, you don't have your body's limitations to stop you."

"My body's limitations?"

"Oh you know you have them."

Tom proceeded to do a few front support swings, then progressed to single and double leg circles.

"Show off." Kaitlyn laughed then lifted herself up to work on her front support swings."

"Thought you may need a coffee." Jonathan spoke as he handed Susan a coffee. Susan woke and stretched.

"Thanks." She took a sip. "How did it go?"

"Kaitlyn's notes and information helped. CovSec is in the process of setting up teams to intersect the shipment. They also send their well-wishes for a speedy recovery."

"You were gone for so long."

"Explaining everything that had happened without mentioning the word telepathy was incredibly difficult."

"You didn't mention the telepathy?"

"I didn't know how I could and not be institutionalized for it."

Susan agreed with his synopsis and this also helped her realize her previous plans were spot-on. Staying on this project would expose her and the ones she loved and the government hierarchy wouldn't care whom it stepped on during its search for the more advanced soldier.

"How much longer?" Susan asked trying to focus her attention on the task at hand.

"Now you're doing it."

Susan smiled as Jonathan stepped from in front of the wall clock. "She's been in there for nearly eleven and a half hours. How do you think it's going?"

"Couldn't tell you. Has he been asleep this entire time?" Jonathan asked looking at Tom still asleep on the couch.

"Asleep yes, resting? Not at all." Susan spoke as she placed her coffee on a nearby table then went to Tom, she pulled back a blanket she had placed over him to show Jonathan, "He's worked up quite a sweat."

"I don't understand. The way you explained it is he isn't even in his body."

"We're not talking about traveling spirits Jonathan, we're talking about telepathic interplay, mind travel. His spirit is still in his body just like Kaitlyn's, but his mind has been in a perpetual exercise routine for the past eleven hours straight. If it were physical exercise he'd be catatonic."

"He could handle it, we've done worse in basic training."

"Right." Susan cooed forgetting how physical these guys were. "Needless to say, I hadn't realized how much of a toll this was going to take on him."

"He wouldn't have done it if he didn't want to."

"You know they dated in high school?"

"Yeah I caught that."

"Their relationship was always turbulent, on again, off again, they were constantly arguing with one another."

"He was training her to defend herself, pushing her to be better than she was. I understand the arguments. I've been there."

"You have?"

"She's a fighter, emotion-packed combatant, uncertain of her own limitations or her own abilities." Jonathan sat down next to Susan. "From the first day she walked into my life, that first day at the White House I could tell by her presence that she was ready for a fight. She was strong, certain she could take anyone, and held that position with every fiber of her being. When I first laid eyes on her my first thought was that I needed to set her straight. She had learned everything she needed to know about being a Secret Service agent except that she wasn't alone."

Susan sat back, listening as Jonathan continued.

"I knew that she needed something, the reason she was there was two-fold. She wanted to do what she could, she wanted the challenge, but she also wanted it to be a step."

"A step? To what?"

"Whom, is the more appropriate question apparently." Jonathan declared as he looked at Tom laying there on the couch. He smiled as he looked back at Susan. "I had a feeling it was something though."

"What do you mean?"

"A man knows when the woman he is with isn't really with him."

"Then why did you...?"

"Why not? I mean, you hope that she'll work through it, that whatever is missing in her life you can fill. You hope that she'll eventually come around."

Susan looked at him sadly.

"At least I tried. At least I was out there and willing to give someone my all." He spoke as he left the remaining unsaid to soak in with Susan. Silence permeated the room for a moment when Tom jolted awake, shocking the both of them. Jumping to his feet the blanket fell to the floor and his sweat covered shirt exposed how hard he had been working.

"She's done." He spoke as he grabbed the coffee on the side table and ran towards the door. He stopped in the doorway and looked back at the two of them standing there, "By the way, you two will make a great couple."

Susan and Jonathan looked at each other as they realized Tom must have heard everything. Jonathan smirked at Susan, then they followed Tom down the hall. They were just turning the corner to the waiting room when the doctor came out the hallway door into the room. Tom ran up to him.

"She came through exceptionally well."

227

Chapter 15

Five weeks later; Kaitlyn was walking, making her way down the path of the parallel bars when Susan and Jonathan walked into the rehabilitation room. Tom was standing at the end of the bars waiting for Kaitlyn. Susan smiled seeing Kaitlyn's progress so substantial since the surgery. The doctors were amazed and baffled at the progress she was making but decided it was her strength training and all of the physical activity she had her entire life that made her body strong enough to pull through this. Her limbs were ready to move, her muscles were course with anticipation, her nerves rendered functionality and surprising ability.

As Kaitlyn looked over at Jonathan and the smile on his face she couldn't help but think back to the moment she awoke from surgery. Jonathan was sitting next to her bed. He hadn't noticed initially her eyes open so she peered around the room quickly. Tom wasn't there. Finding that strange she inhaled to say her first words but the raising of her rib cage forced her to acknowledge the fresh stitches and extremely sore muscles from being clamped open for twelve hours. She choked on the air for a moment, tensing as she held her breath allowing the surge of pain to subside. Jonathan looked up at her and leapt to his feet.

"You okay?"

Kaitlyn nodded her head then looked at the morphine drip next to the bed and pressed the button.

"The doctor said your surgery went off without a hitch. He thinks you're going to be okay."

"He won't know that until I get to rehabilitation but thanks for the encouraging words."

Jonathan sat back down next to her and took her hand into his. "We were all really worried about you."

"We?" Kaitlyn asked phishing for more information.

"Me, Susan... Tom." He paused knowing she was curious, "Even the guys at headquarters."

"What did you tell them?"

"I gave them my report with your research and left out the whole dreams, telepathy business." Kaitlyn raised an eyebrow at him in question. "Hey I didn't need them thinking I was insane and I didn't need them bothering you right now."

"Thank you Jonathan."

There was an awkward silence for a moment as the two of them realized where this conversation needed to go, they both started a sentence at the same moment and stopped with a laugh. Jonathan insisted Kaitlyn talk first.

"Go ahead I insist." Kaitlyn back-peddled.

Jonathan looked at her and smiled. "I had a lot of time to think about things while you were in surgery."

"Me too." Kaitlyn admitted.

"I think, since agent M will be back at CovSec they'll probably go back to pairing you two up to be partners."

"That's what you thought about?"

"Yeah why?"

"I'll be in recovery for at least a month." Jonathan nodded shyly. Kaitlyn continued. "Let's be honest, what you were thinking about was what's going to happen between us now that Tom's back."

Jonathan looked at her expectantly.

"Jonathan," Kaitlyn sighed sadly, "What we had was nice..."

"There it is." Jonathan interrupted, Kaitlyn paused and looked at him curiously. "Had. That's all I needed to know."

"You aren't..."

"Mad? Please. Twelve hours in your head and ten years in your life. I didn't even expect to compete."

"You're taking this rather well..." Kaitlyn paused catching on, "How's Susan doing?"

"She's great. She really is an amazing woman."

"Yeah I know." Kaitlyn smiled brightly. "I hope you take the time to really get to know her."

"I will."

Jonathan made that easier than he needed to but Kaitlyn was appreciative for it. The morphine was taking effect and she was almost ready to go back to sleep again. However, as Jonathan got up to leave Kaitlyn simply wanted to wait and see who was going to walk in next. She may have spent the past twelve hours solid with him with no escape but what they were able to accomplish in that time was more than ten years on the outside.

Kaitlyn landed on her feet, visualized a chair and sat down on it, stretching her legs out to rest. She wiped the sweat from her brow as Tom walked up next to her.

"You can't tell me your tired."

"Hey this may all be in my head but I'm still allowed a short break."

Tom huffed a laugh and sat down next to her and leaned back, reaching his arms up and locking his hands behind his head for support. "We haven't trained like this in a long time."

"Tom darling, we never trained like this." Kaitlyn spoke sarcastically. Tom smiled.

"So what do you want to do next?"

Kaitlyn thought about it for only a moment when the gym scene changed to a beautiful beach scene at sunset, Kaitlyn and Tom laying on lounge chairs with fruity drinks in their hands. Kaitlyn took a sip.

"That's not exactly what I was thinking about." Tom scolded jokingly.

Kaitlyn then changed the scene to a dark cave with shimmery light reflecting off the walls. Tom recognized it as his cave in the Bahamas and Kaitlyn had set the scene for when they made love there that afternoon.

"Yes... we worked up a sweat here but it's still not the kind of activity I was referring to."

Kaitlyn sighed and transformed the scene to the training field. She knew this would make him happy and she knew the fresh air and sunshine would help the monotony of the exercise.

Tom stood and reached for a climbing rope, then looked back at Kaitlyn. "You ready?"

Kaitlyn stood with a shake of her head and also reached for a rope next to him.

"What?" Tom asked seeing Kaitlyn shake her head.

"Is it all about work with you?"

"Of course not but..."

"But what? It's been hours, we've worked harder here than we have in years and haven't really said anything much to each other since you apologized for leaving and left off with something you wanted to tell me."

"You remember that huh?"

Kaitlyn looked at him with scolding eyes and the thought of, are you kidding me? Women don't forget things like that.

"Again, I'm in your head, I can hear your thoughts." Tom chimed up.

"Well then talk to me." Kaitlyn insisted.

Tom lifted himself onto the rope and proceeded to climb. Kaitlyn, with a sigh, joined him.

"I think while we're here we should stay focused on the task at hand. I don't want to cause you any undo stress."

"You don't think dying of curiosity adds undo stress?"

Tom looked to his left and saw Kaitlyn pull herself up to his level. "What do you want me to tell you?"

"I want you to lie to me. I want you to say whatever it is you think will get me to stop loving you." Kaitlyn spat back angrily.

Tom pulled the rope closer to his body so he could hold himself up without undue stress on his arms, Kaitlyn did the same as she waited for his response.

"I don't want to stop loving you."

"Ah so you admit you do!"

"Of course I love you! I love you more than life itself!"

Kaitlyn smiled a small grin as she peered into his eyes. Tom however, looked to the side, averting his eyes from her gaze. "I just don't know how you feel."

Kaitlyn realized they had reached that moment and although she pushed him to this moment she hesitated with her response.

"Tom, ten years ago I saw you walk into the hallway at school and I thought to myself..." Kaitlyn paused trying to recall, "Actually it wasn't words, it was a feeling. It was such a strong a feeling that it really stuck out. My heart danced. I didn't know why, but I knew it was for you and I knew I had to allow it to take me to you."

Tom looked back at her and listened.

"I didn't know how to talk to you. I didn't know if you'd ever talk to me but I felt so overwhelmed with desire to be near you that I literally made a fool of myself."

"You never made a fool of yourself."

"Thank you for being blind."

Tom scowled slightly as he saw Kaitlyn begin to continue.

"I fell in love with you on the very first day and I..." Kaitlyn paused, gripping hold of the rope tighter. Tom saw her eyes close and her face scrunch up in pain.

"Kaitlyn?"

Exhaling a breathy ow, Kaitlyn tried to ignore the pain and get back to the conversation.

"Are you okay?"

Kaitlyn's hands lost grip of the rope for a moment and she slipped slightly but regained control. Dangling from the rope with her arms fully stretched upwards, she held on with all of her might as the sudden jerk swung it outwards. "Oh!" Kaitlyn breathed loudly as the pain continued to distract her. Tom released his grip of his rope to land on the ground under her, ready to catch her if she fell.

"Kaitlyn, why don't you let go of the rope?"

"Tom I think something's wrong." Kaitlyn breathed as she released her grip and fell to her feet. Tom caught her and seeing her face still show her pain, helped her to sit down on the ground.

"Tell me what's going on. What can I do?"

"I... I don't know." Kaitlyn clutched the top left of her shirt with her right fist and gripped it tightly. Her left hand still holding Tom's hand as she clutched trying to release her pain. Gasping for air she began to panic, "I, I can't breathe."

Worried but unable to distract himself, Tom spoke, "Look at me. Kaitlyn, look at me, ignore the pain..."

Kaitlyn slowly raised her head towards him and opened her eyes. Still gasping for breath, shaking her head just slightly. She changed the scene in her head to that of a church. A beautiful church, filled with people, and flowers. There was a picture on an easel in front and next to it a dark wooden podium and he saw Kaitlyn standing there speaking to the people and he was mesmerized by the vision. It was the day of his funeral and as Kaitlyn's words began to ring in his ears he suddenly added the pain and emotions he had experienced with it.

"I wanted to tell you so much. I wanted to tell you how much you mean to me. I wanted to tell you how right you were, how I wish I could turn back time and accept your proposal then, instead of walking away. Why did I let myself ignore my true feelings, ignore you? Please Lord don't do this! Please just give me another chance! I promise I'll try harder! I won't waste my life! I won't continue down this path if you only let me talk to him one more time! Please! Please Lord don't take him from me! I need him!"

Kaitlyn was on her hands and knees praying, pleading aloud to God to give her another chance at love with Tom and Tom remembered the feelings he felt that day, the emotions she sent to him unknowing, he felt her pain and for the first time heard her words and his heart broke. He walked to her. She clutched her chest, panicking, unable to catch her breath. She needed him then more than ever and he couldn't be there for her. She was begging him for another chance and at the time was left unanswered but today, today he was there. He kneeled down in front of her. He took her hand carefully into his palm and kissed it.

She looked up at him, tears streaming down her face, such an intense pain in her heart spreading so quickly and then she saw him. He was kneeling infront of her at that very moment when she needed him the most and the pain immediately disappeared. Taking it in, the sight of him, his chin, his smile, his nose and then his eyes their souls touched at that moment. It was almost as if they had been transported to heaven because there was no more pain, no more tears, no more sorrow and no more fears. Realizing that her prayers had been answered, that Tom was alive and well and sitting directly infront of her, she leaped forward, wrapping her arms around him, pulling him into the strongest embrace she could muster, pulling him as close as she possibly could to her soul.

"Tom," she spoke as she continued to hold him tighter than ever before, "I realized for the first time in my life that I didn't want to lose you. I realized I would never get to see you again or talk to you or hold you again and I was terrified. I prayed for another chance. Another chance to tell you everything I had wanted to tell you but was too scared to, and you know what? He answered my prayer. I didn't realize what I had until it was gone and so I prayed for God to give me one more chance and I said I wouldn't waste it and I did. I lied to God and to myself and I am ashamed of myself. I've been so self involved that I couldn't see through my own pain to see yours and I am so sorry about that." She began to cry. "Tom I don't want to lose you again! I can't. I need you too much. I love you too much. Please, don't leave me again."

Tom felt her in his arms, he felt her trembling and her tears began to soak his shoulder but he had been hurt too many times. She didn't want him to leave but she hadn't given him a reason to stay. He sighed heavily.

"Kaitlyn I can't keep doing this. I can't stick around waiting for you to make up your mind."

"But I have!" Kaitlyn pulled back to look into his face.

"You've decided that you don't want me to leave but that's not enough to get me to stay." He countered.

Tears were streaming down Kaitlyn's face, how could she explain herself? "Tom I love you. I love you with all of my heart, I have since the first day I ever saw you. But I was so afraid of you, afraid of getting rejected by you, or worse, of never getting noticed by you. I wanted you so much, that when I had you, when I finally got you, I felt I'd be able to get anything. I felt if I got lucky enough to get you, I could have anything I ever wanted in this world and I went for it, without you. But I realize now that life without you isn't worth it. You make me whole. I'm not asking you to stay because I don't want you to leave. I'm asking you to stay because you want to. Because you love me as much as I love you and because you want to marry me."

"I asked you to marry me, you refused to answer."

"But now I'm asking you. I'm asking you because I know what I want and now I'm putting the question out there to you. I'm asking because if I don't, then I know, that I'll grow old and die and never again feel the kind of love I feel when I'm with you."

Tom looked deep into Kaitlyn's eyes and felt her sincerity. Suddenly he knew he had his answer. He pulled Kaitlyn into his arms and held her for a moment, when she finally choked out the words through stifled breaths.

"Tom I want to marry you."

"And I want to marry you." He smiled through tears.

When Susan and Jonathan walked up to the two of them in the rehabilitation center they expected to see wobbly feet and unsteady limbs. Jonathan and Susan hadn't been able to come by as often as they would have liked because their duties at CovSec kept them very busy. Tom would call Susan and let her know how things were progressing and Susan always believed he was exaggerating. Seeing her recovery through loves eyes must have given him a bias because no one could recover that quickly.

As Susan walked up and spoke a hello to Kaitlyn, Kaitlyn turned and smiled.

"Susan! How great it is to see you? How is everything going?"

"Everything is so wonderful!" Susan began cheerfully taking Jonathan's hand into hers. Their relationship was prospering.

"I am so happy to hear that." Kaitlyn admitted energetically.

Tom smiled as he looked at Jonathan. He was happy for them but happier for the special trip Jonathan took on their behalf.

A week ago Tom called Jonathan and asked him to meet him outside of the rehabilitation center. Tom was being extra secretive on the phone and even though he knew Jonathan would hear him through telepathy Tom didn't even want to think aloud these thoughts. What he was going to do could potentially put someone he loved dearly in mortal danger and he didn't even want his best friend to know the details.

"I'm going to ask you to do something for me. No questions asked." Tom began in his best secret agent guise.

"What..." Jonathan paused then realized that would have been a question then simply nodded his head."

"Tom put an envelope in Jonathan's hands and spoke. "I need you to deliver this to that address. I don't want any interaction between you and the recipient. I don't even want the recipient to see you."

"Okay."

"I need you to not check on the address, no background check, no research no investigation. No satellite surveillance."

"You're asking me to put a lot on faith here."

"It is not a dangerous mission. I just need this package delivered and then I need you to leave. Do not wait for the recipient to open it."

"No questions asked." Jonathan repeated his understanding. Tom released his grip on the envelope and spoke one last thing. "I'm trusting you. This is the most important mission you will ever receive from me."

"I get it Tom. You can trust me."

"Thanks man."

Jonathan nodded at Tom to let him know the mission had been completed. And as Tom sighed with relief he returned his focus onto Kaitlyn standing in the middle of the parallel bars.

"So you are walking well." Susan interjected excited to see that Kaitlyn wasn't unsteady on her feet or stabilizing herself with her arms.

"Walking, running...."

Susan scoffed in disbelief. Granted she knew Kaitlyn, she knew of her abilities, she was the one who suggested the mental therapy would help to progress her recovery but there was still a small something in her head that didn't believe it was really true.

Kaitlyn smiled as she placed her hands carefully on the bars, aligned exactly parallel. She gripped hold of the bars tightly, took a deep breath and then lifted herself up with her arms. Her feet left the floor and carefully with strength and determination she brought her feet forward. Susan was in awe, excited that Kaitlyn's upper body strength was doing so well. Then Kaitlyn swung her legs backwards. Gripping the bars tightly, she swung her legs forward again and then swung them back so hard she flipped upwards to a standing handstand on the parallel bars. Her feet pointed high up in the air, perfect symmetry, perfect balance. Jonathan and Susan's mouths both dropped as Tom stood there spotting Kaitlyn.

Holding herself in that upside down position, she then bent her arms and slowly brought herself down like a handstand push up. Five pushups was about all her arms could handle at the moment and she swung her legs back down, her feet landing on the floor. Tom steadied her, there to support her even though she was doing just fine on her own and he stood next to her as she walked to a chair to sit down.

Once sitting she looked back over at Jonathan and Susan and caught the dropped jawed expressions still on their face.

"What?" Kaitlyn asked with an innocent yet knowing tone as she waited to hear their responses.

They both seemed to snap out of it at the same time and immediately began talking simultaneously.

"How did you do that? I can't believe the progress... That was amazing!"

Kaitlyn smiled. She was proud of her progress without doubt but she still had a long way to go to get back to the strength and agility she had been in before the accident. Tom knew she was pushing herself but realized she could handle it. He was just happy to be here with her, training her again. Their love was stronger than it ever had been before and whether they returned to CovSec or went on to bigger and better things was still yet to be determined. All he knew was his life was starting and he was thrilled to be able to share it with Kaitlyn.

As Kaitlyn took a sip of water, Susan finally spotted it. Shimmering in the white fluorescent lights of the rehabilitation center it seemed to twinkle with joy. Taking a quick glance over at Tom to confirm then back to Kaitlyn as she screwed the lid back on the water bottle, Susan grabbed Kaitlyn's left hand knocking the water bottle out and nearly yanked her fingers within inches of her face.

"Oh my God!" Susan exclaimed in pure cheerleader valley-girl excitement, her joy billowing out of her vocal cords with an added screech of exhilaration. "Is this what I think it is? Tell me it is! Oh tell me it is!"

Kaitlyn smiled brightly as Tom placed his right hand on her thigh. "It is!" She added after a dramatic pause.

Susan shrilled as Kaitlyn stood and allowed her friend to embrace her in a jumping excited hug. "I knew it!" Susan shrieked as she released her hug to look at the ring again.

"Congratulations." Jonathan spoke as he nodded his approval to Tom who was now standing. Susan hugged him too.

"When is the ceremony?" Susan immediately jumped into wedding preparation.

"As soon as you agree to be my maid of honor." Kaitlyn grinned.

"And you my best man." Tom added to Jonathan.

"Of course." Jonathan spoke as Susan took another longer look at the engagement ring on Kaitlyn's finger.

"It's so beautiful." Susan began admiring the intricate details of the platinum band. "And it looks antique."

"Family heirloom." Tom spoke as Kaitlyn caught his glance out of the corner of her eye. They shared in the secret moment for an instant as Tom wondered quietly if the envelope had been opened yet.

Around 1600 miles away in a northern town a woman was just walking into her home with a bag full of groceries. She dropped her keys in the bowl next to the door, shut the door behind her then carried the groceries to the kitchen placing the sack on the counter. Removing the milk from the sack and placing it in the refrigerator and then the frozen dinner in the freezer, she grabbed the plastic sack, crumpled it up and added it to her ever-growing collection.

When she returned her gaze to the counter top she saw an orange envelope sitting there that she didn't recognize. Her address was on it but there was no return address or postage. Curious, she took it in her left hand and walked through the house checking the windows and doors to make sure they were locked. Once the feeling that the house was secure passed she looked at the envelope curiously and then sat down in a chair in the living room.

She looked at the handwriting on the envelope again and although familiar she dismissed it. She shook the envelope, it was a large nine inch by twelve inch with a bracket closure and it seemed there was something small yet flat inside as she felt and heard it rattle inside. Carefully, she pressed the bracket together to slide it through the hole and open the flap and she examined what was inside. It looked like a Polaroid picture she thought as she flipped the envelope over and let the item slide out into her right hand.

Turning the Polaroid over to face her, then flipping it upright, she took a long look at it. The image was clear, there was no doubt what she was looking at. It was a set of hands, two peoples hands holding each other. One was male large and course, strong looking. The other was female, smaller and delicate looking. Then she noticed the ring. A ring she recognized. A ring so unique it was hand-crafted over forty years ago. A ring with intricate details along the band, a ring that she knew had been inscribed "For the love of my life" a ring she recognized as once her own, handed down to her son to give to the woman he would inevitably share the rest of his life with.

Marge clutched the picture to her chest and released a sob so abrupt it would have woken angels. A relief filled her as the realization, the truth, the secret had finally become clear. Her beloved son Tom was not dead... and Kaitlyn had finally found him.

Read more great books by **Kathleen J. Shields** at *www.KathleensBooks.com*

About the Author:

Kathleen J. Shields is a very creative, highly imaginative and extremely dedicated, hard working individual. She runs her own website and graphics design company, Kathleen's-Graphics, and has published various books; from fully-illustrated rhyming stories for ages 4 and up, children's chapter books for ages 8 and up, and young adult stories with plans for a few romantic mysteries stories as well.

Kathleen has been writing poetry and stories for years; both for fun and for hire in custom greeting cards and for local speaking engagements. She enjoys sharing her stories and talking with children and adults about how they too can write if they put their mind to it.

She has also started a blog with inspirational and educational posts both regarding her endeavors as an author as well as a business woman and Christian. Her views are always light-hearted and thought-provoking and are intended to get the reader thinking.

Her fully-illustrated rhyming children's stories, the Hamilton Troll Adventures, are inspirational as well as educational. These stories are engaging and amusing and provide informative descriptions of various animal characteristics, vocabulary words and definitions, all while incorporating real-life situations that young children can face. Each story introduces at least one additional character, presents new obstacles to overcome, teaches something new, all while imparting a positive impression. This is a terrific series for bedtime stories and young readers, as well as readers who are young at heart.

For more information about the author,
the various books she has written
and plans to write, please visit:
www.KathleensBooks.com
or follow her blog at **www.kathleenjshields.com**

www.ingramcontent.com/pod-product-compliance
Lightning Source LLC
Chambersburg PA
CBHW051453170626
46811CB00002B/464